MW00578505

BEAUTIFUL
NIGHTMARE

DARK DREAMS DUET

GIANA DARLING

To Skye.

For including me in the Midnight Dynasty family.

"All men dream: but not equally.

Those who dream by night in the dusty recesses of their minds wake up in the day to find it was vanity, but the dreamers of the day are dangerous men, for they may act their dreams with open eyes, to make it possible."

—T.E. Lawrence

PLAYLIST

"Blood//Water"—grandson
"Scars"—My Brothers And I
"Once Upon A Dream"—Lana Del Ray
"Wildest Dreams"—Taylor Swift
"Mad at You"—Noah Cyrus, Gallant
"Make Me (Cry)"—Noah Cyrus, Labrinth
"Sucker For Pain"—Lil Wayne, Wiz Kahlifa,
Imagine Dragons, X Ambassadors
"Make Up Sex"—SoMo
"Watch Me Burn"—Michele Morrone
"Game of Survival"—Ruelle
"DNA"–Lisa Marie Johnson
"Lions Inside"—Valley of Wolves
"Filthy Rich"—Evalyn
"Trust Issues"—Olivia O'Brien
"hate u love u"—Olivia O'Brien
"I Have Questions"—Camila Cabello
"sex money feelings die"—Lykke Li

"Open Up"—Gallant

"Lion"—Saint Mesa

"Pretty When You Cry"—Lana Del Ray

"Acquainted"—The Weeknd

"Young And Beautiful"—Lana Del Ray

"Lover"—G Flip

"Sorry"—Halsey

"Knees"—Bebe Rexha

"Out of Love"—Alessia Cara

"Mean It"—Lauv, LANY

"Baby"—Bishop Briggs

CHAPTER ONE

Tiernan Morelli

DREAMS ARE FUNNY things.

For years, I'd dreamed of destroying my father.

I spent hours concocting schemes, planning his demise in so many of my waking and sleeping hours.

It was something I longed for so intensely that the desire followed me into the dark of my subconscious. I went to bed with it and woke up to it, a taste on the back of my tongue, a message burned into the inside of my lids.

I was consumed by this dream and it became my life.

But that's the funny thing about dreams.

They don't always translate well in reality.

As the gun ricocheted in my grip, spitting a bullet into the barrel chest of my father, all my dreams should have been a hair's breadth away, as close as the bullet was to Bryant's black, corroded heart.

Instead, I couldn't seem to blink away the nightmare my life had become in only a few powerful minutes.

Bianca was gone. Ripped from me by the ruthless hands of the truth I'd hidden successfully for so long.

She was gone in a way where I knew she wouldn't come back.

Not willingly.

It twisted up something in my chest so tight I couldn't breathe.

Though, the fact that my father had pulled the trigger a sliver of second after I did might have had something to do with that too.

I staggered back as pain tore through the top of my shoulder, the bullet carving out a path through my trapezius muscle. Through the pain, I wondered if he'd missed his target on purpose from some lingering sense of paternal obligation, or if I'd thrown him off his mark by shooting him first.

"You fucking shot me," Bryant grunted as he pressed a hand to the seeping wound, his breath a wet rasp.

I blinked at him as I breathed slowly through my nose, forcing myself to control the pain of my own wound.

"You'll survive," I said blandly, as if I didn't care.

Inside me though, a storm raged. I wanted him dead on the ground. I wanted the security of knowing he would never come after the Belcantes, after The Gentlemen, after my siblings *ever* again. Six feet of earth and a locked fucking casket could keep Bryant Morelli from exacting revenge against those he thought had wronged him.

And it was irrefutable now.

I was no longer just the black sheep, the disappointing son only good to use as tool for his darkest deeds.

No. Now, I was the enemy.

All because of one angel-eyed girl.

He sneered at me through the pain, his expression curdled with absolute hatred.

"You're a bigger disappointment than I could have imagined, Tiernan. And trust me when I say, I didn't know the bar could be lowered further." He hissed as he shifted to step forward, blood seeping through his fingers, staining the crisp white of his dress shirt like spilled wine. "It was foolish of me to think you could ever be worthy of the Morelli name."

Something creaked and groaned in my chest, the sounds of a structure about to collapse.

All I'd ever wanted was acceptance and unity.

All I'd ever been was alone and a tool of chaos.

I told myself this was different, this was my choice.

But as blood seeped from the bullet he'd put through my shoulder, I felt as if I was losing more than just his acceptance. I was losing everything I'd ever wanted and everything I'd never known I needed.

"I don't need you," I told him, my voice somehow unwavering, as cold as I felt inside. "I never did. It was my mistake in thinking your opinion mattered to me."

"My opinion matters to the most important men in this country for a reason," Bryant snarled as he holstered the gun to take out his phone, fingers trembling just slightly as he dialled. "Yours matters to no one. Not your mother, not your brothers and sisters, and now, not even the pathetic bastard offspring of Lane Constantine."

"You know fuck all about what really matters," I said as fury worked itself like a sliver under my horrified numbness.

I stalked forward so abruptly, he fumbled his phone before he could lift it to his ear. The grin that possessed my face was manic, so wide it was almost painful. I clasped Bryant strongly by the shoulder, ignoring the pain in my own, and dug two fingers into the gaping wound I'd shot out of his hide. He made a horrible, painful keen in the back of his throat and struggled to find leverage to push me off. I stepped closer, pressing harder. His blood poured over my fingers with every pulse of his corroded heart.

"I hope it hurts," I whispered as I leered into his face, watching sweat pop out across his skin, brow crumpled and damp like a used napkin. "I hope I nicked your goddamn heart because it's the only time I'll ever come close to making you feel something for me. You used me like a tool. You made me believe heavy-handed force and negative reinforcement was some fucked-up love."

"That's all you're good for," he grunted, twisting to get away but only increasing his pain. "Killing men and doing dirty deeds for real blue bloods."

"I would have done that and more if you'd loved me," I said, realizing the truth of the words as they fell from my mouth.

I was light headed with pain and blood loss,

with the agony of losing my father and Bianca in one swift blow. It nearly killed me to realize I'd been the orchestrator of my own heartache.

Why was it that everything seemed so clear now—Bianca, Brandon, my true desires and needs—when it was too late to grasp them?

A bitter laugh escaped me like a cough. "Now, I'm done. I'm not yours to use or know or even fucking look at anymore. You'll have to get your own fat, weak hands dirty for a change."

"You still haven't learned. *I'm* the one in charge, not you."

"You'll never learn," I hissed as my fingers knocked against the bones of his ribcage and slid deeper. "So you'll die alone and hated by your own flesh and blood. But I can learn and I will."

"I'll destroy you," Bryant said and even shot through the chest, wobbling on weak knees, he managed to be haughty and threatening. "I'll destroy *them*. That bitch Bianca and her little brother. That disgusting group of miscreants who are the only people you can even *pay* to associate with you. I'll end them all."

"That's an awful lot of blood on your hands," I quipped blandly, but I was a predator and my young had been targeted. Adrenaline surged through me and my hand found Bryant's throat of its own accord, squeezing so tightly, he turned pleasingly purple in the face.

"There are more ways to end a man than death," he rasped.

There was.

I knew all of them because Bryant had taught me well.

Fear skittered down by spine, but I steeled myself and focused.

Leaning so close I could feel Bryant's wet, rattling breath against my scared cheek, I made sure my eyes were all he could see. I wanted him to read the savagery there, the pure, cold intent of the killer he'd created.

"You touch a hair on the Belcantes, I'll finish the job and shoot you through the head, do you understand me?" I said slowly, clearly. "You forget, dear *dad*, I know where all your skeletons are buried. I put them there myself."

"Mutually assured destruction," he whispered, his bloody hand scrambling to peel mine off his thick neck.

"So be it then," I growled. "You come for mine, I'll end you, even if it means the end for me. You took everything from me, Bryant. I don't have anything left to lose, and that is a *very* dangerous thing."

For the first time all night, Bryant looked momentarily unsure, his eyes cutting to the left over my shoulder as he tried to calculated the truth of my words. Even if he wouldn't admit it, he knew of all the people in his life, I was the most capable of destroying him.

That was the problem for people who created monsters, it was only a matter of time before they turned on their creators.

There was something about seeing him across from me like a mirror image that chilled me deeper than his disregard, horrified me more than the violence between us. I felt suddenly sure that I was staring through the looking glass at my future, a villainous man with a black heart and only selfish intentions, corrupted by greed, power, and vengefulness.

How fucking empty it seemed looking a Bryant then, an aging man with a massive family who respected him out of fear instead of love. Who wouldn't give him a fucking *nickel* willingly let alone their love and trust.

It reminded me of Bianca's word about choosing grace over violence.

Done with this, with Bryant and anything associated with him, I threw him away. I dug Eamon McTiernan's old, silk handkerchief from my pocket to clean my hands as I watched him stumble to regain his footing and then land hard on the floor, breath forced from his lungs on a wet exhale.

To my right, still prone on the ground, Carter began to stir.

I stared at him for a moment, the brother I'd wronged who had just tried to exact retribution on me, and I made the first decision borne of grace that I'd made in a very, very long time.

Thankfully, the bullet wound to my upper chest was artificial, because when I bent to pick Carter up in a fireman's carry over my healthy shoulder, he was heavy as fuck.

"Don't you fucking dare," Bryant ordered imperiously as if he reclined on a throne and not the ground over a growing pool of his own blood.

"I never could resist a good dare," I told him with a smirk that was strained with pain.

Using everything in me, I straightened and carefully strode away from the only father I'd ever known as he growled after me. Once, it might have hurt to know he was more upset about me abducting Carter than about shooting me or losing me forever, but now, the only sadness it brought was the truth.

I'd responded with violence for so long, I'd

forgotten the language of love. It took losing Bianca and, potentially Brandon, to realize that maybe I wasn't too old to learn it again. Maybe I wasn't too dead inside to want to try.

CHAPTER TWO

Tiernan

I T WAS A bitch opening the grand, heavy doors of Lion Court. Carter had woken up during the drive. He'd accepted a cursory explanation of the events that happened while he was passed out. He didn't seem particularly shocked, which said a lot for the Morelli ethos. Then he went on to take a call from his mysterious employers in London. I had no idea why a scientific researcher needed high-end encryption on his phone… and I didn't want to know. The Morelli family had enough shit to deal with without Carter's brand of hyperintelligent trouble.

He was busy, which was fine by me. I wasn't in the mood to answer questions or ask them in a way that would compel him to answer.

I needed a drink, but I wouldn't have one. Ever since I lost Grace to a poisonous cocktail of booze and drugs, I'd abstained from both. But fuck me, I could have used them for the insistent, throbbing pain in my shoulder.

Instead, I led my brother up the wet steps through the rain and into my sanctuary, a place he hadn't seen since it was owned by our maternal grandparents. Of all my siblings, they'd left their estate to me. It surprised some people, but then again, Zelda and Eamon McTiernan had always been collectors of broken relics and banned art. They saw things in the unused and unwanted that other people often missed.

They saw something in me. I didn't know what the fuck it was, but a tiny part of me wondered if Bianca had seen it too.

The moment the door creaked open, Walcott appeared at the mouth of the hallway leading back to the kitchen. He took one look at me, turned on his heel and disappeared back down the hall calling to Henrik as he did.

Carter went to a fainting couch and dropped into it.

I ignored him as Ezra appeared at the top of the stairs. He noticed the blood saturating my white shirt and immediately pulled out a gun.

"Christ," Carter muttered.

When Ezra's dark gaze rose to mine, I wearily

BEAUTIFUL NIGHTMARE

lifted my blood-stained hands and signed.

Things didn't go as planned.

His brows cut lines into his forehead. He carefully holstered his gun long enough to sign, *No shit.*

"Where is Bianca?" Henrik asked as he entered the foyer behind Walcott carrying a First Aid kit.

It should have irritated me that he asked after her first. He was *my* employee. My friend. My...family. And maybe, four hours ago, it would have. Now, it only sent a dull echo through my empty chest like a shout in a haunted house.

Before I could answer, Walcott was dragging a chair over to me and pushing me none-to-gently onto it. "Tell me you didn't go through with your stupid plan."

"It was a good plan," I argued mulishly while Henrik bent to peer at my wound. Carter threw himself on an antique fainting couch, looking bored. "Until Bryant shot it all to hell."

"He has a way of doing that to you," Walcott agreed, but his mottled face was creased deeply with concern. "What happened, T?"

I sighed so heavily, it hurt my injury like a bitch. "I fucked up."

"Well, acceptance is half the battle," Walcott

13

quipped as Henrik started to cut my soaked blazer and button up from my body.

"Not this time," I rested my head against the antique headrest of the fucking uncomfortable Queen Anne chair and closed my eyes. "Bianca's gone."

"Where?" Henrik asked.

"I…" No matter how hard I squeezed my lids shut, the sight of Bianca's shocked, broken expression was embedded in my mind. "I don't know." I signed his name. "Ezra?"

Without opening my eyes, I could tell by the tread of his heavy gait that Ezra was leaving the room to find out where exactly Bianca had run away to. Henrik was the tec wizard, but Ezra would find her.

He had to.

"What did you do?" Walcott demanded, an edge to his voice he'd never used with me before.

He was disappointed in me.

It hurt, but he could join the fucking club. No one was more eviscerated by the nightmare of this night than I was.

"I went to that cursed painting and cut it open," I explained as I dug the key out of my pants pocket with a wince.

"Stop moving," Henrik muttered, pouring

water down my bare torso over the wound to gage how bad it was.

"We find what this key opens we find Lane's hidden will." The words should have been triumphant. I'd been working toward exactly this for so long…Even Bianca finding out I was a Morelli had sounded deplorably delightful in those early days when I'd hated her just for being Lane Constantine's spawn. That look of heart-break so clear on her face would have overjoyed me. I would have introduced to her to that crowded ballroom stuffed with plastic figurines of shallow, callous people as Lane's bastard and watched her humiliation and Caroline's like some sick fuck.

And I would have loved it.

Maybe it's too late for you, a voice in the back of my head that sounded like Bryant's whispered, *you are a monster. And monsters don't get to have hearts.*

But I'd been born a man, a boy. I still had vague recollections of happy days from my childhood before my twelfth birthday when I'd been too young to draw Bryant's particular notice and Leo had still protected me like he did the rest of our siblings. When my brothers and sisters had loved me and my mother hadn't yet been driven to drink. They'd lain like half-forgotten relics in the fallow dirt of my soul until Bianca and Brando arrived to unearth them.

And now that I knew I was once capable of love and devotion, I couldn't help but harbor this stubborn hope that I could have those things again.

Sharp pain burst through my shoulder as Henrik dug the bullet out of my muscle with a pair of medical pliers. When I looked at him in reproach, he only lifted an eyebrow as if I deserved the pain.

I couldn't argue with that.

"Bianca found out I'm a Morelli," I said, almost to myself, staring at the innocuous key in my stained hand.

"I figured when you said Bryant showed up. I've no doubt he relished telling her the truth," Walcott muttered bitterly.

"Silly little thing tried to defend me from him at first." My bitter laughter tasted acrid on my tongue. "Can you imagine? A slip of a girl in a feather dress against Bryant Morelli."

"Yeah, I can see her doing that," Henrik murmured softly, as he pulled the bullet from my flesh and dropped it with a *plink* into a metal dish. This wasn't the first or last time he'd retrieved a bullet from one of us. "That girl has got the heart of a lion."

"True," Carter murmured.

I leveled him with a cool look, trying not to wince as Henrik began to stitch me up right there in the foyer. "Thanks for your feedback."

He sighed at me, his temple and jaw already beginning to bruise. "I didn't show up to fight with my fucking father. I showed up to help you. You know, as your brother. Or are you still acting like you don't have brothers?"

Fuck.

Okay, that hit the mark.

But I didn't so much as blink at the barb. "Half-brother," I allowed, because there was protection in being the one to admit it first. "And it's not as if you've ever forgiven me for what happened with the belt."

"According to who?" he snapped. "You haven't spoken to me in years."

I arched a brow. "According to tonight when you put a gun in my face."

"You always were so dramatic," he countered, as if we were two boys insulting each other in mom's garden again. "You have no idea why I was there tonight."

"It seemed fairly obvious," I said drily then

hissed as Henrik pulled taut on the last stitch.

Carter eyed my wound. "How does it feel?"

"One guess."

He winced, an odd reaction. "Gunshots are the fucking devil."

I tried to shrug, but the action was too painful so I only lifted a hand and let it fall into my lap. "And you know about that how? No, don't bother answering. I already know you're neck deep in secrets."

Carter blinked then huffed out a heavy exhale and looked at the ceiling as if beseeching God for patience. "And people wonder why the hell I left all of you for England."

"I never wondered," I offered, because I could still remember the bone deep sense of relief I'd felt when he got accepted to Oxford and moved across the pond.

Carter was the brightest of the Morelli men— and the kindest. Despite what I'd done to him, he'd turned into an upstanding citizen, a man all of the Morellis could be proud of because he was that much better than the rest of us.

"That's your problem, Tiernan." He leaned forward as much as he could with his hands locked behind his back, the face so much like my own open and honest. "You've been Dad's weapon for years—the big, bad, scary Morelli—but you always fall into line so easily."

"You think I wanted this?" I scoffed, resentment churning low in my belly.

He had been coddled by the whole family his entire life. Other than the beating I'd been forced to give him so many years ago, what trials and tribulations had this soft handed man known in his twenty-eight years? He was the golden boy, the one set to do great things. At least, that's how I'd always thought about Carter. I'd always thought he was lucky to get of Bishop's Landing, but now I wasn't so sure. He had returned with lines of strain etched around his mouth, tired lanes fanned out beside his dark eyes. He accepted mysterious phone calls and wasn't afraid to fuck around with a man as dangerous as Bryant Morelli. Who really knew what my little brother had been up to in that last ten years? Most of my trauma was represented by ugly scars across my skin, but I knew how many would never surface and I didn't doubt Carter had earned his fair share of those since he was the kid I'd known.

"No. But I don't think you fought very hard to get out from under Dad," he said, the angle of his chin so familiar from childhood, when he'd dig in his heels until he got his way.

Something inside me ached at the memory and stretched toward him like a flower searching for sunlight.

"You don't know anything."

Carter eyed Walcott and Henrik, who'd both finished up and stood flanking me, offering their silent support even though they had to have questions and doubts about what happened that night.

These men were my family. These men who overcame their struggles every fucking day could inspire me to do the same.

"I know more than you think." Carter rearranged his long limbs on the fainting couch. It didn't look comfortable. "You took in Bianca and Brandon Belcante to use them to embarrass the Constantines and impress Dad."

I pressed my lips together to keep from telling him I'd mostly done it to impress *him*. Carter and the other siblings I'd lost to Bryant's manipulations. For so long, nothing had mattered as much as their love and acceptance.

Now, it felt ridiculous that I'd ever put so much importance on the opinions of people who didn't matter. Sharing the same blood might have given us the same hair color, but it didn't give us the same hearts.

"Now you've lost them because of Dad," Carter continued, a sly kind of look in those dark eyes. "Haven't you lost enough to him?"

"You think I'm going to go back to work for the man who just shot me in the chest?" I questioned drily.

He shrugged. "You went to work for the man who split your face open with a belt."

"I was a fucking *kid*, then," I snapped, immediately irritated with myself for showing how keenly his words cut.

"Exactly," he said, triumphant. "You were a fucking *kid*, Tiernan. So was I. Yeah, I hated you. You were my best friend and then you beat me blue with a belt. It didn't matter to me that Bryant made you do it, that he scarred you and marked you for life at the very same time. I was a kid." He shrugged again, but his expression was as somber as a funeral goer. "I couldn't get my head out of my ass enough to see you had suffered, too. That came later."

I stared at him and wondered if I was a little dazed from blood loss or if I was actually hearing him correctly.

"Dad caused the rift between us, Tiernan. He did it purposefully. He couldn't stand that we were close, and he knew how to drive us apart. He had plans for us both and he didn't want brotherhood coming in the way of that," Carter said, each word strong, perfectly enunciated with a hint of British crispness he must have picked up overseas. "I'm not willing to let it continue. I heard about what you had put into motion. I heard about what he was planning to do. And I decided enough was enough."

"What are you saying?" I asked. "If you came here to help me, can you fucking explain to me why you were at his side waving a damn gun in my face an hour ago?"

Carter eyed Henrik and Walcott, lips pressed tight. "This is Morelli business."

Neither Henrik or Walcott moved an inch.

"I'm not a Morelli," I said for the first time in my entire life. I'd been so worried voicing the words would give them some extra truth, some irreversible power. Instead, they were a release, the value open to release the poison I'd been harboring for years.

I wasn't a Morelli.

I was a McTiernan. Head of The Gentlemen. Guardian to Bianca and Brandon Belcante.

"I'm not a Morelli," I said again with dark relish. "And these men are better brothers to me than you and I have been to each other. So they'll stay."

He considered me for a long moment. "You're different than I thought you'd be."

"You don't know me so that's not surprising. And if you want that privilege, Carter, tell me the truth. What were you really doing with Bryant?"

A fissure cracked through his features, something like a grimace that cut into his cheek and made him look suddenly young and heartbroken. He stared down at the floor, hair falling into his face as he finally murmured, "I stayed away too long. I let things fester between us for far too many years. I want my family back. I want my *brother* back. I came here to try and fix things with you. To repair what he broke."

He sighed then looked up at me with those Morelli eyes in a face that looked so much like mine and said, "When I told Bryant I wanted to come home, he told me I had to earn my place with the family again." A bitter smile. "He told me his darling son, Tiernan, was plotting behind his back and he needed a new right-hand man. So I fooled him into thinking I'd help him, just so I could be there for the confrontation."

I told myself it didn't matter, but Bryant's careless ability to discard me burned through me more painfully than the bullet hole in my flesh.

"I had no intention of harming you or the girl," Carter continued, head lifted high, once more the haughty son of a well-born man. "But I've learned by experience that the best way to build a bridge is by extending your hand, not your fist. Bryant's used you for years. Why do you think that is?"

"Keep your friends close and your enemies closer," I murmured as I thought about Bianca.

God, I'd hated her. Before I even laid eyes on her, she and Brando became the symbols of everything I hated. And then, from the moment she opened the door to that decrepit little home in Bumfuck, Texas, I'd hated her with more passion than I'd ever possessed for a single person, even Caroline and Bryant. Her wholesome beauty, inherent grace and self-assuredness were insult to injury. I'd expected someone meek and easy to hate, young and brash and foolish at the very least.

But no.

Fate had thrown Bianca into my path not to punish me, but to awaken me.

In keeping my enemy close, I'd...

Not fallen.

Not love.

But something like it. Something soft and

foreign that sat in me too large and too heavy. Something that rearranged my insides.

"Exactly," Carter agreed. "Despite what you may think, Tiernan, I'm not in Bishop's Landing to hurt you. I'm here for both of us. Someone told me once that healing starts by admitting your own mistakes. I made one with you. I shouldn't have waited so long to talk to you. I should have been here for you. I'm trying to do that now."

"I'm supposed to believe that you're suddenly willing to help me and go against your own father?" I asked blandly, still not sold on this switch from rival brother to beseeching ally.

Carter stared at me for a moment, gaze hot on the scar bisecting my cheek. "You remember how much we loved to play pranks on Nanny Haus? If I recall correctly, it was your idea to feed her Mom's toy poodle's dog treats."

Beside me, Walcott stifled a bark of laughter with a cough.

I only arched a brow at him.

"You and Lucian loved to wrestle," Carter pressed. "Leo would referee because he was the only one who dared to get between you when you took it too far. You were the only one patient enough to sit for Daphne when she wanted to sketch us. You and me..." he drifted off, looking around the dark interior of the two-story foyer, utterly quiet and still as he searched his memories. "We used to fill the house with our laughter. All of us did. And then Bryant took it all away from us."

"Some things are too broken to be fixed."

"And some things mend," he countered, jerking his chin at me in a way that indicated my scar. "It might not be what it was, but maybe it's stronger for it."

"I tried," I told him coldly, because I could count each time I'd begged him for forgiveness, each time I'd tried to reach him and the others despite Bryant's instance on keeping me separate. "The truth is, I don't need you anymore."

Carter looked skeptical, and Henrik shifted slightly beside me because he thought I was lying too.

But the truth was, I didn't need Carter.

Not the way I thought I did.

If he wanted to form some kind of...connection again, I could do that if he was willing to meet me halfway. But I was done with working hard for people who didn't care about me or didn't love me in the right way.

Done with Bryant.

With the fall of the Constantines to get his

approval or to win back the love of my siblings.

Even with my mother, who loved me like she did her booze and pills, as a crutch and not a child.

"What do you need then?" Carter asked, genuine curiosity in his tone.

"Tiernanny," a small voice cried from the top of the curving marble staircase.

Brando grinned at me as he flew down the steps, his Hulk figurine in one hand and Picasso running at his heels. Blond curls flew back from his cherubic face and his smile was so bright, it made me blink rapidly as if I was looking into the sun. Momentarily blinded, I let him dart across the foyer and crash into my good side, hugging my waist as tight as he could.

I looked down at that halo of hair and thought of the child who'd been stolen from me by Bryant. I thought of the way Bianca prioritized this little man before everything else in life when normal seventeen-year-old girls focused on trendy clothes and school gossip.

And I got it, how she could do that so easily in spite of the demands of her age.

Because this kid was pure sunshine casting light deep into the shadow recesses of my soul.

My throat closed and breath refused to leave

my lungs.

"Who hurt you?" Brando asked, his expression falling as he noticed the bandage Henrik had placed over the round in my shoulder. His little hand brushed the edge of the tape there. "Why'd they do it?"

There was something in the way he asked me that hurt. Not *how did you hurt yourself* but *who hurt you.* This was a boy used to the concept of people hurting each other. The innocence I'd first sensed in him and Bianca wasn't because they hadn't seen the worst of the world, but because they *had* and they still chose hope instead of despair.

Before I could curb the impulse, I reached up and took his hand in mine, engulfing it in my entire palm. He seemed startled, but a little pleased at the contact.

"My dad did it," I told him honestly, catching his gaze and locking it tight to mine. "His name is Bryant and he is a very bad man. If you ever see him, I want you to run the other way and call for help, okay?"

Brando frowned fiercely. Beside him, Picasso felt left out and raised onto his hind legs to lick our held hands.

"You should run away from him too," he

advised me somberly. "Anca and I didn't have a dad for a long time and we turned out okay. Now, we've got you and Ez, Henrik, and Wally."

"Yeah," I said through the emotion clogging my throat. "Yeah, buddy. I'll stay away, too, that's good advice."

"Anca told me the only people worth loving are the ones that love us back," he recited proudly, then looked around the foyer. "Where is she?"

His question echoed in the silence.

I was a killer.

A liar.

A bad man through and through.

But the thought of lying to Brandon felt like the penultimate sin.

I swallowed thickly and looked up at Walcott who immediately stepped forward to sweep the boy up into his arms.

"Bianca was having such a fun time at the party with her friends, I told her to stay and enjoy herself. In fact, one of them asked her to go away for Christmas break. I told her we would miss her, but she should go enjoy herself. What do you think?"

He squinted at me. "Can I go, too?"

"No, buddy, she's on a girl's only trip. But you, me, and The Gentleman will have our own

Christmas holiday, how does that sound?" I asked, a small part of me shocked that I was bargaining with a seven-year-old like I'd been his guardian for years.

The old Tiernan would've locked him in his room until I could drag Bianca home so I didn't have to deal with him.

But Brando had awakened that small part of me that had once yearned and mourned for the unborn child I'd lost when Grace was driven to take her own life. I couldn't look into those clear blue eyes and see anything worth hating in them.

"Can we get a tree?" Brando asked, jumping slightly in Walcott's arms. "Mum never let us get a real one and I want one *so* bad!"

"Sure," I agreed, a reluctant grin tugging at my mouth.

"It should be ten feet tall, at least," Brandon declared, casting a speculative eye around the foyer. "We can put it in here between the stairs or in the living room right in the corner by the fireplace."

"In that case, we better get two."

He gaped at me, little mouth open in a perfect circle.

That mass in my chest, heavy and ungainly, shifted and expanded, pressing against my lungs so it was hard to breathe. Because the kid was looking at me like I'd give him a chest of treasure, something priceless and long-dreamt of.

"It's just a tree, kid," I cautioned for some reason. "No big deal."

"Will you help me decorate them?" he continued excitedly. "If we don't have money for ornaments, I'm really good at making them! We just need to buy some popsicles. Don't worry, I'll eat them all and then we can use the sticks!"

Even Carter coughed around a chuckle at that.

"I think we can do better than that," I said. "We'll get ornaments and lights for outside while we're at it. How's that sound?"

"So fun," Brando breathed, beaming at me. "You're the best."

He turned his focus to Walcott, yammering away about Christmas plans as the man walked up the stairs with Picasso following behind. I watched them go, chest tight, tongue thick in my mouth.

And I knew exactly what I needed.

Not the empty grandeur of the Morelli Mansion or the relationships with my siblings I'd always dreamt of that went unreturned.

I wanted Brandon in his room at Lion Court,

31

filling the cavernous rooms with excited chatter and youthful exuberance. I wanted Christmas with my men, Ezra, Walcott, and Henrik, maybe even Chef Patsy and whoever the fuck else worked around the house and grounds.

I wanted Bianca here in this house with us. Her husky laughter, her witty repartee, the dreamy look she got in her eye when she discovered a new piece of artwork hidden like lost treasure in the nooks and crannies of the mansion.

I wasn't capable of love. This wasn't that.

It was closer to obsession.

A mad desire to possess and cherish the way an art collector revered his most prized masterpiece.

She was *mine* and it was my right to care for her.

No one else's.

That feeling in my chest settled with click like a lock sliding into place and suddenly I was filled with conviction.

I stood up so quickly I almost lost my footing, still lightheaded from blood loss.

"Tiernan?" Henrik touched his fingers to my elbow, ready to steady me.

"Bring the Bentley Bentayga around. The Aston is filled with my blood. I want to be ready to go get Bianca as soon as Ezra locates her."

As if summoned by his name, Ezra appeared in the threshold to the left hallway and stalked forward with a ferocious scowl.

A chill slithered down my spine before his fingers even started moving.

That's going to be a problem, he signed, *because I found Bianca and she is at the Constantine Compound.*

White hot fury flooded my system and for a moment, I was rendered blind by it.

"How the *fuck* did that happen?" I growled low, struggling to contain my helpless rage.

Tilda was at the party. Apparently, Lane's best friend, Beckett, took her to the compound. Caroline just returned home there now.

Self-loathing and bitter regret surged over my tongue. I lashed out, grabbing the delicate wooden chair I'd sat in. It collided against the marble floor with a satisfying crash, splintering into pieces. One of them wedged itself into my palm like a thorn. It reminded me of that first day I'd met Bianca and pressed her hand around the stem of a blood red rose.

Fresh anger sparked through me.

I stalked toward Carter with a snarl on my face, satisfied by the way his eyes widened. He was a dangerous man, but so am I. It wouldn't do for him to forget that.

"Tiernan, I had *nothing* to do with that," he was saying under the roar of blood in my ears.

All I could think of was Bianca, beautiful and pure as a dove caged in the cruel hands of Caroline Constantine.

In that moment, Carter looked too much like Bryant to escape my ire. I lunged forward and squeezed his throat under my grip, watching his face turn vermillion. He thrust the side of his hand against my neck in a martial arts move I was familiar with. It hurt like a motherfucker, but I was used to pain. I stumbled back but remained standing over him.

"You want to to fix things with me, Carter?" I bared down on him with a cruel smile that felt good on my lips. "I'm done seeking forgiveness for something I was forced to do to you eighteen years ago. It's your turn to prove yourself to *me*. Help me get Bianca back from the Constantines. And if they do anything at all to harm her, you'll help me end them forever. Those are my terms."

"You're fucking insane, *brother*," he said, rubbing his neck with a grimace. "Help is what I was offering all along."

"Do we have a deal?" I asked with an arched

brow, extending my bleeding hand to him in offering.

He stared at it for a moment before clasping it tightly in his own. I jerked him forward roughly so he stumbled hard into my chest. Pain seared through me but I wanted my pale gaze— decidedly un-Morelli—to be the only thing he could see when I said, "Prove to me there's more to being brothers than blood."

CHAPTER THREE

Bianca

MOST PEOPLE SPEND their entire lives wishing for their dreams to come true, but no one ever wonders what will happen once they do. When we've reached our goal or achieved our happily-ever-after. Was everything you went through to get there worth it? Does it last?

Was it everything you thought it would be?

I'd dreamt my whole of being enfolded into the heart of the Constantine clan, but the reality was incredibly sobering.

I was heartbroken, lost, and alone in the rambling mansion taking up acres of prime, perfectly groomed real estate in Bishop's Landing. What was left of my heart after Tiernan *Morelli* broke my trust remained back at Lion Court with my baby brother, Brandon.

I'd never, not once in my life, been separated

from him before now.

It was day eight without him.

Caroline assured me her lawyers were working on transferring custodianship of Brando and myself to her, but even her cutthroat, hundreds-of-dollars-an-hour lawyers couldn't strike a compromise with Tiernan.

Caroline seemed almost disturbingly unfazed by the proceedings, but I grew more distressed by the hour.

How could I trust Tiernan to take care of the most precious being in my life? Even though we'd lived there for months, long enough for the entire household to know how to handle Brandon's epilepsy, I worried endlessly. I'd started to pick at my hangnails until they bled, which Caroline told me was a filthy habit, but I couldn't seem to stop.

The only thing that kept me from panicking was that Walcott was keeping me up-to-date on Brando over the phone. Apparently, they'd lied and told my baby brother that I was away on a last-minute holiday so he wasn't even concerned about me, thank God. I wanted to stay happy and oblivious until I could get everything sorted out for us to be together again.

The Compound was disturbingly empty even though Christmas was fast approaching and

Caroline told me most of the kids would be home for the holidays. I was both excited and sick to my stomach at the thought of meeting them.

In my fantasies, Brandon was with me, and they knew exactly who we were to them.

Now, I was alone, and Caroline told everyone she introduced me to that I was a 'friend of the family.' I should have been honored to be taken in by the matriarch of one of the most beautiful and formidable families in the country, but there was something...off about her. A coldness that nothing could permeate. If I hadn't clasped her hand and felt the warmth of blood in her veins, I would have believed she was a beautiful robot.

It was clear, she expected the same behavior from me.

I adjusted uncomfortably in the high-backed wooden chair at the colossal dining room table. Caroline had given me some of her daughter Tinsley's old clothes and they were too tight across the bust and hips, cutting into my skin in a way that made me feel self-conscious. Clearly, I had gotten my exaggerated curves from Aida's blood and not Lane's, because every Constantine I saw in the professional family photos on the walls and in the tabloids was willowy and graceful.

"Stop fidgeting, Bianca," Caroline admonished mildly as she took a sip of white wine, staring at me over the glass. "It's unbecoming on a beautiful young woman like yourself."

"I'm sorry," I murmured, wincing slightly as the engraved wood dug into my spine. "It's a hard habit to break."

"A lifetime of bad habits will take a concentrated effort to fix," she agreed. "We have our work cut out for us."

I wasn't usually an ungrateful woman. Lord knew, in my seventeen years, I didn't have much to be grateful for, but what I did, I cherished with every breath. So, I knew I shouldn't give voice to the lingering suspicion stalking my thoughts, but I'd never been much for impulse control.

"Our work cut out for us towards what end?" I asked, swirling my spoon through the bright red soup in the thousand-dollar China. "I'm so grateful for your help, Caroline, but what is it you…expect from me if I stay here?"

She studied me in that way she had. A cool, almost-reptilian regard. Idly, I wondered if she played poker, because she'd be a shoe-in for success with that unreadable expression.

"Well, I suppose it would be the same things I expect from all my children," she mused lightly. I watched one long, elegant finger laden with diamonds run circles over the rim of her wine-glass. "Decorum, work ethic, and success, perhaps. If you stay here, Bianca, I want you to thrive. I want you to go to the best college and make a name for yourself. If you are connected to this family, you must do right by us."

"Of course."

"And of course," she continued. "Obedience. Above all things, Bianca, I expect you to listen to my rules and heed my authority."

Obedience.

Why did it always come down to that for these people?

For people so moneyed and powerful, you would think they could withstand some descension.

Some of my reluctance must have translated in my expression, but Caroline laughed. "Don't worry too much, Bianca. My daughter Tinsley was an awful rebel, I have no doubt you'll impress me more than she did."

I didn't know what to say to that without insulting anyone, so I just took a sip of my cooling soup.

We ate in echoing silence for a few moments until the servants cleared our bowls and replaced them with steaming plates of roasted salmon and vegetables.

"Have you heard anything about Brandon coming to live here with me?" I mustered the courage to ask for the hundredth time.

A flash of something—irritation?—moved over her lovely face. "Yes, we are working on it. Unfortunately, that horrible scarred man refuses to entertain the idea of giving up guardianship so we have to look for...other means of rectifying the situation."

"Like what?"

A closed-mouth smile. "Why don't you leave all that adult stuff to me? You worry about school and your friends. I know you're close with Elias, but I would urge to make friends with less disreputable peers."

"Elias is lovely," I argued, a little thrown off because he was also her nephew.

She waved her hand dismissively. "Yes, of course. But despite my best efforts, he's made some ill-advised life choices."

"Such as?" I pressed, arching a brow when she didn't seem likely to answer me.

"Obedience, Bianca," she reminded me. "I abhor scandal and I will not abide by anyone, even one of my kin, dragging our name through the mud. Is that understood?"

"Yes, ma'am," I agreed, but I picked at the succulent salmon, something churning in my belly that didn't feel right.

"Now, other than the issue of guardianship, is there anything else I should know? Perhaps your parents left you an estate?" she asked with a beautiful smile. "If so, I could help you find the best investments for any money you might have inherited."

"No, there was nothing," I told her, thinking of Aida's record player, the nearly empty bottle of Chanel Number 5 and an old, scratched Cartier watch Lane had given her back at Lion Court. "Nothing of value really."

Of course, that wasn't really true.

If Tiernan was right, Dad had actually left Brando and me an inheritance hidden away somewhere. It burned in me that Tiernan had the key, but my priority was getting Brandon back and not a key to some unknown, improbable treasure.

"Your father wasn't a wealthy man?"

"What? Oh." I shook my head and laughed a little. "No, he wasn't."

"What did he do for work?" she asked politely.

I shrugged. "He kind of cycled from job to

job."

In truth, Lane's company had so many holdings and interests, it was impossible to list just
one. At the end of his life, he'd been passionate
about green energy. He was the one who took me
on tours of the Texan countryside from oil rigs to
wind farms, showing me how one destroyed and
the other harnessed. It was a passion he'd sowed
in me.

"Was he Italian?" Caroline asked as she placed
her cutlery neatly on her place and lifted a hand.
A second later, a servant scurried forward to whisk
the dirty dish way and another stepped forward to
refill her wine glass.

"I'm not sure what he was."

"Hmm, well, that is a shame. It's good to
know where one comes from."

"Where do you come from?" I asked, genuinely curious. "You married a Constantine, right?
Who were you before that?"

My questions rang through the air between us
like a discordant note. Caroline seemed oddly
disturbed by my question if her stillness was
anything to go off on.

Finally, her lips pursed and she took up drawing rings around the rim of her wineglass again.
The haunting noise was the only sound in the

massive formal dining room.

"No one, really," she murmured so softly, I thought I might have imagined it. Then, with conviction, "I was a Roosevelt. A woman from a prestigious family. You should be grateful I found you, Bianca. I can afford you opportunities you never could have dreamt of."

I didn't tell her the only thing I dreamt of was a safe, happy home for Brandon and the surgery that might stop his epileptic seizures for good. Honestly, I didn't think she would understand the simplicity of it.

"I'm so curious about the family," I ventured with my heart in my throat. I was entering dangerous territory pressing about this, but I was curious enough to kill the cat. "How did you and Lane meet?"

A startled laugh burst from her lips before she clamped them shut and covered her perfectly painted mouth with her hand. "It's a silly story, really."

"I'd like to hear it."

She looked over my shoulder at the past, a soft smile just curving the edge of her lips. "It was in college. I knew I'd have to marry well. That was the role of a society woman in those days. A degree was unnecessary, but I insisted. My parents allowed it only because they knew I would probably meet someone rich and well-connected at an Ivy League school." She tapped her long-manicured nails against the wine glass, peering inside as if it was a crystal ball illuminated with scenes from the past. "It was an entirely new world. New ideas. New people."

"People like Lane." I hung on to every world, feeling momentary shame for supporting their love story when my own mother had loved Lane as much as she'd every loved anything. It felt disloyal, but I also couldn't shake my lifelong infatuation with dad's 'real' family, and my desperation to know more.

Her smile was anemic, a sad curve. "He was the golden boy on campus. Good looks. Good family. He made good grades without effort. He was the life of every party. I was swept away by his interest in me. Flattered by it."

I couldn't help the smile tugging at my lips, thinking of my dad—younger than I remembered him, but just as vibrant, just as strong. He'd had the kind of palpable magnetism that drew people to him in droves. "How did you meet him? Was it love at first sight?"

"Not exactly." She spoke slowly, the words spilling like molasses to the table. I had the sense she didn't usually share insight about her life and I wondered why. "He was a friend of a friend. They were best friends, actually. No one could imagine it now, but I was there. He and Bryant were inseparable."

"Oh my God," I said, as the rivalry between Dad and Bryant came into vivid focus. It made a twisted kind of sense that such a fierce hatred had once started as friendship.

"Love," I said, shocked. I expected that they fought over power or money. The same things they fought over as middle-aged men. I had no idea what love had to do with it. Unless Caroline had gotten between them? It wouldn't be the first time a woman had come between two friends.

She shrugged slightly, looking young and vulnerable for all of one second before she straightened her shoulders and pinned me with a cooling look. "We all make our choices, Bianca. I made mine. And Lane made his."

Internally, I winced. It was such a strange sensation to know my mother had come between the pages of their story. That I was a product of Lane's lies and Caroline's unknown humiliation. If anything, it made me feel tender toward her, as if I owed her my love because my dad had taken his from her.

"Thank you for sharing that with me," I told her, honestly, moved by her words.

"You never told me that, Mother."

We both turned with startled gasps to view the man who had quietly entered the dining room, half obscured in the shadow of an old grandfather clock. I knew who it was when he stepped out into the light though.

There was no mistaking Winston Constantine.

He was in magazines and newspapers, the most famous of the family because he was the head of their company, Halcyon.

The thick blonde hair pushed back from a square forehead, the same cold blue eyes as his mother, a few shades lighter than Lane's. Lighter than mine. In what was no doubt a bespoke suit that fit his tapered frame immaculately, a diamond bright watch on his wrist, Winston was every inch a Bishop's Landing blue blood. He looked more like Caroline than Lane, but I could see our shared father in the shape of his eyes and mouth.

And here he was in the same room as me after all these years.

My breath left my body and my lungs closed up shop.

"Winston," Caroline said calmly, though there was a slight flush in her cheeks that spoke of her embarrassment. I sensed she wasn't usually a very sentimental woman. "What brings you around at dinner time without an invitation?"

It seemed a little formal that her son would need an invitation to dinner, but Winston was unfazed by the question. He sauntered forward as if he owned not only this space, but time itself, as if physics and boundaries had no bearing on his greatness.

"I came to discuss something important with you." He spoke to her, but his eyes were on me. Clearly, he'd inherited that same implacable expression from his mother. "Get rid of the girl and meet me in the office."

"Winston," she said before he could turn on his heel and leave. "I'd like you to meet a dear friend of the family, Bianca." Winston turned to face again, but it wasn't until his mother said, "Bianca Belcante," that his gaze narrowed.

"I'm short on time here," he said flippantly, but he studied me with shrewd eyes before stalking out of the room.

Well.

So.

My first-time meeting one of my half-siblings

wasn't exactly a Hallmark commercial.

Expecting some tender moment was silly and naïve of me, yet I couldn't shake the trickle of disappointment that slid down my spine and made me shiver.

Caroline dismissed me perfunctorily after that, dabbing her mouth with a napkin that probably cost more than some of my coats before she slid out of her seat and down the hallway to her office.

I sat there at the table in the massive room feeling the silence close in on me. Life with Brandon was rarely peaceful and I missed his constant babble, the hum of energy a seven-year-old boy was capable of producing. I resolved to call Lion Court again, hoping Walcott or Henrik might pick up and take mercy on me by letting me speak with him.

My bare feet were quiet on the plush carpet as I entered the hallway and moved toward the grand staircase up to my room. The path didn't take my by Caroline's office, but curiosity compelled me toward the closed door.

I didn't trust anyone anymore.

Not after Dad left us with nothing.

Not after Tiernan tried to use us for his own wicked plots.

So there was no way in hell I was going to blindly trust Caroline, even though once, a long time ago, my dad had. Clearly, he'd lost trust in her too if he'd strayed and fallen in love with Aida.

I stopped a foot away from the door and leaned closer so they wouldn't be able to see my shadow beneath the doorframe if they thought to look for it.

"—This is why it's important you are nice to the girl, Winston." Caroline's voice was muffled through the door so I had to strain to make it out. "You would have known how to comport yourself if you listened to my message."

"I was caught up."

"With work, I hope."

"With Ash, if you must know," Winston retorted sharply. "And I don't have to be anything to your charity case. As far as I'm concerned, this is your mess and I'm holding you responsible for cleaning it up."

The strike of hard footsteps echoed through the door and I scampered away with my heart beating in my throat, almost choking me.

Was he referring to me when he spoke of Caroline's mess?

Why would she feel compelled to take me in?

It certainly couldn't be because she knew I was Lane's illegitimate child. I didn't think even a saint would want to raise their deceased husband's bastard and Caroline didn't strike me as the forgiving type.

So why?

A ripple of unease moved through me as I hurried up the stairs.

It seemed I'd jumped from the pot into the fire and I had no idea how to escape the flames.

Chapter Four

Bianca

M Y BEDROOM AT the Compound wasn't unlike the one at Lion Court. It was wallpapered in a pale gold with scrolling embellishment, the bed an ornate affair with a blue quilted headboard and silk curtains tied off at each of the four posts. The bedroom of a princess, not the pauper I'd been most of my life.

I didn't like it.

In fact, I didn't like the Constantine Compound much at all. It was too well-groomed, too clean and perfectly decorated. I preferred the creative, atmospheric chaos of Tiernan's gothic mansion to the austere perfection of Caroline's wedding cake topper of a home.

It was cold when I opened the door to the room after dinner and stepped into the dark interior. I didn't remember leaving the French doors open to the Juliette balcony, but I walked over to them, grateful for the cold, bracing air over my flushed skin. I wasn't used to feeling so ill-at-ease, so worried about miss-stepping. There was something about Caroline that demanded adherence to her rules, but I felt as though I hadn't been given a list.

A headache started to throb between my temples as I sank onto the edge of my bed. I flipped on the Tiffany lamp on the bedside table so the room was filled with a gentle golden glow before I flopped back against the thick duvet.

"What did you expect?" I asked the canopy over the bed, as if it held the answers. "Real life isn't a fairy tale. These people don't owe me anything and if they knew the truth…"

"If they knew the truth, Bianca," a familiar low and cultured voice purred from somewhere in the room. "You'd be dead."

I jumped up from the bed, searching the dark corners of the room for his presence. My heart beat so loudly I was horrified I wouldn't hear him sneak up on me. I tried to hold my breath as if that would help.

Still, I couldn't see him.

For a brief moment of terror, I wondered if I was going insane. If I couldn't purge myself of

Tiernan Morelli's presence even though he deserved never to be thought of again.

But then something strong and cool wrapped around my ankle from under the tall bed and yanked my foot out from under me. I fell to the ground with a garbled cry that no one would hear in the colossal, mostly empty home. My back hit the plush Persian carpet with a *thud* that sent the breath catapulting from my body.

Before I could orient myself, he was on me.

Crawling from beneath the bed like some nightmarish monster in the night, Tiernan pressed the entire length of his body to mine, hands manacling my wrists and pressing them up above my head. I was too shocked to put up much resistance and by the time it occurred to me to struggle, I was caught irrevocably in the cage of his body.

And then, for a small moment, I forgot everything but the feel of his heavy form crushing mine to the ground and the way that ignited something in my core. The scent of him in my nose, masculine and heady, and the sight of his face, scarred yet so handsome it took my breath away in a different way than my shock had before it.

If I craned my head up just a little, I could lick that ropy scar just as I had only days ago.

It was shocking how much could change in a single week and how fast nostalgia could grow.

"Hello little thing," he whispered with dark satisfaction as he stared down into my face. "I thought it was time we had a talk."

"I called the house a thousand times to talk to Brando, you could have spoken to me then! *This* doesn't feel like talking," I snapped, writhing against him in an effort to buck his weight off me, but Tiernan was two hundred plus pounds of finely-honed bulk. He wasn't going anywhere unless he wanted to.

His thick brows cut into his forehead as he pressed his groin harder into mine, pinning me still at the same time making me feel his half-hard bulge. "If you want to skip the talking, I can be convinced."

"Get off me and get out," I demanded, leveraging my chin in the air so it almost collided with his. "I don't want to talk to you now or ever again."

"And what of Brando? You'll have to talk to me if you want to see your brother again."

Air leaked out of my mouth like a puncture wound as the reality of his power over me settled in. "Would you really use my brother against me like that? That's low, even for you."

GIANA DARLING

"Even for me," he murmured, as if testing out the taste of my hatred on his tongue. "Who do you think I am, Bianca?"

"A fucking *monster*," I growled, rearing up to snap at him. "A lying, manipulative *bastard*."

He stiffened at my words, something dark crossing his features before he could control them into impassivity again.

"Because I didn't tell you who I was?"

"Because you lied to me every single day I lived under your roof. Because you played dangerous games with not only my life, but Brandon's! How could you ever think that was forgivable?"

He stared at me calmly, absorbing my features like an artist trying to render every detail. "Did you not play games, too? When you decided to come to Bishop's Landing, the home of your father's people, and not tell me, the guardian who was appointed to protect you, that you were the daughter of Lane Constantine?"

"I couldn't trust you with that and you proved me right," I spat, trying to wrench out from him again. "Get off me, now, or I'll scream."

"Scream," he invited on a slow drawl. "Draw Caroline and Winston Constantine up here. Let them see how...*close* we are. Explain to them how

56

close you are to them, in ways they never even dreamed of."

"Stop it," I hissed, but my anger was waning into hopelessness. Why was it that I never had the power? How could little old me stand up to these behemoths? These men and women who hadn't taken 'no' for an answer in so long that the word was a foreign language to them now. "I was doing what I thought was best."

"So was I," he countered, dipping to speak the words against the corner of my mouth. "I was wrong then, but I thought I was doing what was right."

I froze, confused and terrified by his admittance. I didn't know what to do with his regret.

I couldn't handle it.

"Don't." I turned my head hard away from that warm mouth on my skin and closed my eyes. "Don't you dare."

"You're wrong now," he continued as if we were having a pleasant conversation sitting side by side at a café and not on the ground of his enemy's home. "Give me a chance to prove it just like you did. Come home with me to Brando and The Gentlemen, sweet little thing. That's where you belong."

"I belong with Brandon," I admitted. "But

not you. Maybe…maybe I wanted that for a minute, but I know better now. All you've ever been is cruel."

"It's all I've known in a very long time," he rasped as he drew his nose along my jawline and pressed a tender kiss to sensitive skin beneath my ear. "Come home and teach me how to be kind."

"It's too late for that," I said, but the words lacked punch.

I was softening, not with acceptance or forgiveness but with pain. Like a bruise. My whole body ached at his sudden sweetness, with the desire to teach him grace like he had taught me violence.

But I wasn't a fool.

I was young and I knew nothing about this twisted, dark world of riches, but I knew enough not to get burned twice.

"If you want to be kind, you'll let Brandon come here with me," I told him.

Whatever gentleness he'd shown me evaporated with my words. He grew hard against me, pressing me almost painfully into the floor. I watched as his features tightened, lips peeling over strong, white teeth into a wolfish sneer.

It shouldn't have aroused me.

That edge of pain and fear, that meanness

shining through.

But I shivered and he felt it, his lids lowering with heavy arousal.

He transferred both my wrists into one punishing grip and used his free hand to tug my hair back sharply. His lips found my hammering pulse point and sucked it into his mouth.

"You can lie to yourself as much as you want, Bianca, but this body became my body the day I took you on the beach and it cannot lie to me. You want me, even if you hate me."

"I'm not controlled by my urges like an animal," I protested, holding still because I could feel his hard shaft against my belly and I didn't want to incite him any further with needless friction. "Do the right thing for once in your life and relinquish guardianship of Brando and me."

"Never," he growled, nipping at my jaw. "You both belong to me."

"Stop being a possessive heathen," I cried out. "Human beings don't belong to anyone."

"They do," he countered, moving his hand from my hair to my throat, collaring it gently so I was immobilised, my eyes forced to focus on his somber, devastatingly beautiful face. "Ezra, Henrik, Walcott and me belong to each other. Children should belong to their parents, but sometimes, in cases like ours, they don't. Wives with their husbands and husbands with their wives. Brando and you. Brando and me." He feathered his lips around my mouth so I was forced to taste his next words. "You and me, Bianca. We belong to each other, it just took me a minute to understand it. Now I do, I won't let you go for anything."

"I don't want to be possessed," I argued, but oh my heart was on fire.

Because this was what I'd wanted all my life.

What I'd yearned for.

Not money or fame.

Not world peace or an end to famine.

I wanted, selfishly and fundamentally, to be loved this way.

Bought and owned with no return policy.

To feel as if I'd never be left behind or lost again.

"It's too late for that," he said simply, his mouth descending to mine. "It's too late for both of us."

And then, he kissed me.

He kissed me in a way that had tears springing to my eyes in an instant.

Those lush lips parted my own and his tongue slid inside to claim my mouth on a low growl of male satisfaction that rumbled up his throat and over my tongue. The hand not capturing my own framed the entire side of my face. It made me feel small in a cherished way, like he could shield my entire heart with a single large palm. His thumb edged the corner of our fused mouths, dipping inside to wet the pad. Done, he traced that wet digit down my throat into the collar of my shift dress and unerringly found my hard nipple, flicking it then pinching it.

Fire arched through me, my chest pressing up into his.

"This," he rasped as we broke for breath. "The way we fit together, feel together, it's not normal. This madness I have for you," he shook his head as if he could clear it of me. "It's in my blood."

I panted heavily, squirming. Only, I didn't know if I was trying to get away or get closer.

"I know it's not normal. It's *wrong*," I said, hoping to hurt him into stopping.

Instead, his chuckle was husky against my closed lips. "Maybe. Nothing about this makes sense except for the fact that I feel like I'm on fucking fire when I'm near you. Like nothing but the wet of your kiss and the wet between your thighs can put it out. Like the wet of your tears when you cry so damn pretty for me."

He licked a tear that had rolled down my cheek and then forced me to taste it, prying my lips open with his own.

"Tell me aren't on fire for me, too," he demanded arrogantly.

And fuck him.

Fuck him for playing me like a maestro, plucking sensations from my body that muddled my brain. Fuck him for playing with *my life* and the life of my brother as if there was nothing at stake.

Fuck him for being *right*.

"You make me cold," I told him firmly, staring into that peridot green gaze that made my heart flutter. "I feel nothing for you but hatred and you bought that, Tiernan."

He glared down at me for a long moment, only the sound of our harsh breath and my own pulse in my ears loud in the cold room.

And then he leaned close enough that we were breathing the same air and the intimacy nearly killed me. As if that wasn't enough, he lapped at my lower lip softly then tugged it lightly between his teeth.

"Then, I'll buy back your admiration," he said, the words so heavy with solemn, unflinching intention that I felt each like a physical blow.

"Impossible," I breathed.

"You underestimate me, little thing," he murmured against my cheek. "I am a wealthy man."

"You can't literally buy me back," I argued, hating the idea that he could think I was like Aida, obsessed with beauty and wealthy. "I'm not that kind of girl."

"No," he agreed, leaning back from me so I could see the full impact of his beautiful, broken face. "I'll buy you back, Bianca, with patience. I'll buy you back with kindness. I'll do it with paintings I know will bring tears to your eyes and I'll do it by putting those damned solar panels on Lion Court. I'll do it by giving you space to make your own decision to come home even though I want to drag you back there by your hair. I'll do it with orgasms that rip you apart at the seams and after, when you're boneless and floating, I'll hold you. Anchor you in a way you know I won't let you go."

"Stop," I choked out, panic roaring through me in wild surges.

I started to thrash against him, so hard I clocked him in the mouth with my chin. He started to bleed, but he didn't let loosen his hold.

"I won't let you go," he repeated almost viciously as he held me like Peleus wrestling the ever-changing form of Thetis, determined to win me and keep me forever. "I won't. Now I own you, I won't ever give you up."

"I don't want you," I cried out, but there were more tears on my face and a keen edge of desperation in my tone that shook my conviction. "I'm not just a thing you can own."

"Such a liar. You are *my* little thing," he reprimanded, darkness crossing his face as he pressed his groin harder into my hips, pushing my legs farther apart so he could cant his erection against my panty-covered sex. "Should I show you how badly you lie?"

"No." I squeezed my eyes shut and turned my face from him.

A part of me wanted it, a large part. For Tiernan to *take* from me. For him to press me open and pull me apart with the hard drive of his thick cock and the punishing hold of those strong fingers all over my flesh.

But another part was terrified. I didn't have anything more to give to anyone, but Brandon. How could I trust anyone after a lifetime of being taken *from*?

I expected him to kiss me then. To take me with the same ruthless savagery he'd taken me on the beach.

Instead, he licked the path of a tear from the edge of my jaw up my cheek before planting a soft kiss at the corner of my closed eye. He smoothed my hair back with a big palm and I could feel his gaze hot on my face.

I didn't dare open my eyes to see his expression.

I knew, whatever it was, I couldn't bear it.

This was the side of Tiernan that eviscerated me. Those small glimpses of a warm heart and kind spirit that razed my resolve to the ground.

So, I lay still and sightless as Tiernan kissed me again. Hot, open-mouthed kisses down my cheek to my neck and chest. Each press of his lips to my body melted my resolve. Atom by atom I sank into the floor, into him, pliant and hungry in a different way than I had ever been before.

This wasn't a flash fire. A burst of lust so intense it burned fast and clean.

This was a slow burn.

A seduction.

And I was helpless against the heat.

"I've barely touched you," he murmured into the hollow of my throat as one hand swept down my side and rucked up the hem of my dress. "But when I put my fingers in your pussy, I bet you'll drench them."

I tried to clench my thighs together, but the bulk of his hips obstructed me. He tsked when his fingers slid over my inner thigh and rubbed over the placket of my underwear.

"Oh yeah," he growled. "You're leaking through the lace."

My face flamed with embarrassment and something dark, headier.

Need.

He stroked me over the fabric, the rough lace abrading my needy clit until a low, keening whine left my throat. He laughed at me.

"So needy," he taunted. "So fucking desperate for me even when you can't say the words."

I swallowed the ones that rose to my tongue. He didn't deserve the validation. He didn't deserve *me*, but I couldn't deny that I wanted this. His fingers, tongue, and teeth on me made so much more sense than anything else.

This could be goodbye, I reasoned.

This could be the end.

So, I gave myself permission to enjoy it—enjoy him—one last time.

"Tell me you want me, Bianca," he demanded coolly as he swirled his thumb maddening over my aching clit. "Tell me you want me to fill you up and remind you who owns you."

"You don't own me," I protested, but I was panting and arching into his hand.

"I do," he argued, eyes flashing. "I own every goddamn inch of you."

And then his mouth was on mine, still bleeding. The rich, iron tang of him panged on my taste buds and ignited a primal kind of hunger in my belly. Wet pooled fast between my thighs, leaking over his fingers like an overturned jar of honey. He growled into my mouth, curled his grip into the panties and ripped them savagely from my sex. Cool air wafted over my heated skin for a split second before his palm was covering me, clit to ass. He cupped me possessively then gave my pussy one, two, *three* short, hard slaps.

My groan burst out between our open mouths.

"Yeah," he grunted, slapping my sticky sex again and again. "You need to be reminded who owns this cunt. Tell me, little thing, tell me who owns this pretty, leaking pussy."

"Fuck," I hissed, pleasure ricocheting through me with every little slap. I never could have guessed how it would feel for him to beat my folds like that. It was pain-tinged pleasure like nothing I'd ever known. "Fuck, Tiernan."

"Yeah, I'll fuck you," he promised. "But I want you to beg me for it."

"No," I groaned, my legs shaking with the effort to hold still as his slippery fingers found my clit and pinched hard.

"Do it," he hissed, plunging three fingers inside me. The stretch and burn singed through me. "Convince me you want me even half as fucking much as I want you."

The combination of his pain-edged pleasure and the rough-sweet demands made my head spin. I didn't know what was up or down, but I could feel Tiernan anchoring me to him, tethering me to the ground, and it gave me the security I needed to shed the last of my inhibitions and doubts.

At least for the moment.

"Do it," I mocked him, eyes flashing up to lock with his glowing green gaze. "Fuck me into the carpet. Split me open and fill me up. Make me forget everything."

"Everything, but me," he growled victorious-ly. "Take my cock out."

My fingers trembled as I obeyed. The click of the belt opening and the metallic rasp of the zipper then my soft gasp married to his dark rumble as my fingers found him naked beneath the trousers. He was so hot he nearly seared the delicate skin of my palms and my fingers strained to hold his girth.

"The thought of this pressing me open…" I whispered, head raised to peer between our bodies at his dick in my grasp. "I feel like I could come just from the first slide of you inside me."

"Challenge accepted."

Done with talk and play, Tiernan batted away my hand and gripped himself tightly before slotting his head at my center.

"So wet," he muttered almost to himself. "So *mine*."

I opened my mouth to protest maybe, or agree, but it was lost to a spine shuddering groan when he wedged his cock inside me in one smooth, slow thrust. At the same time, he bent his head to close his mouth around the side of my neck and suck hard, the twin pain of his bite and thrust cleaving the taut line of my building climax cleaning in two.

I broke apart.

Gasping.

Shuddering.

Almost panicking because it felt as though I'd lose myself to the sensation.

But through it all, Tiernan said, "Good girl.

Good fucking girl taking my cock like that. Coming for me so fucking pretty."

Through it all he was on me, holding me tightly, almost punishingly against his hard body.

In the same moment by the same man, I was both destroyed and reassembled.

Emotion chased the heels of my orgasm, surging through the empty cavities inside me ravaged by pleasure. My chest was too tight, swollen with feelings I didn't understand. I hated this man, this monster who tried to use me for his own gains, who thought two orphan children were tools instead of bleeding hearts.

I hated his cruelty and his selfishness and his inability to self-heal.

Yet.

I thirsted for his body on mine almost feverishly. Even after having orgasmed so strongly, I was already desperate for more. I wanted him to bend me, break me. I wanted to be fucked and swollen and always leaking his cum. I wanted him to mark me up, order me around, taunt me then praise me for all the ways he could make me sin.

It wasn't just physical either.

I longed for his moments of sweetness, so much purer contrasted to his usual bitter brutality. I wanted to heal the wounds that had clearly sat festering so long untended in his soul and teach him how to love again.

Even that cruelty I half-hated, I also loved, even esteemed. To be so strong-willed, so filled with ruthless conviction was admirable and sexy as hell. His attention and praise meant even more because it came from such a brooding, undemonstrative man.

"Stay with me, Bianca," he ordered, changing the angle of his thrusts so my wet clit brushed against the crisp hair on his pubic bone, sparking pleasure so intense I shivered. "Watch me."

I didn't want to and he knew it. It hurt to look up into his gorgeous face and wonder what I meant to him.

He didn't care.

"Watch me fuck you," he rasped, damp mouth open for his panting breath. "Watch me take what's mine."

I couldn't argue with him. Not when tears dripped down my cheeks into my ears and his tongue lapped them up so sweetly. Not when his cock was making a permanent impression inside me, creating an ache I knew would never abate. Not when a small part of me dreaded him leaving me again even though I wasn't sure I wanted him to stay.

"I'm going to come inside this sweet, tight cunt," he growled, the words vibrating against my neck as he sucked kisses into the tender skin. "So you feel me leaking down your thighs long after I'm gone."

My pussy spasmed around him at the thought and he laughed darkly, triumphantly. Taking my chin in his hand, he pressed a savage kiss to my lips then sneered down at me.

"No," he decided, slipping out of me so quickly, I couldn't control the whimper that left my lips.

I watched, mouth open and panting as he crawled farther up my body and straddled my torso just under my breasts. He lowered each thin strap from my shoulders then tugged down the dress, exposing my chest and upper belly to his hot gaze.

"Hold your tits together for me, little thing," he purred as he fisted that deep red cock in one hand. "Use one arm. Touch your greedy pussy with the other. You're going to come when I shoot all over your chest and pretty, tear-stained face."

A low groan wrenched out of me at the utter filth he'd voiced. Before I could consciously decide to obey, my arms were moving, one banded under my breasts to prop them up for him, and the other arrowing through the gap between his thigh and my waist to find my wet, swollen folds. My touch was delicate over my clit because I was already close to climaxing again from his words alone.

Then, he bent forward to wrap his free hand around my throat, a gentle pressure as he braced himself against me so he could set a vicious pace jerking his big cock over my chest.

He was so turned on he was leaking, precum splattering against my skin like wet pearls. His face was screwed up into an intense expression of almost painful desire and I thought he was the most beautiful thing—human, artform, collection of atoms—in the entire world.

And I couldn't hold it back.

The orgasm crashed over me, into me, and submerged me utterly in churning sensation. My vision went black, my breath vanished and I hung suspended in the tsunami of pleasure Tiernan gave to me.

"Watch me," he grunted, his hand tightening on my throat so for one crystal clear moment, I couldn't breathe. "Watch me remind you who you belong to."

I did. Sight blurry, heart pounding so hard I

honestly thought I might pass out, I watched Tiernan Morelli jack himself until he erupted on a masculine growl I felt in my still-spasming sex. He painted in me in cum, my breasts glistening in the low lamp light. A few drops caught my tongue and I realized I'd opened my mouth for him without recognizing it.

He tasted good.

Salty and masculine, like fresh ocean brine.

His eyes were dark as loosened his grip on his shaft and began to rub his seed into my skin. I watched him, mesmerized by those long, tanned fingers and the tattooed rose and cherub on either hand. The way he touched me…it was reverent. Still possessive, still almost heathen, but also *awed*.

When I looked up at his face again, he was staring at me with those eyes like sun-bleached jade under furrowed brows. A charge passed through us both and we shivered, but it had nothing to do with cold air streaming in from the open doors.

Unformed emotions crowded the back of my tongue, but I couldn't find a way to speak them and I sensed the same frustration in Tiernan as he bent closer, almost as if he was searching for the words in my gaze.

A sharp series of knocks cut through the thick silence.

I froze.

"Bianca?" Caroline's voice was clear through the door. "May I come in?"

Thank *God* for her sense of propriety.

"One second, I'm just getting changed!" I yelled, trying to keep the panic from my voice as I shoved Tiernan off of me with both hands.

He chuckled softly, rolling off me to lounge on the carpet propped up on one arm. I was aware of his eyes on me as I did a circle while adjusting my dress, my brain short-circuiting.

"Bianca," he whispered, eyes dancing.

"Get up!" I hissed. "Get out!"

Another soft, almost soundless laugh. He looked so at ease, more so than I'd ever seen him. His smile was crooked, cramped on one side by his scar and it made him look almost dashing. Combined with that humor-filled, tender gaze, even mid-panic, I was arrested by him.

His grin expanded at my reaction. Eyes locked to me, he slowly got to his feet and tucked himself back into his trouser before closing the gap between us. I didn't know what he was going to do, but I was not expecting him to *hug* me.

Only a flimsy door was separating us from his

enemy, from absolute ruin, and he was hugging me.

It wasn't a gentle hug, either. He engulfed me in his long, strong arms, hips flush to mine, back curved like a shield as he bent around my shorter frame. Only when I was tucked intimately against him did he breathe deeply and exhale with relish, the air stirring my hair.

"Um, Tiernan?" I whispered, torn because I loved this moment but I could absolutely not ignore Caroline fifteen feet away. "Why are you being so calm? You need to get out, now! Or hide, at the very least."

"You're the only thing that makes me feel this way," he muttered, a little surprised by his own words. His embrace tightened. "At peace."

"That's the orgasm talking. You need to get out now. Please, Tiernan," I begged, pulling away to shove him toward the French doors. "However you got in, get *out*."

"Promise to go out with me this weekend," he demanded, walking over to the doors leisurely before tossing the words back over his shoulder. "I want a Christmas Eve date."

"Absolutely not."

He arched a brow and leaned against the doorjamb as if he had all the time in the world.

"This was goodbye," I whispered. "I don't forgive you for what you did, especially when you're keeping Brando from me."

A fake yawn seized his face. He covered it with one hand then idly checked his watch.

Another knock at the door.

"Bianca, I do not have all night to linger in the hallway," Caroline called, irritation clear in her tone.

Fuck.

"Okay, *fine*, asshole. I'll go out with you to-morrow, now get out."

"Bianca? I'm coming in," Caroline called.

"No, wait, I'm coming," I yelled back, but I could already hear the *click* of the latch unlocking.

My heart fell into my stomach as I waited for shit to hit the fan.

CHAPTER FIVE

Bianca

TIERNAN'S CUM STILL damp on my chest, I grabbed the robe on the end of my bed and tugged it on, the silk fabric sticking to the dampness. My hair was a mess, even after running my fingers through it, and my mouth was swollen, noticeably red-bitten.

It would be obvious to anyone that I'd just been fucked into the ground.

I just had to hope that Caroline would never suspect I'd sneak a boy in my room when I was a guest in her house. The reality—that Tiernan had broken into the Constantine Compound to hide under my bed and accost me—was far too outlandish for anyone to believe.

Even me, and I'd been there.

I flew to the door, pressing it closed when she tried to open it. Then, I whipped around to check on Tiernan, but he was nowhere in sight. I prayed he'd hidden well or somehow left however he'd once entered.

Taking a deep breath, I pulled open the door.

Surprisingly, Elias was there beside Caroline, his eyebrows cutting into his forehead as he took in my appearance.

Caroline merely frowned. "Bianca, go back inside and make yourself presentable before I allow Elias to enter your room."

Elias laughed, pushing by his aunt in a way I would never have dared to. He knocked me gently in the shoulder as he moved by and then jumped on my bed, crossing his hands behind his head and his legs at the ankles.

"Comfy," he declared.

"Get off the bed, Elias, and try to behave yourself, for once."

"Aye, aye, ma'am," he quipped.

I struggled to hide my smile, but Caroline was too busy casting him a disparaging look to notice anyway.

"It's freezing in here," she declared suddenly, eyeing the open doors to the patio for a moment before she moved into the room.

My heart leapt into my throat.

"No, Caroline, honestly, don't worry, I'm

hot!" The words tumbled out of my mouth, but she was already across the room, pushing the gently flapping curtains aside.

She peeked out onto the balcony and my heart stopped.

Had Tiernan got down in time or was he pressed against the wall out there? Would she spot him sprinting across the grounds like a cat burglar who had robbed my virtue?

But no, she was already pulling the doors closed and adjusting the curtains.

A sigh leaked out the side of my mouth and every muscle in my body relaxed at once.

"You'll send a draft through the entire house, Bianca," she chastised me, knocking Elias's shoes off my bed with swat as she walked back to the door. "I expect this to remain open at all times and if my nephew tries anything untoward, please call for help."

She paused on her way out then shot Elias a cool glance. "Though, I very much doubt you're his type. Curfew is ten pm, be gone before then."

With a swish of smooth blonde hair, she was gone, the clack of her designer heels fading down the hall.

I blinked after her, still discombobulated from the craziness of the last hour.

Elias's husky chuckle was the only thing that finally jerked me out of my haze. I turned to face him to see him holding up my torn underwear on the edge of one shoe. His brows were raised, eyes wide as he laughed.

"I never would have taken you for the kind of girl to rip off her own underwear," he teased.

Heat poured through me, setting my skin on fire. "I didn't."

I stalked over and snatched the incriminating scrap of lace from him before shoving it in my pocket. He was still laughing, a tear forming in his eye that he dabbed away.

"Shut up, Elias," I ordered, but his humor was catching and I found myself shaking my head as I chuckled. "Okay, okay, it's funny."

"It's *hilarious*," he declared. "I wish Caroline had seen them."

"Um, no."

He laughed at me again before laying back on my bed and tapping the spot beside him. "Oh relax, Bianca, she didn't. I'm just saying, it would do her some good to realize women can be lovers not just fighters, you know?"

"No, and I don't think I want to talk about Caroline's sex life." I shivered. "Or mine, for that matter."

"Ah, so you had a guy in your room?" he asked, and a caught an edge of something in his tone. Something hard and bright.

I tucked my hair behind my ears and got onto the bed with him even though I didn't relax back against the array of oyster silk pillows.

"Maybe," I said hesitantly. "What would you say if I had?"

Elias studied my face for a long moment before sighing and looking up at the canopy. "I don't know. Lucky bastard, I guess." He glanced at me. "It is a boy, yeah?"

I nodded, though 'boy' didn't exactly suit the thirty-year-old shady billionaire that was Tiernan Morelli.

"You shouldn't assume," he said in explanation.

"Do you like...boys?" I asked, because I'd wondered sometimes if he was gay, if that might be why Caroline had such a problem with him.

"Sure," he agreed with a flippant shrug. "I like girls too."

"Oh." That made sense, it was only that Elias was so at ease with it that shocked me for a moment. He was a seventeen-year-old guy in a fairly traditional family. "That's cool."

He peered at me from under a lock of blond

hair that fell into his eyes. It was obvious some of his coolness was an act, because he seemed relieved by my nonchalance. "Well, that's a better reaction than it's garnered before."

I shrugged. "I don't hate people for who they love."

Besides, who was I to judge?

I'd just had rough sex with my family's arch nemesis under their very roof.

I had no moral high ground to stand on, especially when the rug burns on my ass still stung as a pleasant reminder of my sins.

"That's a nice sentiment," he said, bitterness creeping into his tone.

I sighed, reaching out to squeeze his shin. "Truly, Elias. You've been nothing but a friend to me. Why would that change now?"

His eyes shone with moisture, round and vibrant blue like marbles. "You're a good person, you know that? Everyone in the damn family pretends to be good, but they're not. Not when it counts. You know what Caroline said when her watchdog Ronan found me fucking a man and woman together one day? That if I didn't break it off with them, if I didn't toe the line and end up marrying a respectable woman one day, I'd be disinherited and erased from the family."

"That's awful," I murmured, taking his hand in both of my mine as if I could heal his emotional wounds with only a touch. "I'm so sorry, Eli, no one deserves that, but especially not you. You're a good man and a good friend. I don't know what I would have done if I hadn't met you my first day at Sacred Heart."

His stare was filled with tortured, vibrating energy as he chewed over my words. Then, he leaned forward suddenly, smoothly dipping into my space and cupping my cheek. I was so startled by the movement, I didn't hesitate when he pressed a soft, chaste kiss to my lips.

Oh my God.

Elias was my *cousin*.

I tore away from him and jumped off the bed, my trembling fingers over my lips. "You can't do that!"

Two stripes of red decorated his cheeks, an embarrassed flush he couldn't hide even though he tried to hide the shame from his voice. "If you aren't attracted to me, you only have to say so."

"It's not that," I bumbled, pushing my hair way from my face as I let out a shaky sigh. "I mean, it kind of *is*, but it doesn't even matter because we can't be kissing."

A wicked grin edged the corner of his mouth.

"Why not?"

"This isn't a game, Eli," I snapped.

"I like that nickname from you," he murmured, eyes soft as he went to his knees and face me squarely. "I like you, Bianca. Is this about me being bisexual? Fuck, everyone always thinks guys who say that are really just gay, but it isn't true and honestly, it's insulting you'd believe that."

"I like you too," I told him honestly, waring with myself.

He deserved to know why I didn't want him, but could I trust him?

I'd trusted Tiernan and look what had happened there.

But Elias was a Constantine.

Not only was he my people, he was my friend.

So, I sucked in a deep, steadying breath and whispered, "We can't kiss because we're cousins."

He blinked at me owlishly for a moment then burst out laughing, slapping his knee with one hand and holding his belly with the other.

"I'm serious," I hissed.

"Yeah, yeah," he crowed between fits of laughter. "And I'm a magical unicorn who shits fairy dust."

"Elias," I insisted, stalking forward to take his hand and jerk him forward so he was forced to brace on his other hand. Only when he was looking into my eyes did I repeated myself somberly. "We are cousins. My father was Lane Constantine."

Silence dropped like a bomb. A nuclear wave of energy rippled between us, rocking him back onto his knees his hand slipping out of my grip. The air felt pressurized, weighing on me so heavily my knees shook.

"It's true," I said through numb lips. "Lane had a decades long affair with my mom, Aida, which produced Brando and me. We used to live Upstate and we saw him all the time, then he moved us to Texas because he didn't want anyone to find out about us and use us against him."

"Shut up," Elias said, suddenly lurching forward to wrap his big palm around my mouth.

I mumbled into his skin, struggling to break away from him. Fear skittered up my spine. I'd never been scared of Elias, but suddenly he emanated the same cold, domineering energy Caroline and Winston did.

"Shut up," he repeated on a low, angry growl. "You stupid, *stupid* girl."

I stilled, blinking at him over his hand.

"Don't say one more word," he threatened before slowly removing his hand.

He glared at me for one long moment then cursed quietly as he scooted off the bed to check the hallway. Satisfied no one was lingering there, he closed the door and pressed his back to it, gaze searching the room.

"What are you doing?" I whispered, because the tense atmosphere wouldn't allow for anything else.

"Making sure no one was listening," he muttered. "But with Caroline and this lot, you can never be sure. C'mon."

He powered over to the French doors and outside into the freezing December air.

I followed slowly, my heart beating hard and hollow in my throat.

Snow was falling, muffling the sound of everything in Bishop's Landing. Lights twinkled on the houses and sprawling lots laid out at the feet of the Compound like cheaper models of the Constantine mansion. The dark sheet of ocean glittered like unpolished metal, corrugated where it met the shore.

It was beautiful, but I couldn't enjoy it with Elias practically shaking beside me. I tugged my flimsy silk robe closer around me and hugged myself.

"I can't believe you told me that," he mum-

GIANA DARLING

bled, almost to himself. "Please tell me no one else knows."

"No, I mean, no one in the family."

"But someone else knows you're Lane's daughter?"

I hesitated, Tiernan's scarred face flashing across my vision followed by The Gentlemen of Lion Court. "Yes, a few people."

"Jesus *Christ*, Bianca, how stupid are you?"

"Hey," I protested. "Stop saying that!"

"I'm sorry," he said immediately, cracking his knuckles. "I'm only saying it because I'm shocked and processing. And fucking *worried*. Jesus, Bianca, you can't stay here."

"Why not? No one knows about me and Caroline invited me here herself."

I didn't tell him it was my dream to be included into the heart of the Constantine family. That I'd played pretend as a child at imaginary tea parties with the whole family as my guests.

"That's what concerns me," he said, his tone implying I was still being stupid. "She's...she's not a good person. If she invited you here, it's for a reason. I wondered before if it was just to have control over me, but I'm not that important. Uncle Beckett didn't like it either."

"Uncle Beckett?" I asked.

"Huh? Oh, yeah, the man with Aunt Caroline at the party? He was Lane's best friend as an adult. His sister, Emelie, is my mother."

I frowned as I struggled to map out the family tree and history. Okay, so Beckett was the man in the red scarf I'd seen at Aida's funeral and he'd been best friends with my dad.

It was obvious he knew exactly who I was and how I was connected to the family.

My heart seized with horror.

"He was there," I told Elias, reaching forward unconsciously to grip his hand. "He was at my mum's funeral months ago. I never talked to him, but if he was there…"

"He knows," Elias concluded flatly, but his hand grasped mine tightly back. "Shit, Bianca."

"Maybe he didn't tell Caroline?" I asked optimistically even though there was a lead weight in my stomach that suggested otherwise.

"Maybe," Elias allowed. "They're pretty close, though, especially now that Lane is gone. There were even some rumors…"

"Rumors?"

"That they're *together*."

"Fuck." The curse escaped me on a sharp exhale as I dragged a hand through my tangled hair.

Questions raced through my mind on a continuous loop.

Why was Beckett at the funeral?

Could Caroline know that I was her dead husband's daughter?

If so, why the hell had she taken me in?

"It just doesn't seem possible that she would know," Elias decided at the same time I did. "What would she have to gain from it? If anyone found out the truth, she would be ridiculed for unwittingly taking in Lane's love child. Caroline wouldn't stand for any risk to the family reputation. If she knew…well, let's just say I'm afraid of the woman for a reason. No. I think it's more likely you are one of her 'charity cases' to make herself look good."

"Yippee," I said half-heartedly, which drew a laugh from him.

"It's better than the alternative."

"True."

"Still, this is dangerous, Bianca. I don't think you get that. Caroline is absolutely *not* someone to fuck with. She's ended people's lives in worse ways than killing them, do you understand? She will eviscerate you if she finds out the truth."

I bit my lip as I fought an inner battle. It was impossible to truly divorce myself from the lifelong dream of being a proper Constantine, especially when Caroline had been nothing but kind to me so far. But the naive girl that had first moved to Bishop's Landing was dead, stabbed in the back by Tiernan Morelli. I knew better than to blindly trust anyone, even if my dad had once loved and respected her.

I couldn't imagine Caroline would react well if people discovered the truth of my lineage, but I also couldn't help hoping that if that happened, it would be far down the line after she might have fallen in love with me for who I was instead of the circumstances of my birth.

"You have dreams in your eyes," Elias warned me. "Kill them now. I'm going to ask Mom and Dad if you can come stay with us for the rest of the year. You aren't safe here."

Warmth and tenderness bloomed in my heart for this beautiful boy who had taken me into his heart so effortless. *This* was the kind of love I'd always wanted. Uncomplicated and unconditional.

A little voice at the back of my head whispered that that was a *lie*.

The love I wanted was crooked and kinky, bent into the shape of a tall, dark, and scared man who wanted to fuck me and own me, not coddle and tend to me.

Even as I shut that line of thinking down, it spurred a new truth.

I wasn't naive anymore.

I wasn't enamoured with the wealth and glamor of this world.

I knew better.

So instead of cowering—from Tiernan, from Caroline—I would take the bull by the golden horns and make it my own.

Tiernan wanted something from me, that much I knew. To use me as the tool of Caroline's humiliation, though I wasn't sure why he harbored such animosity toward her.

And Caroline wanted something too.

Maybe it was just to better her image, a benevolent benefactor for the poor, little orphan girl.

Maybe it was more nefarious.

But I resolved right then, standing in the cold, dark night on the balcony of the Constantine Compound with the world seemingly laid at my feet, that I would find answers. My entire life had been filled with mystery and skeletons rattling around in closets. I was determined to bring them into the light once and for all, regardless of the consequences.

"I'm staying," I told Elias, clutching both his cold hands in mine and raising them between us as I stepped closer. "They invited me, Elias. I want to know why."

"You want to die?" he countered brutishly.

"Don't be so dramatic. Besides, staying here is the best shot I have of getting Brando back from Tiernan."

"Why don't you just resolve whatever the hell happened between you and go home?" he protested. "I know he's a Morelli, but you seemed…happy with him."

Home and happiness.

Yeah, for a brief moment, like a star falling through the sky, I'd felt both at Lion Court with Tiernan and his motley crew.

But like most wishes made on a shooting star, it hadn't lasted.

"I'm done with other people dictating my life," I told him, fury and resolve casing the words into bullets. "I'm almost eighteen years old and I've been through…a lot. I'm old enough and strong enough to take this on."

"Take what on?! The Morellis and the fucking Constantines? People more powerful than you have tried and failed, Bianca. What in the world makes you think you'll be the exception?" he demanded.

The smile that claimed my face was sly and triumphant, because for the first time in my life, I felt like *I* had the edge.

"Because everyone will underestimate me, they always have," I reasoned. "Only this time, I'm only going to *act* the naïve ingenue. They expect a lamb, and maybe I was before, but now, I'm going to give them a lion. While they're lulled into a false sense of security, I'll discover the truth."

Elias stared at me, eyes hard, almost inanimate, for a long moment. I flinched when he finally raised his hand to push away some of the hair on my right shoulder. He pressed his thumb into the skin of my neck, pushing into the bruise I'd forgotten Tiernan had left with his teeth and lips like a scarlet letter.

"Be careful," he whispered. "Sometimes, the truth hurts more than the lies."

"I'm tired of being clueless and taken advantage of when I don't even know why I'm being used like a pawn." I felt filled to the brim with conviction, with righteous purpose like Joan of Arc on the eve of battle. This was my fight, so why wasn't I fighting? It was about time I figured things out for myself and no one, not even Elias, was going to stop me. "I'm doing this, Elias, and I'd like your help, if you'll give it."

He squinted at me before sighing, a long ribbon of air that brushed my cheek because we were still standing too close.

"Fine," he finally said, the one word filled with resignation. "But you have to know, I'm not doing this because we're cousins. I'm doing it because we're friends. I don't want you to get hurt and if I can do something to stop that happening, I will."

His words washed over me like warm spring rain even in the cold winter night. I pulled him into a hug and held him so tightly, I could feel the bones creak in his spine.

"You know, my whole life that's all I ever wanted," I whispered as I pressed my nose into his neck. "Someone to fight for me. With me."

"Well, you've got your wish. Let's see what we can do about making some of the others come true."

CHAPTER SIX

Tiernan

IT WAS FIVE in the morning and I hadn't slept.

How could I?

Everything in my world was *wrong* like some interloper had entered my home and put everything askew.

Bianca was with Caroline.

Bryant was too quiet, licking his wounds while he no doubt planned his revenge.

And I had the key to the Constantine's ruin and the Belcante's fortune in my possession with no idea where the locked treasure even lay.

It was a peculiarly lonely exercise to watch your life fall apart and know you were responsible for the destruction.

I wasn't used to such chaos and it ravaged my insides, dredging up emotion and inner reflection, both of which I hadn't practiced in years. Since the day Grace took her own life and that of our child.

My fist hit the black bag with a solid series of thwacks that vibrated up my arm into my shoulders. I went easy with my left hand because of the wound to my shoulder, just tapping the bag with my knuckles, but I overcompensated with my right. It was a painful exercise, but it grounded me. After a lifetime of being beaten physically and emotionally, I found comfort in the ache and sting.

Ezra held the bulk for me so it didn't swing back into my body as I let loose, arms swinging in a flurry of punches that made my knuckle aches. Sweat poured off my face and naked torso in rivulets, soaking my bandage, the wraps on my hands and the waistband of my black athletic shorts, but I didn't pause even to wipe the stinging wet from my eyes.

There was a devil inside me I needed to purge before I dared pause to draw breath.

Because I'd taken Bianca just hours before, had her sweet body beneath mine, those soft, velvet blue eyes looking up at me like I was half-devil and half-deity, the taste of her in my mouth and stuck like a burr in my mind, and walking away from her had taken everything inside me. I hadn't been joking when I told her I wanted to drag her back to Lion Court by the hair.

I was dangerously close to doing just that.

Oh, I wanted to own her and control. That desire was born in me and would never die. But that was our sexual dynamic and I found I didn't want the same power discrepancy in our relationship.

I was already older, wealthier, more experienced. Legally and sexually in control of her actions. If I took away her ability to make decisions, I was no worse than Bryant. Nothing short of a tyrant.

So, I left her there in the viper's den.

It was the right decision, maybe, but it set my teeth on edge in a way I couldn't shake.

Hence the early morning session in the gym, battling my demons with my fists because my mind was too exhausted and my heart too inexperienced to make any sense of it themselves.

"So, what's the plan, boss?" Walcott asked from the matts a few yards away where he was doing his usual morning stretches. Maintaining mobility in his extensively scarred tissue was a daily battle for him that he combatted with yoga, frequent massages, and moisturizing.

"He doesn't have one," Henrik drawled as he

hulled his bulk over the chin up bar.

"Fuck off," I ground out as I pummelled the bag in a quick series of punches that rattled the chains attaching it to the ceiling.

Walcott sighed. "That means he doesn't have a plan."

A growl worked itself loose from my tight chest as I landed one last upper cut that made Ezra shifted his weight to keep from losing his balance. I stepped back, chest heaving, eyes stinging with sweat, and glared at my men.

"There is a plan," I growled. "It's just...changed form in the last few days."

"So, we aren't out to take down the Constantines?" Henrik asked, dropping to the ground with a heavy thud. "Somehow I doubt that."

I glared at him. "If Caroline touches a single hair on Bianca's head or mistreats her in anyway, you better fucking believe we'll take that bitch down. But it's not the priority. There's no doubt in my mind Bryant will try to put me in my place for turning against him. We need to attack before he fully recovers to put him in *his* place. A dark, cramped place like the inside of a coffin or a jail cell."

Walcott stopped his movements to frown at me. "You're serious about this? Your own father?"

"Aren't you the ones who told me he doesn't deserve the title?" I countered, remembering the twisted delight on his face when he revealed who I was to Bianca. It was the last in a series of so many misdeeds against me that I couldn't believe it had taken me this long to reach the breaking point.

Only, for most of my life, he'd been one of my only sources of validation and love, however perversely it presented itself. I'd been so young when he took my family from me, young still when he took Grace, that I'd been programmed to believe he was all I had left.

All I was good for.

Not anymore.

There was a boy upstairs in his Spiderman bedsheets that deserved more than a villain for a role model and a girl across Bishop's Landing in another house that would never be a home who deserved more than that.

So, I'd find it in myself to give more to both of them.

And that started with eliminating the enemies who stood against us.

"How the hell are you going to take down the head of your own family?" Henrik pushed, wiping his bald head with a Santa towel he'd picked up yesterday after taking Brando shopping for Christmas paraphernalia. They'd returned with dozens of bags stuffed with tinsel, holly, cookie cutters, ornaments, and Santa only knew what else. "How do you hurt him without hurting the entire family name?"

"He isn't the head of Morelli Holdings anymore," I reminded them. "Lucian is. Bryant's exerted his control over me for too long. It's time he retired. The only thing that matters to him more than power is money."

You go after his private holdings, Ezra signed.

I nodded, signing along with my words for him even though he was brilliant at lip reading. "At the end of the day, Bryant is a greedy motherfucker. If we dangle something enticing enough for him, he'll take the bait."

The low keen of the doorbell interrupted our conversation. We looked at each other, obviously wondering who the hell would visit Lion Court at five fifteen in the morning.

Walcott got up without a word, ascending the stairs to check out the situation. We listened to the faint sounds of the door opening and indistinguishable voices floating down the staircase.

What is the end goal? Ezra signed.

"Yeah," Henrik said. "Death or prison?"

"Neither," a masculine voice said from the top of the stairs, hidden from view.

But I didn't need to see him to know who had spoken.

Lucian Morelli had been the worst kind of bully to me after what I'd done to Carter. It wasn't the same as Leo's reaction, which was one of hurt and betrayal. There was something different about my eldest brother, colder and less prone to empathy. I'd wondered over the years if he could have been on the psychopathy spectrum and that question was rekindled when he finally appeared on the stairs, pinning me with his black gaze. Those eyes were as cold and soulless as twin black holes, sucking up every ounce of confidence I'd shored up in the years since I'd lived with him.

For a brief, painful moment, I was an over-large, ungainly teen again watching as my brothers laughingly locked the door to the media room so I couldn't join their antics each night after dinner. It hadn't really mattered, not when Bryant gave me extra homework and a variety self-defence and weapons training every evening, but it was still one among many countless hurts he'd instigated over the years.

Behind Lucian came Leo.

He walked with a nearly imperceptible stiffness, his shoulders carefully square in a way that most people probably couldn't notice. Otherwise, he was still the formidable, fierce-faced man that had earned the moniker 'Beast of Bishop's Landing.'

It hurt to look at him, and it had since I was twelve years old. I might have betrayed Carter and my sibling bond when Bryant forced me to take a belt to him, but it was Leo who had betrayed me. He had been our protector, the brother who always found ways to get the rest of us away from Bryant's wrath, but he'd been nowhere in sight that day or the days following. Some trip for school he'd been happy to escape to.

In fact, by the time I saw him again, the cold front had already settled in between my brothers and sisters and myself. I was already being homeschooled so I wouldn't embarrass the family with my scar, already being trained in ways the others never would to see out Bryant's wicked deeds. I even ate separately from them every night but Sunday when we had our requisite Sunday dinners.

That restless, gnawing energy inside me that had begun the moment I left Bianca at the Compound roared with new life.

Carter trailed behind both, but he stepped in front of them when I started to stalk forward with my fists clenched.

"Now, Tiernan, just wait a second—" he appeased, holding up his hands like dual white flags.

I ignored them.

Morellis weren't known for their mercy.

Leo was closest, so it was him I went to first. To my surprise, he just watched me as I surged toward him then didn't so much as lift a finger in defense when I reared back and socked him in the jaw.

His head snapped up and to the side, breath exploding from his lips.

I shook out my hand because the asshole had an iron jaw.

He worked his mouth, the hinge of his mandible creaking as he turned his head back around to pin me with his angry gaze.

"Feel better now?"

I glowered at him. "Not even fucking close."

Leo nodded slightly, opening his arms in invitation. "You want to do this properly, brother mine? Just know, the first punch was free. If you come at me again, I'm hitting back."

"Leo," Lucian said blandly, but it was enough

to still us both. "There is no need to lower yourself to Tiernan's childish antics."

"Fuck *you*." I bared my teeth at my older brother, the man who should have loved and protected me but instead became my biggest tormentor. "How dare you set foot in this house. Get out before I rip your goddamn throat out."

A small part of me was shocked I felt so hostile. For years, I'd just wanted their praise and acceptance. I'd never dreamed of them visiting Lion Court, because the idea had been so outlandish. Now that they were here, it felt like a violation of my haven. Sure, it was a haunted mansion filled with eccentric, artistic debris, and a crew of scarred survivors, but it was *mine*.

No one had the right to enter these walls and disrespect me or mine.

Lucian just blinked at me, boredom filling every inch of his face.

"Get. The. Fuck. Out," I growled, shoving him with my good hand. "Why are you even here?"

"Carter texted us," he said, blandly, checking his phone as if I was utterly unimportant. "He said you wanted to reconcile. Is that not true?"

"You think I'll just get over the shit you did to me?" The words shot out of me like blood from a bullet wound.

Another lazy blink as he lifted his inscrutable gaze to me. "I didn't do anything."

A bitter, barking laugh. "Okay, you want to follow that logic, asshole, we can do that. You did nothing. You ignored me. Shunned me. Set the example for everyone else to do the same. You think Leo and Carter would've done that without you? You think the girls—" My voice fucking cracked, but I surged on. "You think Eva and Sophia would have done that? Daphne? Lizzy?"

"So you were left out," Lucian shrugged. "Worse things have happened to better people."

Through the roar of blood in my ears, I saw Carter adjust uncomfortably and heard Leo murmur something to Lucian about backing off.

"Left out?" I mocked. "Yeah, I was left the fuck out of the bond you all share, forced out because Bryant beat me until I agreed to beat Carter. One time, I buckled to the pressure and hurt one of our family. *One fucking time.* But you hurt me every day after that. I didn't get it before, I didn't get it until last week when our dad put a bullet through me for disobeying him, but emotional neglect and abuse is still abuse. You want to pretend you didn't take part in that, you're fucking delusional. Now, get the fuck out of my house, Lucian. The next time I see you, you better fucking run, because I'm a grownass man and I won't be bullied ever again."

My chest was heaving by the time I finished. I wasn't used to speaking so much, so passionately, and it had taken more out of me than the hour-long boxing session I'd just had.

In the silence that followed, Walcott started slow-clapping.

Henrik and Ezra followed until the sharp rap of hands meeting filled the air.

Giddy, relieved laughter bubbled in my too-tight throat.

These men were my men.

I didn't need these assholes because we shared half of the same blood.

"That was a good speech," Carter said, stepping forward to clap me on the shoulder with a genuine smile. "Didn't think you had it in you."

I shrugged off his hand. "You don't know me. We made a deal to work together, but I'm rethinking it. Why the fuck did you bring these two here?"

Carter's playfulness transformed swiftly, easily into a soothing a smile. "Because they want to reconcile with you as much as I do."

I glared at Lucian, who only raised a cool

brow, and then at Leo who winced slightly.

"You weren't the only one hurt, little brother," Leo told me, his eyes stale with old pain. "Bryant's given all of us a lifetime of pain. You don't want to be bullied anymore? Thank fuck, because neither do we. We're moving on without him. Together."

"How can you expect me to trust this? Suddenly, after years of distance, you want to hold fucking hands and sing kumbaya?" I demanded. "What the fuck's changed?"

"We grew up." Leo put his hands in his pockets. "We gained a different perspective."

"They're happy now." Carter snorted. "Hell, they're also both happily in *love*, now. Don't you know love changes people, Tiernan?" His tone was gently mocking, but his eyes were too shrewd as he stared at me, as if he had a direct line to my heart and who laid claim to it.

I wanted to make light of his words, but how could I? Loving Bianca and Brandon had set off a chain reaction of life events and emotions that I was still reeling from every single fucking day.

Leo rolled his eyes at Carter, then stepped closer to me. "Come on, Tiernan. I know there's been bad blood, but we're honestly here to make amends."

I crossed my arms over my chest even though it pulled at my wound. "I don't hear any apologies or see any fucking flowers."

Walcott snickered.

"You want an apology?" Lucian asked, his eyes suddenly flashing. "What if I want one from you? You've been working for Bryant and against *us* for years. Should I list the ways you've helped him? Should I unlock the closet hiding all the skeletons?"

"I did what I had to survive," I told him. "I won't apologize for that. I didn't have the luxury of being the first-born incumbent to Morelli Holdings; the heir or the spare. I was just the hammer."

We glared at each other, the energy crackling so palpably the hair rose on the back of my neck and arms.

"Tiernan wants to settle it the way we used to," Leo said, his voice powerful and absolute, the voice of a highly successful CEO. "Fight it out. Winner apologizes first."

"No way," Henrik said, stepping forward into our circle. He ignored the way my brothers glared at him as if he was the intruder in this house and not them. "Bryant just shot your brother in the shoulder nine days ago. He's not fighting."

"I'm in," Lucian said, a sly, mean grin slicing across his face. "I'll fight for all three of us."

He began to shed his blazer and roll up the cuffs of his shirt.

"No need to fight for me," Carter said, hands in the air. "Tiernan and I sorted our shit already."

Leo stared at me so hard, I felt the weight of his gaze divot the skin of my cheeks. Finally, his rigid posture relaxed. "I don't need an apology."

"Yeah, well, I do." I stepped toward him, even though Lucian put a hand on my shoulder to stop me. I shrugged it off and bared my teeth at him before facing my second-oldest brother. "You were everyone's champion but mine. You left for a fucking trip for school and we were all defenseless. You think I'm going to let that slide without an apology or explanation, you're not as smart as you think you are."

It seemed the lid I'd kept locked and tightly sealed on my emotions over the years had been punctured irreparably by the bullet Bryant had put through my shoulder and the loss of Bianca from my home. I was seething with them until my skin felt it would tear at the seams.

I wanted to fight. That was a language that made sense to me. I could land my sorrow in an upper cut, my rage in a single jab. And the opportunity to ring Lucian's fucking entitled, arrogant bell would settle something deep and dark inside me that had be thirsting since I'd been scarred at twelve years old and left for dead by all of them, led, as they always were, by Lucian.

"Get in the ring," I growled to Lucian before turning on my heel and stalking over to the ropes.

Ezra was there to lift them for me to step between and then he, Henrik and Walcott followed me onto the platform.

"You've always been good at bad decisions," Henrik drawled as he poked at the fresh blood seeping through my bandage. "But this has got to take the cake."

"He's a paper pusher. Even injured, I can take him," I argued as I kept an eye on my brothers.

They huddled together to speak quietly as Lucian rolled up his sleeves, toed off his thousand-dollar loafers and rolled his shoulders in preparation. Leo had found a spare pair of wraps and methodically wound them around our brother's hands. Finally, they broke apart, Leo looking tense but resigned, and Carter with something like an awkward smile on his face, a cheerleader who wasn't sure which team to root for.

"He's a big guy," Henrik pointed out as Lucian ducked between the ropes and into the ring, taking up his corner. "And he hasn't been shot or spent the last few hours pounding on a bag. He's fresh and he's fucking mean."

"I'm not going to lose," I said easily, and I wasn't.

There was no way I was going to lose this fight.

I was owed an apology and I might have been tired and wounded, but I had a tank fueled with years of poisonous history to fuel me.

"I'll referee," Walcott decided loudly, then softly to me. "You've got this, T. Can't wait to see you make that motherfucker bleed."

He stepped into the middle of the ring, producing a whistle from his pocket because Walcott was like a boy scout, always prepared.

Lucian and I met in the middle of the ring, my perfect brother in his deconstructed bespoke suit facing me like the polished version of my rough draft.

He grinned at me, a manic, excited look in his eye that I felt mimicked in my own heart.

We were going to enjoy this.

The moment Walcott released our hands, it was on.

Lucian attacked first, which I knew he would

do, snapping a tight jab at my bad left shoulder. I slid past the punch, ducking to deliver my own to his exposed kidneys.

He barely seemed to feel it, already driving forward with another series of hits.

It became obvious, immediately, that Lucian was both very strong and very smart.

But he hadn't spent the last eighteen years of his life being trained by Bryant Morelli and his league of martial arts specialists. He hadn't had to physically fight for his life against someone who had no regard for it. Or maybe he had, I didn't know.

I was going to win, but it wasn't going to be clean, because Lucian was a ruthless asshole.

Because he was a Morelli.

And as with all things in our family, this was about revenge.

Mine, of course, but also his.

He knew he wasn't going to win, I could see it in the way he took each punch and almost blindly powered on. He knew it. But he would wreck the utmost damage on my person before he finally went down.

One of his uppercuts caught me on the chin and my skin split under his knuckled force. Another pounded me just under my bullet wound, sending pain wheeling through me so that I lost my sight to black spots for a vital moment. Then, one to my other shoulder, another to my gut.

He seemed frustrated when I just grinned at him, blood spilling down my chin.

Of course, he didn't understand that the pain cleared my exhaustion and surged through me like battery acid. This was what I knew, I wanted to tell him, this is what *he* did to me.

But I didn't say the words.

It was time for the language of violence and it flowed through me as sweet a wine.

I kicked into high gear and finally went on the offensive with a series I'd picked up from Hardy Hayes, the world champion boxer, himself. Lucian tried to defend himself, but I was an unstoppable force. Hatred and misery, bitterness and the triumph of revenge crackled like kindling in my heart. My brother hit the ropes and raised his hands futilely.

I didn't know I was laughing until the last blow landed, glancing off his cut cheekbone so his head went reeling to the right, spit and blood flying in a wide arc.

I stepped back, breathy laughter leaking from my mouth as Lucian struggled to stay standing then collapsed into the ropes.

Silenced echoed through the huge basement. I never knew quiet could be so big, impossibly loud. It pushed against my eardrums painfully, like pressure too deep underwater.

Lucian stared at me as he sagged heavily against the ropes, eyes so black they were blank, cheek cut and dripping blood, suited body slicked with sweat and apostrophes of spilt blood.

I knew I looked a mess, my chin split, bullet wound reopened and aching, seeping beneath the bandage.

But I felt incredible.

It wasn't often a man got the opportunity to beat down two demons in the span of a week.

Black, sticky vengeance and righteous indignation roared through me.

Then, something shifted.

Lucian.

He waved away Leo and Carter who were behind him, outside the ropes, and rose to his own feet without wincing even though the tightness beside his eyes told of his pain. When he started forward on heavy steps, Walcott almost intercepted him, but I jerked my head slightly and watched my brother come to me.

If he took a swing, I was ready.

The idea that this fight might turn deadly was a real possibility.

Every muscle was strung taut as a bow, my fists quivering like notched arrows.

But Lucian didn't take a swing at me.

He stopped a foot away, close enough I could smell him, the tang of sweat and musk of some no doubt ungodly expensive cologne. Close enough I could see the faint difference between the dark of his pupils and the dark of his irises, the sweat beading out of each pore.

I hadn't been so close to him since I was a boy and suddenly, the proximity made me feel sick, nauseated to the very pit of my stomach.

He studied me for a long, quivering moment and then raised his hand, still shaky with adrenaline.

At first, I didn't know what he was doing, just hovering between us. It didn't make sense when I'd been expecting violence. As always, expecting the worst.

Then I realized he was offering a handshake.

A gesture of truce.

My bloody chin canted into the air as I gathered my anger and indignation around me like a shield. He read it in my eyes, my refusal to bend.

I wouldn't have anything less than a spoken

apology.

Lucian's jaw spasmed as his hand still floated untethered between us. When he opened his mouth, it was with an audible creak, like opening an old, unused box.

"I'm sorry," he said and the words were surprisingly quiet, soft. "I'm sorry for what Bryant did to you." A hesitation that vibrated. "I'm sorry that I stood by and let it happen. And let Leo—" He shakes his head. "I'm sorry that I was a cold motherfucker afterward. I should have stood up for you. I should have stood up for all of you."

The words struck my heart like a fucking gong, every inch of me shaking minutely. It rattled lose the last of the secrets and emotions I'd hidden away so long ago and they all spilled into my chest with a clatter that set my teeth on edge.

It made breathing difficult so my voice was strained when I demanded, "Are you genuine or is this only because you lost?"

He bared his teeth at me and it occurred to me that was something I would have done. We might have only been half-brothers, but the similarities between us were stronger than I'd remembered.

"I wouldn't be here if I didn't mean it," he grunted. "Why the fuck do you think I came?"

"I take your hand, it doesn't mean we're best friends," I warned him. "It doesn't mean we're brothers in any way that counts."

"No," he agreed, cocking his head, the impression of a smile on his lips. "But you want to get there, we'll get there."

Without waiting for me, he snapped forward and grabbed one of my hands, enfolding it in his own. Before I could wrench away out of instinct, he was jerking me forward into a brutal hug. I slammed against his torso, shoulder aching, and his free hand gripped my neck, almost too tight. It was a claiming hug, almost the same way I'd hugged Bianca on the floor of her room at the Compound. As if I could absorb her, as if I could imprint all the words I didn't know how to say from my skin to hers.

Automatically, I struggled to push away from him. I didn't like to be caged and it was impossible not to feel trapped.

Lucian didn't expect it, so I was able to push him off and clock him in the face, right in the mouth. He recoiled, neck twisting, but when he recovered, he did it calmly.

He faced me again, brought a thumb to the blood, and then, he laughed.

Bright, long and loud.

Laughing so hard, his eyes started to tear.

And it broke something inside me.

Something that needed breaking.

The idea that revenge always trumped for-giveness.

That violence ultimately won out over grace.

That everything Bryant had taught me—no—*programmed* in me was wrong.

It was all a fucking lie.

And this?

The laughter, the forgiveness of a bad blood between brothers, the coming together after so many years apart, *that* was exactly what Bryant wouldn't want.

Because it felt good.

It felt good to feel an echo of Lucian's laugh rumble through my chest. To hear it mimicked awkwardly at first and then louder in Carter and Leo. The Gentlemen didn't laugh, this wasn't their feud, their moment, but they smiled at us as if we were lunatics. As if they liked that we were lunatics.

"What a fucked-up family we are," Carter said through his laughter, shaking his head and slinging an arm around Leo.

Leo stiffened, but his shoulders relaxed and he grinned again. "If those assholes are done beating each other up, let's try being brothers again. I'm game if you are."

"I'm game," I said with a casual shrug, as if I wasn't deeply and secretly relieved to have my brothers back the way I'd dreamed of since I was twelve years old with a fresh scar on my face.

Leo ducked out from Carter's arm and stepped toward me, offering his hand to shake. I swallowed thickly as I gripped it.

He tugged hard, bringing me in to hug around our clasped hands as he thumped me on the back. When I tried to pull away after a moment, he surprised me by pressing his forehead to my skull to whisper in my ear, "I never would have left you, T. Never would have let him hurt you that way. I would never have gone on a fucking trip for school." His voice was shattered as he spoke, aching with remorse I felt echoed in my own chest.

"Then where were you?"

"In the hospital."

"For fucking *what*?"

"I'll tell you another time. I wouldn't have gone if I could avoid it. I didn't have a choice."

"Was it Bryant?"

"No."

What the hell happened to him? Who else got

to him? I guess now that we're brothers again, there's time to find out. I patted him on the back, slightly awkward, more than a little relieved that he hadn't left us like that because he didn't care. "I'm sorry to fucking hear that. I didn't know." I hesitated then asked, "You're happy now?"

Leo pulled back, a small, private smile on his face. A smile meant for someone else. "Yes."

Leo and Lucian left then, though Carter lingered, picking up a pair of gloves to spar with Henrik as if he did so every day.

I watched him spar and joke with my men as something broke free of the previous fallow soil in my soul and grew leaves. This was what I'd always wanted. My brothers back and hopefully, one day soon, my sisters, too. I wanted family and peace, an end to the tragedy and violence Bryant had forced on me my entire life.

I wouldn't ask Lucian and Leo to help me strip Bryant of his lingering power over me. That was something I was prepared to do alone. But it meant the fucking world that they had my back all the same. Now, I wasn't just putting Dad in his place for me, I was doing it for what he'd done to Leo, what he'd no doubt done to all my siblings. I'd face our tormentor and I'd take him down myself.

CHAPTER SEVEN

Bianca

THAT NIGHT, I had nightmares of Tiernan I didn't want to wake up from because I knew I wouldn't see him when I opened my eyes and how fucked up was that?

He was this contradiction only my heart could decipher.

A lovely monster.

A beautiful nightmare.

I was fascinated by his cruelty and savagery as much as I was by his hard-won loyalty and infrequent but brilliant flares of tenderness and humility. Even in the depths of slumber when the mind untangled itself in long ribbons of vibrant dreams, my consciousness couldn't make sense of my feelings for the man.

And then, as if in answer, that morning when I woke up, there was a gift on the vanity.

The French doors to the balcony were closed, the curtains barely parted, but I knew without question that Tiernan had broken into the Constantine Compound again to leave me the immaculately wrapped present tied with a crimson red bow. A red rose was slotted beneath the satin fabric and, like the one he'd had on the day he showed up on my doorstep in Texas, this too was resplendent with sharp thorns.

I smiled despite myself as I carefully brought the bloom to my nose and inhaled the rich floral perfume. The small white envelope wasn't addressed, but the cramped hand-written words written within the blank card were undoubtedly for me.

I've made you bleed since the moment I met you, but now I'm bleeding out without you.

It wasn't signed with a name. Instead, a neatly pressed bloody thumbprint marred the bottom of the cardstock.

Maybe to another girl, or a Bianca from an earlier time, the words would have been too dark or too cliché, but in that moment, I was certain I'd never read, seen, or conceived of anything more romantic than that proclamation. That beautiful whorl of a blood-stamped finger print.

This was how a violent man proclaimed his affection.

With blood.

This was how a man without the proper vocabulary to express his love made his intentions clear.

I'd doubted his sincerity when he'd spoken about buying me back on the floor of my borrowed room. How could he be believed after everything he'd done? When I knew he'd sought out Aida then taken Brando and I solely to suit his own needs for revenge against our Lane.

I still didn't know *why* he felt the need for revenge or when he had decided not to go through with his original plan. Why he hadn't gone through with it.

But staring at that thumbprint, feeling the shifting of my something fundamental in my soul like shifting tectonic plates, I knew something with absolute and terrifying certainty.

My fingers were numb as I pulled out my cell phone and swiped through my contacts to Tiernan's number.

It only rang once.

"Little thing," he practically purred. "Did you have sweet dreams about the monster under your bed?"

Normally, I might have laughed and rolled my eyes, but my entire focus was on the card pinched in my trembling hands.

"I hate you," I declared with surprising conviction even though my heart was turning over in my chest like a key in the lock of a heavy door that pushed open suddenly at the pressure and sent me falling.

Falling for him.

The enormity of the revelation threatened to consume and the only thing keeping me anchored was that card, that print, the hushed murmur of Tiernan's breath through the phone line.

"I think you understand me too well too hate me," he countered calmly.

In the background, I could hear the low murmur of one or more of The Gentleman and the high octave of Brando's trilling laugh.

"Is that Brando?" I whispered through the cataclysm rocking through my chest cavity.

"He bullied me into making getting two trees," Tiernan admitted ruefully. "Ezra's just set one up in the entry hall and the other in the living room. We're making..." he paused and I could picture the look of self-mockery on his face, "popcorn to string from the boughs."

A startled laugh burst from me like machine

gunfire. "You aren't."

"This is not something I'd brag about," he drawled.

In the wake of my laughter, I felt hollow and alone, a tumble weed blowing across a barren landscape. "I wish I was there."

"Come home," he said and I could hear the effort it took him to play casual, to form the words without ordering me. "Stop the bleeding, Bianca, and come the fuck home."

"No."

"Why the fuck not?"

"A single rose and a thumb print aren't going to erase all the lies you've told," I countered, relieved to feel a surge of anger. Anger I could understand more than this bone deep ache for a man it wasn't permissible for me to love. "I don't even know why you did it. Why you took us in to get revenge on a man who has been dead for five years."

There was a long pause punctuation with Brando screaming in delight in the background.

Missing my brother deepened my aching and yearning so acutely tears bloom along my lower lids.

"I won't forgive a man I know nothing about," I warned him, but what I really meant was

'*I won't* love *a man I know nothing about.*'

His sigh crackled over the phone. "I've kept secrets for some many years I've become a vault. It's not in my nature to share things, but to hide them."

I could relate to that in a strange way.

I was Bianca Belcante because I had to hide who my father was. I spent the last ten years in Texas then lied to Tiernan about my history for the same reason. Even with Aida, I'd been a false sense of self. Someone harder, more somber and bitter than the woman I wanted to be.

Ironically, it was only heated by the flame of my hatred for Tiernan I'd begun to discover what it was like to truly be *me*. To fight for who and what I wanted and deserved.

"I can't say I don't understand, but I still need answers if who want anything more to do with me."

"I want everything to do with you," he replied instantly, easily, and it was so shocking to hear such sweet words in such a habitually cruel and filthy mouth that they hit me like hammer strikes. "I'll answer your questions, Bianca, but I won't do it on the phone. When I see you on Friday, I'll tell you what you need to know."

"What about what I *want* to know?"

A soft exhale that was almost a fond laugh. "I'm sure you can find a way to…coerce me into revealing all my secrets."

Heat flared in my cheeks and pooled in my groin at the fantasies that prompted.

"I'm sure I can," I agreed because I knew it would make him laugh and despite my turmoil, I was starting think I'd do anything to see Tiernan's scarred smile or hear his rusty laughter.

He rewarded me with a husky chuckle then sobered. "Don't misunderstand me, little thing. I'm not playing a game with you. The stakes are much higher than that. I'm hunting more than just your body, now. I'm a greedy man and I won't stop until I have your soul."

I breathed deeply, trying to keep my equilibrium. "Well, that's not easily won or bought."

"It wouldn't be worth anything if it was."

Another silence, but this one was tender somehow. I had the sense that Tiernan wanted me there just as desperately as I wished I could be there.

Still, I clung to the fact that even if he wanted me, maybe even loved me, he had proven himself to be untrustworthy.

And what was love without trust?

Something, I decided, like a wish without

hope.

"Brando is beckoning so I'll let you go," Tiernan said. "But I want you to think about something before you do. I hated Lane and Caroline Constantine because of someone they took away from me when I was young. But it's not revenge against them that will right that wrong, because the truth is my own father took something from me long before anyone else did. He ripped away from me what I should have loved most."

"Who?" I whispered, as if Id break the spell of his vulnerability.

I don't know who I thought he'd say, some lost lover or his clearly estranged family, but it definitely wasn't what he uttered next, in a voice razed to the ground of his soul.

"Myself. I realized after thirty fucking years, I still didn't know myself or like myself very well. There was an entirely undiscovered part of me partially unearthed by the curious, innocent hands of two orphaned Belcantes." He paused to allow me to digested the tremendousness of his words. "Now that I've discovered what I really want, do you think I'm the sort of man who would ever allow it to be taken from him? At least not without one hell of a fucking fight?"

"Who are you fighting for exactly?" I asked, trying to mark the shakiness of my voice.

Fight for me, I wanted to plead. Please, God, for the first time in my life, let someone fight for me.

"Brandon. You. Myself. The family we could have together if you're forgiving enough and brave enough to come home."

I blinked sightless at the mirror, at my wet, wavering reflection in it.

His voice gentled as if he could sense my utter shock and inability to process anything further. "I hate knowing you're in a house with a madwoman like Caroline Constantine, but it's your choice and as much as I'm fucking desperate to, I won't take that from you. Just be careful. For me and for Brando. I'll have him ready for you daily call tonight. Oh, and Bianca? Open the rest of that present when you hang up the phone."

He ended the call before I could respond, but I didn't lower the cell for along moment. My entire chest was a writhing mass of slippery emotions, some of them snakes and some ribbons. I was too terrified of the former to sort between the two so I just sat them feeling everything all at once.

Five or ten minutes later when I could breathe

properly again, I dug my thumb nail beneath the tape of the present and rent the paper open in a clean line.

A silver frame slid out of wrapping and landed on the marble vanity top with a clatter, almost falling over the edge into my lap. Instinctively, I caught the cold edge and looked down into the glass covered center.

Someone, probably Walcott, had taken the photo one morning in the kitchen at Lion Court. In it, Tiernan was wearing one of his partially dismantled bespoke black suits, the jacket discarded and the sleeves of the black button up rolled to expose his corded, tattooed forearms. He was bent nearly double to look into Brando's wide eyes as he explained something to the older man, his hands open and raised passionately. His face was in profile, one cheek sprinkled with flour, one hand coated in. On Tiernan's scarred cheek, a small palm print of white powder appeared in stark relief on his tanned skin from where Brando had obviously patted him. I stood behind my brother, my hands on his shoulder, partially leaned over his head so I could see Tiernan's expression as they spoke. It was a candid photo. No one was looking at the camera. And somehow, that heightened the intimacy of the moment.

Tiernan and I were curved over Brando like two parentheses.

And, despite the space between us, we were curved into each other, our awareness of the other somehow obvious in a million little physical tells. The way I smiled softly at both him and my brother, the hand he had braced on the kitchen counter right beside my hip, his fingers close enough to brush my school skirt, the way my hair made a curtained backdrop for both our bent heads.

We looked in every sense like a family.

A happy one.

Pain and longing cut through me like a thousand knives, snapping sinew and carving through bone, until I was slumped over the vanity unable to hold up my weight. I clutched the photo in one hand, the card with the bloody thumb print in the other, and I cried until the entire vanity was covered in my tears.

When I was done, eyes aching and chest sore, I peeled myself off the marble and forced myself to place the gifts face down beside me. The small, childish part of me wished fervently I could just call my mother or father and ask them for advice, but that hadn't been a powerful option long before they'd passed away. As usual, it came down to me.

I was lost in a maze constructed between the Morelli and Constantine houses and I had to find my own way out. The question was whether I would end up with the Constantines who hid their secrets and lies behinds silks and saccharine smiles, where I had always assumed I'd belong, or with the blatantly cruel Morellis and their black sheep third born son.

Chapter Eight

Bianca

L ATER THAT MORNING, Caroline insisted on taking me Christmas shopping.

I'd been to Fifth Avenue and perused the ritzy offerings of Manhattan with Tilda, Tiernan's cousin, when I first moved to Bishop's Landing, but nothing could have prepared me for the experience of shopping with one of New York's more elite figures.

There was a personal shopper waiting for us at the entrance of Saks with two glasses of champagne waiting on a gilt tray. She treated Caroline as if she was true royalty, deferring to her on all things, readily accepting the matriarch's sometimes acerbic comments about the clothes that had been pulled for us beforehand. When I mentioned that I was getting hungry, the woman even offered to call out for food for us. Everywhere we went, jewellery stores I'd never dreamed of seeing, clothing stores where a single garment was as much as a down payment on a house, Caroline was greeted with revered awe.

For a small-town girl who had spent most of her life favoring anonymity, it was…surreal.

But it was also pretty damn fun.

Caroline had certain expectations of how I should dress, but she also let me pick outfits that suited my style and coloring. Once, after trying on a velvet, navy blue dress just a shade darker than my eyes, she had even stopped emailing on her phone long enough to stare at me.

"You look…" she paused delicately. "You look very fine in that shade of blue. It compliments your eyes."

I beamed at her. Since my mother's death, I hadn't had much female influence in my life and I'd almost forgotten how much fun it could be to just be girly with another woman.

I twirled, the skirt flaring out around me as I laughed. "It's just beautiful. But truly, Caroline, I have clothes at Lion Court that Tiernan has to give back sometime. I can just wait for those."

"Absolutely not," she'd sniffed as if the idea was insulting. "I will not be seen with a woman dressed in anything less than the best." Turning to the poor woman helping us, she waved at the pile of discarded clothes I'd accumulated in the dressing room. "Pack everything up and send it to Bishop's Landing. She will wear this one with the Chanel jacket right now."

Which was how I ended up dining in one of the most exclusive restaurants in the city wearing an outfit that cost more than my entire wardrobe back in Texas. Even the gentle noises filling the ornate interior were somehow expensive: the clink of real silverware, the chime of crystal glasses undercut by the low murmur of cultured voices and barely discernable classical music. I felt like an imposter sitting there with Caroline, who was greeted by almost every diner as if she owned not only the restaurant but the very chairs they sat on and cars they had arrived in.

"It was a nice day, Caroline," I said as we were served heaping salads topped with fresh seafood that made my mouth water. "Thank you so much for this. For everything really."

Unlike the polite smile she had given to everyone else that day, Caroline gave me a small, genuine grin that curled her pale pink painted lips. She had been quiet for most of our lunch, contemplative, her gaze pinned to memories cast over my shoulder.

"I am glad you enjoyed yourself. I was hoping you would, because, you see, I have grown quite fond of you over the last week. My lawyer dropped these off last night and I really believe this is the right choice. Not just for you, but for myself. I've been lonely since my husband past away and my kids are older now, fair too busy to spend time with their mother." Her expression was wistful, but her eyes were still a sharp, pale blue, cutting as the edge of an icicle. "It will be nice to have you as a true companion."

I watched silently as she reached into her Hermes bag and produced a collection of papers that she placed beside my plate.

A guardianship agreement.

I looked up at her with wide eyes, hope and misgiving lodged in my throat.

"You're old enough to make the decision for yourself, so if you no longer want to be the ward of Tiernan Morelli, all you have to do is sign the papers, and you'll be mine," she assured me, her manicured fingers curled around a Mont Blanc pen. "Here, Bianca. Take your life back."

The pen was cold and absurdly heavy in my hand as I grasped it. My vision swam as I tried to make sense of the legal jargon presented to me. It was hard to reconcile the terror I felt staring at those pages that represented a lifelong dream when I'd always believed this was exactly what I wanted. But my heart pounded hard enough to crack a rib and cold sweat crusted my brow.

"It's very standard," she guaranteed with that plastic smile she was so practiced at.

Still, I tried to read more of the document. I couldn't shake my father's voice, telling me more snakes lay hidden in silks and furs than in the long Texas grasslands.

"Here," she pressed, leaning forward to pick up the papers and flip to the second page where my signature was needed. "Sign just here, here, and here so we can wrap this matter up for good."

I bent to read again when her cool fingers gently grasped my chin and raised it until my eyes were level with her own. Her expression was soft in a bid to express her sincerity, but there was a tension in the fingers that held me, a vibrating kind of energy that made it obvious she was coiled tightly around something.

Some secret she was trying to keep hidden from me.

"One day," she murmured, her voice as cool and smooth as silk. "If you're with us long enough, we might even see what we can do about giving you the Constantine name."

Each word shot through me like bullet to the chest. A twisted cocktail of hope, longing, and suspicion threatened to drown my lungs, overloading my system until I couldn't breathe.

How was it possible that a name could mean so much?

It was a short collection of consonants and vowels. Pleasant enough to speak, but hollow without the meaning attributed to it by others.

Constantine was almost a brand, one synonymous with wealth, prestige and glory.

If I asked anyone in the restaurant today if they wanted to be a Constantine, most of them wouldn't think twice about saying yes.

Of course, the name meant even more to me.

My dad had been a Constantine. He had been the one to take that name and reputation and forge it into steel, something unconquerable and eternal.

For all his flaws, I'd loved him and admired him. Brando had his superhero obsession, but I'd only had one my whole life. Lane.

So the idea of finally sharing his last name after so many years of having to hide it, of feeling ashamed because I didn't have my dad's surname or permanent residency…it elated me.

The word 'yes' sat on my tongue pre-formed,

ready to spring from my lips.

But I swallowed, thickly, painfully, dragging it back down my throat into my belly.

Tiernan might have broken my heart by lying to me, but he'd also taught me a valuable lesson.

To blindly trust kindness was as dangerous as trusting bold-faced lies.

I looked into Caroline's perfectly symmetrical face at the diamonds and pearls in her ears, the Dior lipstick and Botox-smooth skin and I knew I couldn't trust anything I found in her features. They were a mask she had spent years painting into the masterpiece it was today.

I had to look deeper than that, the way I did with paintings. Beyond the surface into the detailed depths.

And there was that palpable tension in the way she held her mouth, a tightness beside her eyes that spoke of *need*.

She needed me to sign these papers.

I just didn't know why.

Carefully, I moved my head back out of her grasp and let a sheaf of hair partially veil my face as I looked down at the papers once more.

Caroline waited in a mushroom cloud of toxic silence.

It only took me two minutes to realize the

problem.

"There isn't anything about Brandon in here," I said, sickness blooming in my belly, curdling the expensive food there. "Why isn't there anything about my brother?"

She sighed, a long, dramatic expression that was more eloquent than words. "Tiernan Morelli isn't willing to give him up. We can fight him on it, but it will take *time*, Bianca. The least we can do is get custodianship of you away from that monster."

"Monster?" I echoed, catching the flash of true disgust on her face.

A stillness settled over her and when she spoke next, her words were slow and perfectly articulated as if she measured them first. "Well, you don't know anything about this world, Bianca but the Morellis are unprincipled heathens. The lowest of low. Any association with them is absolutely forbidden, is that understood?"

"But why?" I pressed. "Why do you hate them so much?"

"Hate is such a strong word. They aren't worthy of my hatred. Quietly simply, they are below me and they should be below *you*."

I thought of being below Tiernan on the floor of my bedroom and squirmed as arousal prickled down my spine.

"What did they do?" I asked again, even though Caroline's face was growing so cold, I worried it would fractured into ice chips.

She looked down at the papers than back up at me, calculating. "They have always wanted what is mine. What was Lane's." Her left eyelid twitched. "They don't seem to understand that I will not be taken from. I have earned what I have, every ounce of it, and I will always do battle to keep it."

I blinked slowly, feeling as if I was being given the Cliff Note's on a much larger, more complicated story.

"Is that why you want to take us in?" I asked, steeling my shoulders against her tangible irritation. "To take something from the Morellis?"

"Maybe they never should have had their uncouth hands on you in the first place," she suggested, relaxing carefully into her chair to address her almost uneaten salad. "Look at how they hurt you."

"Tiernan never laid a hand on me," I defended, even though I knew it was stupid, even though I didn't want to.

She raised a thin blonde brow. "There are many ways to skin a cat."

The metaphor was said flatly, in a way that signaled she was done with the conversation until I signed the documents.

"I won't sign without Brandon," I told her, my voice surprisingly strong even though I was faintly worried I'd be homeless after this lunch.

The truth was, I already felt homeless without Brando by my side.

"You will do as I say." Caroline didn't even lift her head as she daintily ate her salad. "Obedience, Bianca."

"Fuck, obedience," I said, ignoring her startled look at the glances from the table beside us. "I've been obedient my whole life and it's only ever gotten me shitty second-helpings after everyone else took exactly what they wanted. There is one thing that matters to me more than anything else in this world and it's my brother. Whatever I am, orphaned Belcante, fostered Morelli, or adopted Constantine, Brando is with me."

"Bianca," Caroline said in a low voice that clinked like ice against her teeth. "You will sign these papers and we will deal with getting Brandon together after that."

"Absolutely not." I glared at her, refusing to be cowed. "I don't mean to be rude, Caroline, but

I think you can understand that family comes first. Brandon is all that I have left of mine."

After a second, her mouth moved into something like a smile that was really a grimace. "Yes, I understand what it is to put family first. You are being foolish and ungrateful, though, which I will not understand. You should be thanking me."

"I just did," I reminded her of the beginning of our lunch. "I will again, when you help me get Brandon back."

Another eye twitch as we stared at each other across thousand-dollar china. I was nothing and no one, an orphan from Bum Nowhere, Texas, but I was done letting other people attribute my worth. I was smart and capable and I could carve out a life for Brando and me, even if everyone else stood in our way.

Even if Caroline Constantine forbade it.

"Eat the rest of your lunch and we will discuss it again *like adults* after you've had some sustenance. Clearly, you have low blood sugar," she said dismissively, turning back to her salad.

And that was it.

When I knew Caroline wasn't the kind benefactor I'd hoped for, when Elias's words of warning finally sunk in.

Because it was obvious she wanted to use me

just as badly as Tiernan had wanted to and I was going to find out *why*.

Right fucking now.

I stood, tossed my napkin on the table, and leveled Caroline with my own cold gaze. "I'm going for a walk, I'll make my way back to Bishop's Landing myself. If you open the gate to me, I'll be grateful. I want to stay with you, Caroline, and I'm thankful for your graciousness, but you clearly don't understand me." I placed my fingers on the table and leaned over so I looming slightly over her. "I may be young, but I'm not stupid. I don't know what's going on between you and the Morellis, but clearly, you're using me in your war against them and I won't be a pawn. You want to use me, fine? But first, you get me my brother back."

I turned on my heel and stalked out of the restaurant with my head back, the speculative gazes of the other diners rolling off me like water off a duck's back.

CHAPTER NINE

Bianca

I CALLED ELENA Lombardi, Tiernan's lawyer, on my way to the subway.

She didn't seem surprised to hear from me, but I had the impression she was a hard woman to rattle.

"I need help," I told her honestly as I shifted through Tinsley Constantine's old Prada purse to find some change. Instead, I found a condom, a tube of lip gloss and a crumpled hundred-dollar bill. "I didn't know who else to call."

"Well then, I'm glad you called me, Bianca. That is why I gave you my card." There was a pleasant smile in her voice along with the trace of an Italian accent. It made my heart pang to hear it because Aida had spoken to us in broken Italian from time to time and I hadn't heard it since she passed away. "How can I help you?"

I explained my situation leaning against a traffic pole at the mouth of the subway station. She listened without interrupting until I was through, somewhat breathless even though I hadn't moved an inch.

"You want to know how to get custody of Brandon for yourself," she repeated thoughtfully. "I'm afraid that's going to be impossible until you are eighteen and even then, improbable unless you have a full-time job and a permanent residence of your own."

Frustration burned away my lingering politeness. "Fuck that. How is that fair, Elena? I've been taking care of Brando since he was born and now, I can't even see him because Tiernan won't let me."

Silence.

"I don't truly believe Tiernan would keep you from your brother," she said slowly, as if she was still processing her thoughts. "You have to understand, Tiernan is a man who has never gotten what he wanted. At every turn, it's been ripped away from him. Now, it seems he feels very passionately about having you and Brandon in his life. Sometimes, when people feel threatened, they lash out and threaten others. I'm not saying it's the same, but that feeling you have because someone is trying to take Brandon from you? Is it possible Tiernan could be feeling a little of that, too?"

I hadn't thought about that, which shamed me a bit. It was easy to look back at our time in Lion Court, even before those weeks Tiernan visited our home in Texas, and see the bond he and Brandon had formed. The memory of the big, bad scarred man making pancakes with flour on his face for a little boy because he'd thought he'd missed his birthday. The Hulk figurine that had appeared on Brando's bedside after his seizure. Picasso, and the date for surgery set in January that might actually stop my brother's seizures permanently.

It seemed almost like Tiernan loved him.

I stood there in the masses of New Yorkers bustling past as if time had stood still for me alone. It seemed cruel to say I'd thought Tiernan was totally heartless, but I certainly hadn't thought he was capable of genuine, compassionate love. How ridiculous of me when it had been staring me in the face this whole time.

Just because Tiernan wasn't capable of loving *me* didn't mean he wasn't capable of it at all.

He'd been good to Brando since the beginning.

Because he loved him.

For whatever reason, my beautiful baby brother had found his way through Tiernan's fortress of solitude into his heart.

My own panged in my chest like the chords of an old harp, brittle, close to breaking under the strain.

"I think you understand me," Elena said softly into the silence.

My answer was a long-winded sigh that prompted her to laugh.

"I want to help you, Bianca, I will help you. But I need you to understand that Tiernan is my client so if what you need or want is in direct conflict with him, I can't be involved."

"Yeah, I figured," I said sullenly. "But I understand."

"You said Tiernan told you that your dad left you an inheritance and he was trying to find it," Elena mused allowed. I could hear the clack of long nails thrumming on a desk in the background. "Let me quietly ask around to figure out which lawyer handled Lane's estate. Maybe he or she can give us some answers."

"Thank you, Elena," I said, hope bubbling in my chest. "I only need one more thing from you."

"Anything," she said instantly, and if it was

possible to love someone you barely knew, I did then.

"Where exactly does Tiernan work in the city?"

✧   ✧   ✧

INEQUITY WAS IMPOSSIBLE to find unless you knew exactly where to look.

It was down a short flight of stairs like so many other businesses in Soho, but the blue door was nondescript, not even a sign to mark its contents. Just a keypad to one side housed in a black box affixed with a golden lion symbol on the front.

Elena had hesitated to give me the code, but she'd told me where to go.

Happily, a simple phone call to Henrik revealed the combination.

Apparently, it rotated every week to keep members and unwanted intruders on their toes, but that week the six-digit code was my name.

Bianca.

242622.

I tried not to feel that like a punch to the throat, but I was disorientated as the door swung open to reveal a small, almost cramped reception and coat check. Everything seemed almost in a shambles, old and tired, including the older Black man sitting on a stool behind a partition like a coat check attendant.

"Name?" he said, his long, beautiful eyes squinted as he peered at me.

"Bianca Belcante," I said even though I knew I wasn't on the list.

To my surprise, the man broke into a wide, toothy grin as white as gum squares. "I've been waitin' for you."

"Oh?"

He chuckled deeply. "Oh yeah, Miss B, Henrik called me not ten minutes ago to say you were on your way. Charity is waintin' for ya. Go on in."

I blinked at him for a moment, trying to understand exactly what the hell this place was. It seemed like the entry to a theatre but even though Tiernan was like something straight out of Shakespearean tragedy, I couldn't see him associating with theatre or drama in anyway.

The man laughed at my confusion. "I'm Chuck Bentley. I've run this door since Tiernan opened ten years ago, you'll find a lotta shenanigans behind that door, but none of it should kill ya."

Heartening.

I braced my shoulders and went to the next blue door.

"Password for that one's 200204," he called out.

My birthday.

February 20th 2004.

Something in my chest crashed and crumbled into motor and brick filled dust. It felt, terrifyingly, like a section of the walls I'd been trying to build and maintain around my heart.

I punched in the code and opened the surprisingly heavy door.

It was heavy, because it was something like the door to a *vault* with steel reinforcements and heavy locking mechanisms.

What the hell?

Noise spilled into the little room before I could even fully open it. Sounds of laughing and chatter, a hollow, clanking *ping*, and technical sounding rattle. The air was warmer there, my new heavy winter coat suddenly suffocating.

And then I saw it.

The lobby.

The ceilings soared above me, golden accents and beautifully rendered designs pulled from various mythologies. There was Zeus with Leda the swan and there was Odin with one eye and his two Ravens. Chandeliers sparkled in domed pockets throughout the massive space, their shine so bright I had to squint when I looked at them.

Below it all was chaos. Sumptuous, sinful chaos.

It was clearly something of an underground casino, but I'd never seen such beautiful slots machines, such lush velvet on the mahogany table tops where poker and Black Jack and whatever else people who gambled played. It wasn't the blatantly expense of the furnishings and aesthetic that made me draw breath though.

It was the people.

I recognized some celebrities, an older female popstar I'd listened to since I was a kid, a retired soccer player who'd married a famous actress, even a politician or two I'd met when Caroline hosted a charity brunch last weekend. They were all dressed impeccably, expensively, in outfits that put my new nine-hundred-dollar velvet dress to shame.

And it was only five o'clock in the evening.

I had no doubt the group would swell in numbers as the night went on, too.

The opulence and energy went straight to my head as if I'd had too much champagne.

It was magical.

A smile split my face as I stood in the entry surveying Tiernan's den of inequity like a glutton faced with an endless feast.

When a gorgeous, model thin woman appeared at my side, she was smiling too.

"I see you like it here already." She had a thick Russian accent that made it seem as if she was speaking around marbles tucked into her cheeks.

"It's unlike anything I've ever seen," I admitted, watching as a staff member in a slinky gold dress served a tray of champagne to gamblers at a roulette table. "I feel a bit like Alice through the Looking Glass."

She frowned at me, not understanding the reference. "Well, Mr. Wagner asked me to see that you were settled."

"I'm looking for Mr. Morelli."

"He isn't in yet. May I suggest you wait at one of the tables? Mr. Wagner suggested it himself."

I was guessing Mr. Wagner was Henrik and it was difficult to imagine pink nail polish wearing, prank-loving Henrik as the stern Mr. Wagner in charge of *Inequity* beneath Tiernan. At the same time, I loved the dichotomy of it. Of Henrik and Tiernan and everyone in Lion Court.

Even, I was coming to understand, in myself.

Giddiness bubbled up my throat and erupted

in something like a giggle. "Lead the way," I suggested.

I learned the Russian woman's real name was Inga as she led me to one of the lower stakes poker tables where they were playing Texas Hold 'Em. The dealer was also beautiful—I was sensing a theme—and he carefully explained the rules to me while Inga disappeared for a moment. When she returned, it was to settle a massive stack of chips in front of me.

When I gaped at her, she laughed.

"An early Christmas present," she said. "From Mr. Wagner."

I grinned as I picked up a thousand-dollar chip. "Do you know, I've never held so much money in my hands before?"

She grinned at me, knocking me in the shoulder in sisterly solidarity. "Enjoy it while it lasts. You know, the house usually wins."

I knew that even though I wasn't a gambler (I'd never had any money to spare to risk it on anything). But Inga didn't know what I did.

If this house was Tiernan's, technically, it was my house too.

So, when I settled in to play, I did it channeling my scarred guardian's cool arrogance. I found it wasn't difficult. I'd always vacillated between a potential career in art or one in environmental business, so math was a proficiency of mine. Before I knew it, I'd forgotten my original intention in seeking out Tiernan and there was a group at our table watching our game.

I'd just won *seven hundred dollars* when a dark-haired man switched out for a woman beside me at the table. I didn't look at him, at first, but the hair on the nape of my neck stood on end as the air was filled with static.

"You play well for a beginner," a low, smoky voice practically purred. "It must be luck."

I grinned as I stared at my cards, a pair of pocket Queens. "Whatever it is, I'll take it."

"Or perhaps you're just distracting everyone else at the table with your beauty," he suggested, but the words weren't an effort at seduction.

They were sharp-edged as knives.

A threat more than a compliment.

I tossed my chips in to call then carefully put my cards down so I could face the newcomer.

The moment I did, my heart stopped.

He was older, maybe early or mid-thirties, but his age only heightened the planes of his symmetrical perfection, roughening the beauty in a way that was utterly masculine. Swarthy, with the olive tinged skin I shared due to my Italian ancestry, and five o'clock shadow as dark as spilled ink across his jawline, he was both striking and vaguely menacing, like something out of an old school mafia film.

But his beauty wasn't what stole my breath away and left icy panic in its wake.

It was the fact that I *knew* him.

Remembered him.

How could I ever forget who abducted me as a girl?

He stared at me calmly, almost impassively, but his entire body was turned to me, attuned to me, and when he saw the panic in my face, his lips twitched with triumph.

"Hello Bianca," he said.

And a second later, I screamed.

CHAPTER TEN

Tiernan

"**T**IERNAN? DO YOU have a moment?"

I looked up from my computer to see Beckett Fairchild lurking in the doorway to my office. He was a handsome older man who carried himself the way any man born into an American legacy of money and power carried himself. As if he expected people to bow when he entered a room.

I didn't bow.

In fact, I didn't give him more than a cursory glance before I went back to searching for business opportunities we could lay like bait in a trap for Bryant.

"I do not," I said.

Still, he lingered.

When I watched the monitors or walked through *Inequity's* casino floor, Beckett struck me as a self-possessed man with a quiet, smug kind of grace, but whenever he sought me out, there was a nervous energy he couldn't quite hide in his hands.

I wondered with dark pleasure if my reputation frightened him, or if it was just that he had a long association with the Constantine family and I was a Morelli. I didn't give a crap who he associated with as long as he kept frequenting my illicit businesses.

"Only, I wanted to talk to you about something rather important," he continued, as if I hadn't effectively dismissed him.

"I highly doubt there is anything you could tell me that I'm dying to hear," I said, honestly, without sparing him a look. "I'm a very busy man, Beckett."

There was a thread of humor in his tone that set my teeth on edge when he said, "You're very like your father sometimes."

"If you knew anything about Bryant, you'd know better than to say that to my face," I said softly, the threat buried in my low voice.

He held up his hands in surrender. "I meant nothing by it, I apologise. I came to talk about something very pressing, Tiernan. I'm going to have to insist you give me a moment of your time.

I've been trying to get in touch with you for weeks, now."

I knew that, of course. But there was something about Beckett that put me on edge. It could have been his close relationship with the Constantine family, but it was something deeper than that. There was something in his pale gaze that unsettled me and the feeling had never faded, not even when he as he became one of the biggest patrons of *Inequity* over the years. I avoided him as often as possible and pawned him off on Henrik.

Only Henrik wasn't in tonight because he, Ezra, and Walcott were taking Brando to see the new Marvel film at the cinema. The kid had begged me to go too, but there was no way I was going to sit on my ass when Bryant Morelli was no doubt racing to take me down as soon as he could.

Instead, I'd given Brandon a hundred bucks to gorge himself on sweets at the theatre and promised him fucking pancakes tomorrow morning as well. Brando had seemed to find my reluctance to indulge in the holiday spirit amusing and he'd somberly dubbed me 'Grinch' with a three-foot-long candy cane Ezra had bought him earlier.

My lips twitched as I thought about it, but then I remembered Beckett was staring at me with that acute gaze and I schooled my features into a scowl.

"Well, what is?"

He seemed surprised then hesitant, rubbing a hand over his dark brown stubble in an obvious nervous gesture.

"Well, out with it, man!"

Beckett finally opened his mouth to speak when a scream tore through the casino, filtering through the door Beckett hadn't fully closed behind him. Icy fear clutched me by the throat.

No one screamed in my casino.

Not ever.

I was on my feet, the gun pulled from the holster under my injured arm in an instant.

"Wait here," I barked to Beckett, who'd frozen, as I jogged around the desk and yanked the door open. "Lock this behind me. Only open it for six staccato knocks."

Before he could answer, I was out in the chaos. Patrons scurried for the exits guided by my calm employees. Even though the casino seemed like one long uninterrupted space without windows or exits, there were secret passage and doors faded seamlessly into walls throughout for exactly this reason.

I followed the calamity to the far right of the casino space, keeping an eye on the lockdown procedures as I went.

"Sir, get back to your office," Gerard shouted over the constant murmur of shouts and cries from scared gamblers.

I ignored him and surged forward.

A ring of employees, guards with bullet proof vests worked into their uniforms, blocked the scene around a Black Jack table. They had their guns trained on a dark head barely visible through the tight security.

When I pushed between two men, they parted instantly.

I hadn't been expecting anything. My mind was a cold, empty chamber just waiting for whatever moronic asshole had thought to hold up *my* casino to stumble into my cruel keeping. I'd show him ruthlessly why no one else had ever dared to fuck with *Inequity* and in doing so, I'd send a clear message carved into that man's flesh why no one should ever dare to fuck with it again.

But I hadn't been expecting this.

The sight of Bianca Belcante held trapped against a man with a gun held to her temple.

Her eyes found me instantly, too blue in the

bloodless expanse of her horrified face.

She clawed at the arm around her neck, blood trickling from the deep wounds she had inflicted on her attacker. It did something to allay my fear, to see that small sign of her courage and fight. To know that maybe I'd given her the courage to stand up for herself when she'd never known how to do that before me.

But that small pleasure was lost in the avalanche of cold rage that blurred my vision momentarily and eradicated whatever logic I'd thought to shackle my fury with.

I was all wrath.

All violence.

My entire body vibrated with it, finger clamped too-tightly around the trigger of the gun as I brought it up to aim at the face of the man who dared to touch what was *mine*.

I'd burn *Inequity* to the ground myself before I let another man get away with touching what was mine.

And he wasn't just touching her.

He was threatening her.

The barrel of a Ruger GP100 grinding into her temple. The brutal, almost suffocating hold on her neck.

I wasn't just going to kill this motherfucker.

I was going to dismantle him.

Piece by fucking piece.

Atom by goddamn atom.

So he felt every single inch of his incremental march toward death.

So he begged me, fucking wept for me to end him.

And oh, that would be sweet.

Not sweet enough to eradicate this brutal fury, this crushing fear, the kind of which I hadn't felt since the day Bryant found out about my romance with Grace Constantine when I was seventeen.

But it would go a long way to making me saner.

To making Bianca safer.

"You're a dead man." The words tore up my chest, savaged my throat and cut through the air like knives.

The man holding my woman shifted his face out from the shadows, from the cloud of her golden hair and I saw with shocked clarity that it was Santo.

The gun in my hand dipped, dropping almost impulsively, because I knew this man.

I almost trusted him, as far as I ever trusted anyone.

And he was not someone I ever would have guessed would hurt what was mine.

"Tiernan," he growled. "Tell your guard dogs to lower their damn weapons."

"Not a chance," I returned coldly, stepping forward with my gun once more trained dead center in his forehead. "If you release Bianca now, maybe I'll kill you quickly."

"Tiernan," he said flatly, as if I was being unreasonable.

"Release her right this fucking minute!" I roared, the words echoing in the now near-empty casino.

Above us, the mammoth chandelier rattled gently.

Santo's dark brows cut high into his forehead, clearly shocked by my outburst. "I wouldn't hurt her," he said slowly, almost condescendingly.

"He's the one," Bianca countered and her voice was calm, so calm.

Pride surged amongst the fury in my chest and ebbed.

"He's the person who abducted me when I was a girl," she told me, wincing slightly as my men stepped closer and Santo pressed the gun hard enough to her temple to blanch the skin.

Fury so bright, it whited out my vision.

Through it, I was only vaguely aware of growling, "Drop the damn weapon or I'll drop you right now, Santo."

Something changed in Bianca's face, something important, but I couldn't see beyond the veil of my own feelings like a red curtain hanging between us.

"I wouldn't ever hurt her, you fucking *stronzo*," Santo gritted out. "I've spent most of my life trying to protect her."

"Prove it then," I goaded, jerking my chin at Hank, who stood directly behind Santo, giving him the signal to put the man down if he didn't immediately obey.

I was done fucking around with Bianca's life.

Each second she spent pressed close to potential death made me feel dangerously close to my own.

"Drop it," I demanded for the last time.

Santo had never been an idiot, far from it, and he'd never had a death wish.

So, after a fierce curse in Italian, he loosened his hold on Bianca, shockingly pressed a brief kiss to her temple, and stepped away.

My men were on him in an instant, shoving him to the ground and wrenching his hands behind his back to cuff them.

But I was only distantly aware of it, because my focus was on Bianca.

It took me two steps to reach her and when I did, I hauled her into my arms roughly, unable to gentle the ferocity of my need to feel her against me. One hand cupped the back of her head, feeling the smallness of her and a resulting echo of panic in my soul. She was so fucking young, so slight and untried in the ways of this horrible world.

The cruel irony was obvious to me. Once, I'd so deliberately put her in harms way when now, all I wanted to do was protect her from everything, even something so slight as a fucking papercut.

My relief at holding her was compounded by the intensity of her own embrace. She clawed at my back as if she could press closer, her nose tucked into the side of my throat, her lips stamped to my hammering pulse.

"My sweet little thing," I realized I was saying, the rough proclamation a mantra. "My sweet little thing."

Bianca just squeezed me tighter, locking her legs around my waist in a fully body hug.

"Sir?"

I ignored Hank, smoothing my hand down

Bianca's silken hair, pressing a kiss to her forehead. I wanted to lay her out on the nearest surface and check every inch of her skin for injury.

"Sir?" Hank tried again.

I adjusted Bianca so I could look over her head, pressing her cheek down on my good shoulder. "What?"

Hank blanched at my tone. "What do you want done with the attacker?"

"He's not an attacker," Bianca surprised me by saying, pulling away and squirming so I was forced to put her down.

"For fuck's sake, you can't possibly be so naïve to believe I'll forgive the motherfucker for pressing a gun to your head."

She glared at me, all softness and gratitude forgotten. I'd never tell her that the sight of her familiar scowl was almost as welcome as her smile after days without her presence in my home.

"If you call me naïve one more time, Tiernan, it'll be the last," she warned, drilling a pointed finger into my chest before casting a wary glance at Santo who was being hauled unceremoniously to his feet. "I'm ready to forgive him for more than just putting a gun to my head." She sucked in a deep breath and expelled it so harshly it stirred her hair. "But he's not just a random attacker or the man who abducted me when I was a kid. If he's who I think he is, that man is my uncle."

CHAPTER ELEVEN

Bianca

"TAKE HIM DOWNSTAIRS," Tiernan growled to his group of employees as he snuck an arm around my waist and tugged me hard into his side. "I'll be down shortly. And someone get Beckett Fairchild out of my damn office."

"Yes, sir." A man with a name tag that pronounced him as 'Hank' barked a sharp series of orders to the crew and they immediately dispersed as quickly as they'd appeared.

In moments, Tiernan and I were alone on the massive casino floor.

A fission of fear scoured through me, different than the kind I'd felt with a gun trained on me for the second time in two weeks.

Palpable fury emanated off Tiernan's large body in waves that buffeted against me and alchemized something in my gut. Something base, almost animal, that got off on fear and transmuted it into pure molten desire.

"He is the last man who will *ever* touch you." The words rumbled through Tiernan and into me.

I gasped when he carted me up into his arms and took two brisk steps to the same table I'd only recently gambled on. He deposited me roughly on the felt, his body carving out so much space between my splayed thighs that the muscles burned from the stretch. His big hands splayed on my ass and tugged me even closer so our bodies were fused through our clothes.

"I won't let you go," he warned, his voice ravaged by fury and something like agony. His fingers flexed compulsively, almost too tight. "Not after this. You can't expect me to let you out of my goddamn sight when there are too many people out for my blood. Out for the secret of who you are."

"Tiernan," I said, just his name, as if that was enough to explain the multitudes of reasons why I wanted to be with him at Lion Court but didn't trust him, why I wanted him with enough passion to sear through my soul but couldn't let myself have him.

"You want to see me beg for your forgiveness,

Bianca? I'll do it on my knees between your thighs and by the time I'm through with you, you won't remember anything but pleasure." His eyes were all black, his pupils' thin frames for the ferocity of his intent. He shook me slightly in frustration. "Do you want me to carve your fucking name into my chest to prove to you that I am mad for you? Lost to you? Nothing will ever fucking do again except for *you*?"

"Yes," I said, my throat raw from the honesty of the word. "Yes, I want all of it. Just once, I want someone to fight for me!"

Tiernan's hand came up to grasp my chin, holding it steady so he could lean forward and press his forehead to mine. He was so close all I could see were those green eyes as pale and warm as diffused light through trees.

"I've been fighting my entire life, Bianca." That rough palm traced the edge over my jaw and framed the entire left side of my face. "So I know, this is one fight I won't lose. You know now, the kind of man I am, I'll kill anyone who tries to hurt you, who even thinks about taking us from each other. Do you understand?"

I kissed him, then. Surging up to claim his firm mouth with my open, to sweep past those satin lips into the hot cavern of his mouth and lay claim to every inch of it.

Because I understand exactly what kind of man Tiernan Morelli McTiernan was.

He was a monster. One who wanted to swallow me whole. Maybe a smarter girl would have tried to run away, but it seemed that whenever I picked up my feet, it was toward him I ran.

I wondered—as Tiernan gathered my hair in one strong fist and tugged my head back to kiss me deeply, a groan captured between our mouths—if the difference between a monster and savoir was a matter of perspective. Because the truth was, even when Tiernan had sought to use me, he'd protected me in equal turn. He could have left us to rot in foster care or locked up in the attic of Lion Court and forced us to do his bidding like some 18th century gothic fairy-tale gone wrong. Instead, he bought Brando Spiderman sheets and made his pancakes, he gave me carte blanche on a shopping spree and sent me to the best prep school in the Tri-State area.

There was a deep river of kindness flowing through the arctic tundra of Tiernan's heart and I was fairly sure Brandon and I had stumbled into it much earlier on than I'd originally thought.

I wondered if the moment Tiernan made me bleed around the thorny stem of that rose, if he hadn't begun to bleed a little for me himself.

"Stop thinking so loudly," he murmured against my damp lips. "It's insulting when I'm trying to kiss you senseless."

"I am senseless," I promised him, raking my hands through his luscious dark hair, loving that I was allowed to do that. "Any girl with sense would run the other way."

A smile played over his mouth, that ropey scar on his left cheek flaring white with the tension. The expression fell when I touched my fingers lightly to the mark, feathering it from the edge of his full mouth to the bottom of his ear. His hand snapped up to grab mine in a tight grip. A current of fear chase down my spine, but he only pressed a kiss to my palm and then pressed it again to his face, tight over his scar.

"I'm not a good man and I have no desire to ever be one," he admitted in that rough, sex-heavy tone that made my belly tingle. "But I don't think you want a good man between these pretty thighs. For such a sweet little thing, you love to be owned and used."

"Maybe, I'm not as sweet as you think I am," I countered.

His hand dipped beneath my skirt to cup my entire underwear-clad sex in his palm. I watched as he brought damp fingers to his mouth and sucked on the tips. "I beg to differ."

A shiver ripped through me like a rusty zipper and when Tiernan slipped both hands beneath my skirt to tag the edge of my panties and slide the down my thighs, I lifted my ass without struggle.

"Enough talking," he declared. "I believe I was in the middle of groveling."

Before I could process, he was down on his knees. He was so tall, even on kneeling he was at eye level with my groin. Without waiting for permission, he tugged me farther along the edge of the poker table, flipped up the flared velvet skirt of my dress and fixed his mouth over my pussy.

I fell back to the felt table, landing hard on my elbows, head falling back between my shoulders as I let out a ragged moan.

"Tiernan," I panted as his mouth did delicious, wicked things to my throbbing clit. "Someone could walk in any minute."

"No one would dare," he growled into my inner thigh before nipping at the sensitive flesh there. "And if they did, they'd enjoy a very happy last sight of my gorgeous little thing in throes of passion before I knocked them out."

"Such a heathen," I admonished, but the

effect was lost as I knifed up, my hands burying themselves in Tiernan's hair as he started to fuck my clasping entrance with his tongue.

I loved him like this, raw and brutal. The sight of the big man forcing my thighs apart with the width of his suited shoulders, his dark head bent to feast on me almost savagely, chin coated in my juices, his tongue wet and loud in my folds was almost too much to bear.

"Fuck yeah," he rasped as he pulled away to watch two fingers stretch me open and begin to fuck me. "So gorgeous for me. Do you forgive me yet, sweet thing?"

"No, but maybe if you make me come, I will."

His laugh was pure smoke. "Oh, be careful what you wish for."

A second later, a third finger was wedging itself inside me, working me open in a way that stung and throbbed pleasantly at the same time. His hot, satin mouth sealed over my clit and began to trash it mercilessly with his tongue.

My orgasm reared over me so suddenly, I couldn't breathe. I couldn't even see as it descended, just blackness in my vision and then, as the climax boke over me, wheeling whorls of color and blinding light. I was vaguely aware of the broken groan and gasps falling from my mouth, of the way my pussy spasmed around his thick fingers, wetting him down to his elbow, but I was too far gone to even imagine being embarrassed by my wantonness.

When my vision clear, he was still between my legs, a dark, triumphant grin curling the scarred side of his mouth.

"Again," he declared and then bent once more to pay his penance on my swollen pussy.

This time, he was ruthless, curling his fingers against a spot inside me that made me see so many stars I thought I was witnessing the entire galaxy unfurled around me. He made me moan and keen like an animal, begging for more and for mercy at the same time. When his teeth rasped ever so gently over my hypersensitive clit, I burst open at the seams, thoughts and inhibitions escaping into nothingness.

"Tiernan," I cried again and again, his name echoing in the massive empty casino. "Tiernan."

"That's it, little thing," he murmured, eyes glittering when I finally found the energy to lift my head to look down at home. "Such a good girl coming all over my hand. You taste so fucking sweet."

A moan rattled loose in my chest and fell out my open, panting mouth. I wanted to beg him to stop, but each orgasm seemed to carve a path out inside me that led to *more*. Greed trampled through me, eviscerating my concerns, my exhaustion and shame.

"Fuck me," I begged, "Please, Tiernan, I need you inside me."

"It might hurt," he warned on a low rumble as if the idea pleased him. "You're so swollen and you're still practically a virgin. I haven't had the time to fit you to my cock properly yet."

"Oh my God."

He chuckled as he lazily toyed with my swollen pussy, running his fingers through my wetness as if swimming laps in a pool.

"I think one more and I should really be forgiven," he mused, sucking at the inside of one thigh.

"I forgive you," I promised. "Please, I forgive me. I don't know how much more I can take."

"Let's find out, shall we?" His voice was dark as his hot gaze as he fixed it between my legs.

I shuddered violently as he gently started to work his mouth over me again. He was softer, aware of how sensitive and swollen I was, but still ceaseless. It took longer to build the heat inside me, kindling laid piece by piece. By the time I was sweating, writing on the table under the punishing grip of Tiernan's hands as he fought to keep me still under his tongue, my entire lower body felt as if it was on fire. I wanted to put it out nearly as desperately as I wanted to give in to the heat and luxuriate in its sweet-sharp bite.

"Tiernan, please," I whispered scream, nearly sobbing from the intensity.

"You ask so fucking pretty," he praised as he suddenly stood up and stepped away from me.

Cool air wafted over my overheated sex and I groaned then groaned again as I watched him teared open his trousers. His thick cock was almost purple with lust as he took it in his fist and gave it one vicious stroke.

"Do you need this, little thing?" he taunted. "Do you want to come all over me?"

"Yes," I gasped as he stepped forward, the hot tip of his erection like a branding iron on my wet folds. "God, yes."

"Then, do it. Come for me," he ordered magnanimously as he gripped my hips and impaled me completely on one brutal thrust.

I screamed soundlessly as my pussy clenched all around him, pulling him even deeper, desperate for *more, more, more*, even as I felt myself shatter with overwhelming pleasure. There were tears on my cheeks and the filthy, wet slap of

Tiernan's cock sawing in and out of my tight folds while he held me still through my orgasm. My elbows were abraded by the felt table and my thigh were weak from the strain of spasming through so many orgasms.

And still, somehow, when I emerged from the depths of my pain-edged climax, I wanted more. Honestly, the depth of my insatiability almost scared me.

Tiernan read the fear in my eyes and grinned like a demon. "Hush, sweet thing, don't worry. I'll keep fucking you until you're ruined for more. You'd like that, wouldn't you?"

When I whimpered in response, he placed a hand in my sternum and pushed me flat to the felt. Leaning over me, he kissed me softly, soothing the edge of pain thrumming through my body with the sweet press of his lips. The high frequency energy tingling through every inch of me gentled, mellowed, as he curried my torso with strong strokes of his hands.

"You can take more," he promised me, hooking an arm around one of my limp legs to raise it up over his shoulder. "Tell me, Bianca."

"I want more," I answered immediately, my voice threadbare from screaming and moaning. "I always want more with you."

Pure masculine triumph lit his face and his handsomeness took my breath away.

He pulled me up into his arms, hugging me tight as he thrust up into me. His rough pubic hair abraded my clit in a way that had my nails scrabbling at his back through his suit, my teeth sinking into his corded neck to anchor me to him as I threatened to float away.

But no matter how hard he fucked me like that, I couldn't seem to orgasm again. Frustration built inside me along this intense, itchy need to climax again.

"Please," I begged incoherently, clawing at Tiernan's head as if I could force him to break me open around this burning energy inside me one last time. "Please."

"I know what you need," he promised, pulling away from my grasping hands.

I watched blearily as he moved to the nearby craps table with his trousers hanging open around his wet, red cock. He grabbed a glossy wooden stick with a flat golden end from the felt top that I'd seen the dealers use to push chips around on the table. He tested the weight of the implement against his palm and then glanced over at me with dark intent rich in his eyes.

"Tiernan," I said in warning.

"Hush," he encouraged as he stalked back to me.

Quickly and easily, as if I was a ragdoll, he flipped me over on the table so my torso was pressed to the felt and my legs dangled over the edge, bottom thrust into the air. He was inside me the next second, his air-cooled dick soothing inside my sensitive pussy.

"Brace against the table, little thing. This one is going to end both of us," he promised as he wrapped one hand around my shoulder for leverage.

On his second thrust, I discovered what he had grabbed the stick for. It slapped down against the bare skin of my ass, lighting my tired nerve-endings in a way that made me gasp and clutch fruitlessly against the felt table top.

"Tiernan," I ground out between my clenched teeth as he fucked me and beat my bottom with the dealer's stick. "Oh my God, it's too intense."

"Do you want me to stop?" he asked, his civilized veneer crushed beneath the heel of his savage desire. "Or do you like the pain? Does it make your swollen pussy ache for me?"

"More," I sobbed, crying as sensation crashed through me, obliterating everything I had left. The sting of the improvised crop on my ass ricocheted through me like a battering ram. "More, please, more."

"Fuck," he groaned long and low. "I can feel you milking me. Do you want my cum inside you, little thing? I'm going to fill you up until your leaking down your thighs and then I'm going to feed it to you."

My fifth orgasm overtook me like a predator in the night, overpowering me with ferocious teeth and claws. It tore me apart piece by piece, until I was a shivering, gasping mess hanging over the table like slaughtered prey. The sound of Tiernan's victorious shout and the feel of him pumping me full of his cum, cock jerking against my clenching cunt, made me nearly pass out from the pleasure and for a moment, everything went blessedly black.

When I came to moments later, Tiernan was gently cleaning me up with a silk handkerchief, his touch light between my ravaged folds. He hushed me and murmured little words of praise as he tucked his softening cock away and gently collected me off the table into his arm. I settled in his hold easily, utterly boneless and spent.

When he pressed a kiss to my forehead and then another to each cheek, I was too tired to tease him for his sudden loveliness.

"Am I forgiven?" he whispered against my lips, and that wasn't a tease, but an aching vulnerability.

I forced my eyes open so I could look up into his equally shattered expression. "Carve my name into your chest and we'll see, but you're getting there."

He chuckled, kissed the top of my head and started walking us through the casino. "Rest, my sweet thing. I'll keep you safe while you sleep."

"We still have to talk," I warned, but the words were slurred with exhaustion.

"We will," he promised. "For now, you've earned some sweet dreams."

And even though there were still countless questions that needed answering, pasts that needed decoding and futures to plan, I believed him and fell swiftly in my first deep, dreamless sleep in weeks.

CHAPTER TWELVE

Tiernan

FOUR LEVELS BELOW street level, there was a room I liked to use for situations like these. Concrete floors and walls, the former stained with faint rust-like splotches around the center drain from years of spilling enemy blood.

I had Santo hanging there now, suspended over that middle drain by chains manacled to his wrists. His arms were wrenched nearly out of their sockets, blood streaming down his torso from the split in his right cheekbone where my knuckles had cut through flesh.

I studied my false friend as he hung like a side of meat from the ceiling. I'd known Santo for years. He was often called in to do the work too dirty and dangerous for Bryant to pass off on even his least favorite son. In recent years, he'd joined the Belcante crime family under *capo* Monte

Belcante, but before that, he'd been a thug-for-hire the Morelli family put to good use.

In the past, we'd strung up men exactly as Santo was now, and the irony wasn't lost on me.

Hank had gagged him before I entered the room, and I took my time laying into him. His entire torso would be one large bruise tomorrow, but he deserved that and more for threatening and terrifying Bianca. I didn't care if he was her uncle or fucking God himself. Anyone who raised a hand to my little thing deserved to nothing but pain and misery.

Santo took it like the man and mafioso he was, barely groaning as each of my brutal hits landed, but now he hung, swaying slightly, as if in a coma. My own body was aching from the beating, my fight against Lucian the day before, and the bullet wound still healing at the top of my shoulder so I decided he'd had enough and ripped the gag from Santo's bleeding mouth.

I rolled my shoulders back, ridding myself of the last of the tenderness I'd felt when I was with Bianca so I could face Santo as the cold motherfucker I usually was. It was hard, after the last thirty minutes I'd spent with Bianca, with the taste of her still on my tongue even though I'd washed my hands and cock in my office bathroom like a whore after setting her sleeping form on the couch.

My old friend lifted his head slightly and glared at me from under the tangle of sweat drenched hair falling into his face.

"There was no need for this," he told me blandly. "If you wanted to fight, I'd have been happy to have a go in the ring."

"You put a gun to the temple of my ward, my need is for more than just a fight." My voice was mild as I stalked over to Hank and took a bludgeon from his grip. "Do I need to extract my pound of flesh now or will you tell me what the hell you were doing first?"

Santo's chuckle was hollow and bitter. "Your ward? Fuck." He squeezed his eyes shut. "I look away for a few years and this happens."

"Look away from what?" I demanded, even though I had Bianca's voice in my head saying '*my uncle.*'

"From my sister." He shifted in the restraints even though it hurt so he could fix me with a level glare. "From her children."

"Bianca mentioned she thought you were her long-lost uncle. Funny, in all the years I've known you, you never one mentioned family. The orphan taken in by the Belcante family, that's how the world knows you."

"You never wondered about her last name?" he countered.

"Belcante is a common enough Italian surname. It would have been a pathetic stretch to assume a widowed mistress and her two kids living in Bumfuck, Texas had any association with the New York crime family."

"Maybe so, but it's true." Santo spat out a wad of blood saliva. "I'm not an orphan old man Monte took in out of the good of his heart. Aida and I were his bastard children. I think you know a little about being born out of wedlock?"

I snarled at him in response, but he only smiled thinly.

"Our mother got the hell out of town when he rose in the ranks and he couldn't find us for years. When he did…" he shrugged. "He intended to marry off Aida for connections and make me his successor because he didn't have a legitimate heir. Instead, Lane Constantine met my sister one day when he was negotiating with Monte and within a month, he'd taken her away."

My brain was slower because of the recent orgasm, but I found myself connecting the pieces of the story in quick succession.

"Monte didn't like that," I speculated, because

the recently deceased Italian-born mafioso was notoriously jealous and possessive.

For the last five years since Lane Constantine had died under a cloud of suspicion, most people had assumed Bryant (and me by extension) had had something to do with his death. But this offered a second, even more intriguing option. If Lane had taken Monte's daughter out from under his nose, he would have painted an enormous target on his back.

Italians didn't often forgive and forget.

Hence the Morelli family motto: *et vindictam retribute in alis nigro.*

Vengeance on black wings.

"He sent someone after them a few times," Santo confirmed. "I was able to intercept them the first couple, but someone finally found them Upstate. They abducted Bianca from school."

"She said it was *you.*"

"She was a kid and it was a fucking traumatizing experience. It's not surprising she doesn't remember the details." He had the audacity to roll his eyes at me. "A guy named Bruno Puglisi kept her in an abandoned house for two days even though he was ordered to bring her back to Monte." Santo's jaw went white with strain as fury transformed his face. "He was thinking about taking her away for himself."

His fury echoed through me like a gunshot in an empty room. "Tell me you killed him."

"I carved him up like a Christmas ham using his own knife," Santo promised with a gleaming smile, white against the blood on his chin. "When I found her, she was locked up in a room using a fucking pan as a toilet. When Lane showed up, he had his own go at Bruno."

It stirred something in me to know the perfect Lane Constantine was as vengeful, corrupt, and deceitful as any Morelli. The man had done dealings with the mafia, stolen one of their women as his mistress, had two children out of wedlock and hidden a fortune from his wife in their name. In a way, I admired his ability to keep his dirty deceptions as far removed from his public persona as he had.

Us Morellis hadn't been so successful.

"I told them I wouldn't be able to help them again without jeopardizing my position." Santo's voice took on a faraway quality as he looked into the past. "I wanted to make something of myself so I could take care of Aida and the kids myself."

"You were a kid yourself," I noted, because Santo was even younger than me, only twenty-seven years old.

He shrugged. "Sometimes, being a kid's got nothing to do with your level of responsibility."

I thought of Bianca laying upstairs, how innocent and young she looked in sleep. It was such a contrasted to the wisdom she wore on her soul like battle scars and the slope of her shoulders carrying too much weight from too young an age.

My heart stopped and restarted in my chest as I thought how lonely she must have been all her life.

Almost as lonely as I'd been.

"How did you lose touch?" I asked, shaking myself momentarily loose of Bianca's hold on me. "Obviously, you weren't around of I'd never have been next in line for guardianship."

"When they moved, Lane decided not to tell me where he'd placed them just in case my loyalty to Monte outweighed my loyalty to my own sister," he spat the words.

"So, no one knew where they were in Texas until I found them," I concluded.

"Not quite. Lane told his best friend—"

There was a knock at the door then that had me glowering at Hank when he stuck his head through the opening.

"Sorry to interrupt, sir, but Mr. Fairchild is still here and he's asking to speak with you urgently."

"Tell him to fuck off," I barked, before turning back to Santo. "If you're so loyal to Bianca and Brando, where the fuck were you when Aida died?"

"I didn't realize she'd passed away until a few weeks ago," he admitted. "I found them a few years ago and had a man check in every few months, when he went this time, he reported they'd been taken into foster care. I was still searching for them in Texas until Gabriella told me her new friend Bianca was a ward of Tiernan Morelli." He glared at me. "I think it should be *me* playing the protective older man here, Morelli, what the fuck have you been doing with my niece and nephew?"

Sudden exhaustion settled into my bones. I sagged against a metal table set against the wall and crossed my arms. "Making a fucking mess of things, of course."

He continued to glower at me for a moment before humor twitched in his upper lip. "You always were good at that."

I shrugged. "I'm humble, but you're right."

This prompted a laugh from my old friend before he sobered. "These kids are all I have left of my sister. They should be with me, Tiernan. Even you should understand, kids are off-limits in our games."

"They should be, but they aren't," I said darkly. "You and I are both examples of that. It doesn't matter, they're in it, now, and they're in it with *me*. I won't give them up for anyone, even their uncle."

"Do I have to fight you on this?" he countered, as if he sat in a throne and wasn't hanging suspended in my interrogation room.

I shrugged. "You can, but I'll win. For the first time in my life I've got something I'm fighting for *myself* instead of for Bryant or the family. Have you ever seen me lose a fight over anything less than that?" When Santo's lips thinned, I flashed a predatory grin. "Exactly. They're mine. And before you say something fucking asinine about being their blood, need I remind you that you abandoned them for years? That you're a known criminal without even the veneer of a civilized family like the Morellis to protect their reputation? That you can't protect them from harm either, not when you're a member of the Belcante Outfit?"

To my right, I was aware of the door creaking open, but Santo's next words stole my attention.

"Are you insinuating I can't keep my own

family safe?"

"I'm stating it as fact," I said mildly. "I got to them, didn't I?"

"They should be with family," he stated like the stubborn Italian he was.

"They should be with someone who will make them happy," I exploded, stalking forward to grab Santo fiercely by the throat. "They should be with someone who bleed when they bleed, who will put them first for the first goddamn time in their lives. No one, and I mean not a goddamn, motherfucking person, will do that better than me. So, if they should be with family, Santo, you better fucking believe that family is with *me*."

"As entertaining as it is to see to grown men having a pissing contest like animals, I think I should have a say in who I belong with, don't you?"

I stilled at the sound of Bianca's voice, only an undercurrent of sleepiness in the strong tone. When I looked over at the door she stood with her arms crossed over her pretty velvet dress, her hair a cloud of tangled white golden around her face and her pouty mouth red-bitten by my own. The sight of her alone hit me like a sucker punch to the gut.

Would I ever get used to looking at her? Was

this how she felt about her art? That no matter how many times she might study it or look upon it, the subject would continue to fascinate her, even with her eyes closed, even far removed from it.

If I felt anything less for her than this all-consuming passion, I could have let her go. But the intensity of my longing for her drove me to madness. After all, only a mad man would think to take on the two most powerful families in New York for one lowly teenage girl. Only a mad man would threaten an underboss in the notorious Belcante crime family for the right to call her his own.

And there I was, mad and happy with it.

I stepped away from Santo and crossed my arms in a mimicry of her pose, raising a brow. "Do I need to remind you that you belong to me?"

Even at a distance, I could see the delicate shudder roll through her.

"No," she said primly, tucking her hair behind her ear. "I don't think that's necessary. I just want to remind you that I'm not going back to Lion Court with you. And I just want to say to you," she said, frowning at Santo for a moment before she went to stand beside me, in front of him. "I haven't seen you since I was a girl. You're not even a stranger, you're a danger to the life Brando and I should be able to choose freely. So, if you care about us at all, I hope you're step out of the ring, because you aren't even a part of this fight."

"Fight for custody?"

"Fight for our freedom," she countered. "To pick our own family and circumstances. We've been shuttled here and there, hidden and taken against out will, but I won't let that happen again. I might not be old enough to drink and vote, but I'm old enough to decide what's best for my little brother and me. And, Santo, you aren't it."

A triumphant voice inside me pronounced, *I am*, but I had the sense not to crow about it. Instead, I grinned cruelly at Santo from over Bianca's shoulder.

When she twirled to face me, I schooled my features into impassivity, but she still peered up at me suspiciously.

"And you," she said, drilling a finger into my stomach. "You said we would talk later. Later is now. But first, get my uncle down from there."

"Bossy," I quipped, trying to swallow my laughter when her eyes narrowed further, but I did as she asked and motioned for Hank to lower the pull Santo was attached to.

Bianca stepped forward to help him out of the shackles, rubbing her hands over his arms to chafe the life back into them. It turned something over in my chest to see her with him, to know she forgave him and gave her love to him even though he'd abandoned her. This girl was the purest, gentlest soul I'd ever known and she awed me every single fucking day. Men like Santo Belcante and I didn't deserve her, but I didn't give a fuck about that.

There was something in her that was drawn to the dark like a moth to a flame. I knew she would venture again and again over the course of her life into the shadowy underworld and I was the perfect partner to shepherd her through the blackness and keep her safe at the same time.

She was too good and I was too bad, but life wasn't black and white, and somehow, together, we made more sense than we did separately. Night and day. Ice and fire. A matched set.

So, for the first time in my life, I was ready to spill all of my secrets and put my complete trust in someone other than myself.

Something about seeing them together dislodged an idea at the back of my brain. A way to take down Bryant that suddenly seemed so clear.

"Santo," I drawled, waiting until he looked up from righting his shirt to continue. "There is a way I believe you can make nice with Bianca and I."

He snorted. "Let me guess, it's dangerous."

"Life threatening," I promised with a feral grin. "You're going to love it."

CHAPTER THIRTEEN

Bianca

H E TOOK ME to the cemetery.

It wasn't exactly a place for romance, but after he parked his Aston Martin in the parking lot, he told me to wait while he got out and walked around to my side to open my door for me. It was gallantry from a villain and the contrast combined with the night-dark creepiness of the cemetery satisfied some need for duality in my soul.

I was exhausted from the turmoil of the last twenty-four hours, but I would've followed him to the ends of the earth if it meant knowing the last of his closely guarded secrets. In fact, there was an awful giddiness in me at the idea of being able to share in his pain.

Like he'd said in his note to me, I bled for him as he bled for me. If he had to carry the weight of trauma, I wanted to be able to shoulder some of it myself. To have the privilege of giving such a powerful, proud man some relief was a heady thing.

Tiernan's silence had an intensity that seemed to vibrate in the air between us as he took my hand and led me up the snow crusted hill to the rows of grave stones dotting the long plot. We stopped deep along the far outer line of markers before a large tombstone engraved with curling vines of flowers and a smaller matching one to its right.

The name on the large one read *Grace Priscilla Anne Constantine* and on the smaller, *Our Baby*.

My heart froze inside my chest, the fierce winter wind cutting through my flesh and bone to calcify the organ in ice. When I looked up at Tiernan with wide eyes gone wet, his were unfocused and fixed on the graves.

"When I met her, my first thought was *of course her name is Grace*," he said so quietly I had to sway closer to hear him. "She wasn't a great beauty, not like the rest of the Constantines. They made sure to remind her of that whenever they could. But she had this energy, this bubbling over of happiness and kindness that washed over everyone like sunshine. I fell in love her the moment I met her."

"Where was that?" I whispered, afraid to break his confessional.

"I wasn't allowed to go to school after this." He ran a gloved thumb over his scar. "And I had no time for extracurricular activities outside of the martial arts training Bryant insisted on. Actually, I rarely left the fucking house. But I started to go for runs in Bishop's Landing just to get away from the lunacy at the mansion. I met her on the beach one day."

I thought about our interlude on the beach and tried not to feel jealous.

As if sensing that, a ghost of a smile whispered over his mouth and he squeezed my hand. "I was seventeen, Bianca. And she was the first girl outside my family I'd ever had a meaningful interaction with. It's not surprising I fell in love with her."

No, it wasn't.

It was heartbreakingly easy to imagine Tiernan at seventeen, sheltered in some ways and utterly broken by the brutality of life in others. Scarred and ostracized by his family, I could almost feel the echo of awe in joy in my own heart at the thought of him faced with a kind woman who could see beyond his brusqueness and shallow disfigurement to the goodness that lay beneath like buried treasure.

I leaned into his side, offering him my silent support and warmth.

"We were careful, but we were kids. Bryant was a controlling, obsessive parent. It's no wonder really that he caught us." He shrugged woodenly, but I could feel the tremble of fury through our clasped hands. "Six weeks. Six weeks with Grace was all I got before she disappeared. I met her at our spot on the beach for three weeks before I heard the rumors that Caroline had sent her away."

He stepped forward until his expensive loafers sank into the mound of snow over her grave and crouched down to wipe the snow off her gravestone.

"I tried to find her, but I didn't have the resources I do now." He shook his head as if to clear it. "She must have been fucking devastated, lonely and afraid. She found her escape in booze and filthy street drugs."

"She killed herself?" I whispered through numb lips, shaking from more than the cold as I hugged myself.

He jerked his head in some semblance of a nod as he stood and stepped back into line with me. When he grabbed for my hand, I latched on just as strongly.

"We'd just found out she was pregnant," he admitted in a voice like gravel. "We were meeting to make a plan."

Agony cut through me, splitting me straight down the middle. A headache pointed at the center of my skull and my heart threatened to spill out my throat.

"I'm so sorry, Tiernan," I said, hugging his arm to me because I didn't know if he would accepted more and I didn't want to intrude on his sorrow. "That's...that's just fucking tragic."

"Yeah," he agreed, scrubbing at his face with his free hand even though he wasn't crying.

His eyes were red-rimmed, but dry, his mouth pinched and his scarred stark white. There was so much pain in every inch of him, I wanted to latch onto him and suck it out like a leech.

"This is why you hate Bryant and the Constantines," I surmised.

"Bryant must've told Lane and Caroline about our relationship. They ripped her away from me and it killed her."

And with her, any dream Tiernan might have kept safe from his brutal father at the deepest corner of himself that he might one day have love and family.

Fuck, life was brutal.

It didn't matter if you were born wealthy or poor, beautiful or scarred. Tragedy was the great equalizer.

It hurt to admit I could believe both Caroline *and* my dad capable of doing something like that. Caroline with her need for obedience and perfection, and my dad with the ability to put himself and his loved ones above all else. It had always been something I admired him in him, but now, I was horrified to see its dark side.

"I'm so sorry this happened to you," I told him, deciding against caution as I embraced him fully. He was broad and tall, especially in his black overcoat, but I did my best to wrap him up in my arms before I canted my head to look up into his haunted eyes. "I'm not sure if there's any part of you that believes you deserved that, maybe some part that Bryant forced you to believe, but if there is, it's absolutely not true. No kid deserves to be hurt like you were hurt."

Tiernan just stared down at me, still and handsome as one of Michelangelo's statues.

I reached up with one hand to cup his cold cheek, fingers curling around his ear so I could tug him farther down to me. When he was close enough, I went to my tiptoes and pressed our foreheads together the way he had done in *Inequity*.

"I get that you would want revenge on Bryant, even on the Constantine family for their part in it, whatever it was. I understand the need for it, Tiernan, and I forgive you a hundred times over for seeking it with Aida, Brando and me. It led us to where we are now, and I have to believe everything happens for a reason." I sucked in a deep breath and locked my gaze to his cold green eyes. "But I think the best way to get revenge against your father is be everything he isn't, to show him that even when he tried to take everything good away from you, you still found your way to love and peace."

Suddenly, his arms wrapped around me like a vice. "I know I didn't deserve Grace. I know I don't deserve you. The difference is, I'm a grown fucking man now and every fucking thing in my life has wielded me into a weapon. I won't let anyone take you from me, Bianca, that's a fact I'll die for."

"I believe you," I promised, because how could I not when he showed me the collection of fragments his heart had been reduced to as if they somehow made him less worthy. Instead, like a painting that had been eroded and stained with neglect and rough hands, I saw only the unmitigated beauty in the wreckage. Tears started track hot paths down my frozen cheeks as I stared up at the man I couldn't believe I'd once thought to be a villain. "And please, don't say you don't deserve me. It's so far from true. You're a survivor, Tiernan, and you know what a survivor deserves most of all?"

He swallowed thickly, once, twice, as if trying to force down a lump in his throat. Finally, he gave up and shook his head, his forehead rolling against mine.

"A happy ending," I whispered, the words a hot plume of white between our mouths.

Our kiss was soft, closed-mouth, but I could taste the brine of my tears in it. He took more slowly, as if realizing his hunger. When we finally parted, our twin breaths cast billows of white clouds in the air.

"You're forgiving me," he said slowly. "But are you asking me to give up my hatred for Bryant? Because Bianca, I'm beginning to realize there isn't much I wouldn't do for you. For Brando. But that... I've lived with it so long, I don't know how to carve it out of me."

"No," I said immediately, letting the anger in

my belly spark into flame. I clutched his face in both my hands and snarled over the words that poured from that fierce place inside me, the same place that ignited when someone tried to fuck with Brando. "Bryant has taken from you your entire life. He deserves to *die* for what he's done."

For one crystal clear moment, Tiernan didn't blink or breathe as he looked into my probably manic expression, and then, shockingly, he threw his head back and *howled* with laughter. It rumbled through us both as he shouted his mirth to the cloud-covered heavens and he didn't stop for long moments, not even when it started to snow.

Finally, he dropped his head to smile down at me, moving my hair out of my face with a gloved palm. "You are a contrary girl, Bianca Belcante."

"I told you I wasn't as sweet as you thought," I countered with a cheeky smile, relieved to see the deadness faded from his eyes.

He squeezed me tightly and leaned back, taking my feet off the ground. I wrapped my hands around his neck and laughed into his mouth as he kissed me again.

When he put me back on my feet, he grasped my chin and studied my face. "So, little girl with the fierce claws, are you ready for a fight? Going up against Bryant will mean danger and bloodshed. I learned to be a monster from a man even more monstrous than me."

"Your fight is my fight. Everyone underestimates me because of my age and maybe the blonde hair, but I'm clever and I don't ever give up. Not when it comes to my family."

I watched as the word *family* rocked through Tiernan like a physical blow. In the wake of the hit, his face softened, the brackets carved around his mouth and between his brows smoothing. He looked younger than I'd ever seen him.

"Oh, I know it," he teased drolly. "I'm just glad to finally be on the same team. Your claws fucking hurt, little thing."

I rolled my eyes at him, but he just laughed and hugged me tighter.

❖   ❖   ❖

OF COURSE, IT was Tiernan and I, so the peace didn't last for long.

In fact, it ended abruptly as soon as we arrived back in Bishop's Landing.

"Absolutely *fucking not*," he roared, slamming on the brakes at a stop sign. "No way in goddamn hell, Bianca."

"What happened to letting me make decisions

for myself?"

"Make all the *smart* decisions you want," he countered. "This is not that. We kissed and fucking made up. You need to come home. Not just for me, but Brando."

"Don't you dare use Brando against me," I snapped. "You don't think I'm doing this for him too? Caroline *needs* me for something, Tiernan."

"Don't tell me you want to help that bitch," he asked incredulously.

"No, of course not." Between Tiernan and Elias's stories, I had no doubt Caroline was a beautiful painting rendered by a despicable artist. The dreams I'd had for years of being accepted into her home were hollow enough to cave in when I was faced with the truth of who she was. "But I want to know what she knows."

"And if she knows you're her deceased husband's daughter? You think she'll take that well."

"She hasn't hurt me yet," I argued, even though it was a fairly weak argument. "I haven't had a chance to look through the house yet, but I know she keeps Dad's office locked up the exact same way he left it. If I could get inside, maybe I could find a clue to what that key opens—"

"Oh, fucking great idea, you go snooping around the Constantine Compound," he jeered, then caught a glimpse of my face and tried to soften his tone. "Fuck, Bianca, you cannot expect me to be okay with this after everything I just fucking shared with you."

"No, I can't. But I do hope you'll trust me enough to do this because I feel strongly that I have to. I know you're technically my guardian, Tiernan, but if you want to be more than that, I need to know you can respect my decisions."

"Fuck me," he said to the roof of the car as if speaking to God. "Sometimes I can't believe you're only seventeen."

"Thank you," I chirped happily.

"I'm not sure that was a compliment," he muttered darkly.

I chose to ignore the comment, reaching over to the gear shift to tangle my fingers with his over top of it. "The first sign of trouble, I'll come home, okay? I just...I need to see this out. If Dad really did leave something for Brando and I, I need to know. I've spent the last five years thinking he just abandoned us."

Tiernan's silence was stony, a cement wall-built brick by brick between us. I let him stew though, knowing I'd said my piece and he would either trust me or not.

Outside the windows, Bishop's Landing

blurred past in streams of winter white and bright Christmas lights flaring across ornate entry gates and opulent homes. I remembered driving through the city the first-time months ago and feeling awed by the grandeur. Now, I knew the expensive bricks and mortar hid people just as horrible as anywhere else in the world.

When we stopped moving at another stop sign at the crossroads between Lion Court and the Constantine Compound, I noticed the static current of electricity filling the car and turned to look at Tiernan. His knuckles were white around the steering wheel, his lips peeled back over his teeth in a feral kind of grimace. He was breathing hard, but slowly, as if struggling to control the pace.

When he finally spoke, his tone was sliced to pieces by resentment and anger. "I don't like this at *fucking* all. Is that understood? You've backed me into a goddamn corner and that's not a place I feel good in, do you understand me, Bianca?" His gaze cut to mine. "I'm not used to being afraid of anything."

"You don't need to be afraid, I'll be fine," I promised, taking his stiff hand in both of mine.

He tugged on our hands to place mine over his heart pounding hard in his chest. "It's an animal response. My fucking mate is going into danger *deliberately* and I can't follow."

My mate.

I tried not to smile at that and failed. Tiernan might not have told me in exact words that he loved me, but I didn't need him to. Not when he called me his mate, not when his heart beat furiously in fear for me.

"Trust me, please," I beseeched softly.

His furious gaze scoured my face for a long moment before he sighed heavily and grumbled. "You have two days. I want you home for Christmas Eve, understood?"

"Yes, Lord Tiernan," I sassed as I lounged across the console to pepper his face in kisses. "Thank you for trusting me."

"Against my better judgement," he muttered like the old grump he was. "Don't do anything I wouldn't do. Or really anything I would, either."

I laughed through the kiss I pressed to his mouth then opened my car door before he could change his mind.

"Wait," he said, snagging my hand to pull me close again. His face was fierce mask of intensity as he looked into my eyes and pressed something small and cold into my palm. "I've done countless things in my life that I should not have done, but loving you is the best mistake I ever made."

He closed my hand around the key he'd placed in my palm and I knew without asking that it was the key we'd found behind *Child with a Dove* at The Met. He was trusting me with his trump card, telling me with words and actions how much I meant to him.

Tears flooded my eyes, but I didn't let them fall as I look into the most beautiful face I'd ever seen and told him the easiest truth I'd ever known. "It's funny now to think I ever hated you. The truth is, I think I knew the moment you found us that my heart had found a home, I just didn't trust it yet."

"And now?" he asked, dipping forward to clasp my lower lip between his teeth and give it a sharp tug he soothed quickly with the lash of his tongue.

"Now, I'm not just fighting for Brando and me." I didn't tell him I was fighting for him, for us.

Instead, I kissed him until there was no breathe left in my chest and my heart was pounding like an insistent knock at the door waiting for him to answer. When I pulled away, his face was flushed with heat and his eyes were all dark, all desire.

"If you don't come back to me whole by to-morrow night, I'll burn Bishop's Landing to the ground and rip Caroline Constantine apart with my fucking teeth," he swore, tugging a fistful of my hair as if to drive his point home.

"I don't doubt it, you heathen." I pressed another kiss to his lush mouth, wishing life was simpler and I could just go home with him then. Instead, I pushed the door wider and got out into the snow. "You take care of Bryant, I've got Caroline," I promised. "I owe you a happily ever after, don't I?"

✧   ✧   ✧

THE HOUSEKEEPER ANSWERED my knock at the door, but she disappeared silently as soon as I entered the foyer and knocked the snow off my Prada boots. Even though it was well after dinnertime, I was surprised by how quiet the house was. Caroline had told me she'd expected her youngest son, Keaton home from Europe tonight.

Instead, silence seemed to echo through the cavernous entry hall. My socked feet were soundless against the marble foyer and then on the plush carpet as I walked under the twin staircases into the first sitting room then through the rooms after it in search of the matriarch. All the lights were on, a sign of wealth I wasn't sure I'd ever get used to, but Caroline was nowhere to be found.

Finally, just as I was about to give up at go to bed, I found her in the library at the back of the house. Flickering firelight caught my gaze from the hall and the twin doors swung smoothly in when I pushed through into the warm room.

She sat in a wing-backed chair before a fireplace enormous enough for me to stand in. Even though she must have heard me, she didn't look away from the flames as I approached and for a moment, pure fear clamped its hands around my throat.

Did she know my secrets?

That I was a closest Constantine?

That Tiernan's cum was dried on the inside of my thighs?

That I intended to take whatever Lane might have left for Brando and me for myself no matter what the cost?

It was only when I drew up behind the side table between the two chairs that I noticed what Caroline was twirling in one hand.

A red rose.

When my gaze snapped from the familiar

bloom to hers, I found it seething with dark shadows and firelight.

"Bianca," she said, my name like an incantation, the first line of a curse. "You're home late. Out cavorting with the scum of Bishop's Landing?"

"I told you, I wanted answers. I went to find them." I was surprised and proud of how strong my voice sounded.

"Mmm, and what did you find on your wanderings?" she asked silkily as she brushed the rose over her mouth, back and forth like a pendulum. Despite everything, I found myself entranced by the movement. "A scarred Morelli perhaps?"

I didn't say anything because I had the sense every word I uttered would lead me into a trap she'd laid out for me.

She stood abruptly then, so quickly I took a quick, stuttered step away from her. Before I could do anything more, she was in my space, taller than me in her high heels, her pretty face peeled back to reveal true viciousness.

"Bianca, I am going to make one thing very clear to you and it is the absolute last time I will do so, is that understood? After this, if you disobey me, you will not be welcome in this house…" She paused and I couldn't see her eyes in the deep shadows because she was facing away from the fire at her back, but I could sense them digging into me, trying to unearth whatever I might be hiding from her. "You will not be welcome in Bishop's Landing. You will not be seen in polite society in this country ever again. Is that understood?"

I didn't want to nod, but her hand not holding the rose latched out to grip one of mine so fiercely, my skin burned.

"Is that understood?" she repeated placidly as she ground my bones together.

"Yes, Caroline."

"Excellent. You will not see Tiernan Morelli again. Not ever. In fact, you will never fraternize with a member or associate of that filthy family again so long as you wish to be harbored under this roof. If I hear of you doing so, I will be incredibly displeased."

"He has Brando," I argued, even though self-preservation urged me not to. "If you can't get Brando back for me, I have to visit him at Lion Court."

"Oh, I'll get the boy back," she said lightly as if he was a misplaced possession and not a vulnerable child. "I'm a kind woman, but I don't do anything for nothing. When the time comes,

Bianca, I expect certain things of you. Great things in the name of this family. Do you we understand each other?"

"Yes," I hissed, wrenching my hand out of her grip. "There is no need to threaten me, I'm grateful for your help and I'll happily repay you anyway I know how."

A thin slice of a smile carved her face into two perfect fragments. I'd never known beauty to be so ugly as I did in that moment looking into Caroline Constantine's face.

"That's a good girl," she praised magnanimously, turning from me as suddenly as she'd come.

I watched as she casually dashed the rose into the roaring fire and then adjusted the already perfect alignment of the family portrait on the mantle place before resuming her seat.

I hovered for a moment, unsure of what had just happened and how to approach it. I'd just turned to leave when Caroline voice called out over the crackling flames.

"Oh, Bianca, I'm having my lawyer redraw those papers for you. When you're ready, I expect you'll be happy to sign them."

I hesitated as anger flooded me. It was interesting how alike Bryant Morelli and Caroline

Constantine were, both bullies who felt shielded by their wealth and reputation. As I stalked out of the room without replying, I knew exactly what I needed to do in regards to Caroline.

It seemed Tiernan had rubbed off on me more than I thought.

Because the only thing I could think of to rectify the cruelty of Caroline was to get revenge for Tiernan, Elias, and anyone else she'd no doubt wronged myself.

And I thought I knew exactly how to do it.

CHAPTER FOURTEEN

Bianca

IT PHYSICALLY HURT to lay in bed and try to sleep that night after everything that had happened, all the things that had fundamentally changed in a single day, after talking to Brando on Facetime, lying about being away with friends on vacation when all I wanted to do was run the twelve blocks between the Compound and Lion Court and hug my baby brother into next year.

But somehow, I was able to eek out a few hours of sleep in between planning with Elena Lombardi and laying awake thinking about Tiernan and Brando.

When I woke up, the Constantine Compound was in an uproar. Keaton had returned home with his girlfriend and it sounded as if Winston and maybe Perry were also talking in the foyer, their voices drifting up the stairs to my room. I stood in the doorway in my pajamas, yearning to go down and meet them but also knowing I needed this morning to search the house for anything pertaining to my father's hidden will.

I almost jumped out of my skin when the clack of shoes on the stairs reached my ears and I scrambled to jump back into bed to feign sleep. My heart pounded as I tried to control my breathing moments before the door opened after a short knock.

"Bianca?"

I breathed a sigh of relief hearing Elias's voice.

"Hey," I sat up and smiled at him. "What're you doing here?"

His face screwed up with distaste as he leaned in my doorframe. "We always go to this charity Santa's breakfast on Christmas Eve morning. It's a huge publicity thing and Caroline gives them a big cheque. It's dead boring, but it should be better with you at my side."

I winced, thumbing the silk thread of the bedspread. "Actually, Eli, I need to stay here."

His scowl was instantaneous. "No way, what's the good of you staying at Aunt Caroline's if I can't drag you to these God-awful functions?"

"I won't be here much longer," I admitted,

jumping out bed to tug him into the room and close the door behind him. When I faced him again, I couldn't help the smile that tore across my face. "Tiernan only gave me last night and today to find something about Lane's will. I'm expected back at Lion Court by this evening."

He rolled his eyes once, then again ever harder when I giggled at him. "So, the lovebirds are back together?" At my grin, he just shook his head. "Well, at least one of us is happy, I guess. What do you need from me?"

I bounded forward to smack a big kiss on his cheek. "You're incredible, do you know that?"

"I've been told," he said drily, but there was a smile hidden in his cheeks.

"Can you tell them I've come down with something? Make it gross so no one wants to check on me."

He laughed. "Okay, I can do that. I'll text you when we're all on our way back, too."

"Thank you," I said, grasping his hands to pull him into a fierce hug. "You're the best friend I've ever had."

"Yeah, yeah," he muttered as he squeezed me back then gently pushed me away. "You're just trying to butter me up so I forgive you for ditching me on this boring ass outing."

"Is it working?"

He shook his head at me again, but winked when he turned to open the door. "Be careful and get some rest if you can, when the family gets back it's Christmas tea and opening presents early. Utter calamity."

"I'll look forward to it." And a part of me did. It would be strange to take part in a Constantine family Christmas tradition without truly being a member of the family. While knowing finally, after all this time, that they, or Caroline at least, was my enemy and would never be my friend.

"I wish you could stay, it would be good to have you part of the family," Elias said before he closed the door behind him.

And something about that resonated with me.

Part of the family.

That was what Caroline had dangled before me like a carrot on the end of her stick, leading me toward something I couldn't see in the distance.

She seemed almost desperate to make me her ward, but why?

Obviously, because she needed something.

Why had Tiernan done the very same thing?

To get revenge on the Constantines.

But why me? Why was it important to be my

guardian?

Because of Lane's hidden will.

It took everything in me to wait until the commotion downstairs died down, until I saw the cars peel out of the circular drive. Only then did I finally cave in and call Tiernan.

"Sweet thing," he answered warmly. "I hope you're calling to tell me you are coming home earlier than expected. The Gentlemen and I were going to take Brando ice skating, but you and I could always stay behind and I could show you even more inventive ways to use a croupier stick."

"A croupier stick?" I asked, momentarily side-tracked by the husky intent in his tone.

"My makeshift crop at *Inequity*. Check the marks on your sweet ass in the mirror, I'm sure it will spark your memory," he said, drily.

Heat burned in my cheeks. "Stop distracting me. I called for a reason. Why was it important that you became our guardians?"

"Bianca—"

"No, I'm not mad or anything, I just need to know. It has something to do with Lane's supposed hidden will, right?"

"Well, now we know there probably is a will if that key he left in your painting is anything to go on. But yes. My private investigator found a gap in Halcyon's history." I knew the name of the Constantine's Fortune 500 acquisition company and my heart started to pound even harder. "They'd acquired a company near the end of Lane's life called Colombe Energy Investments—"

"Dad's green energy company," I supplied, mind whirring. "He named it after me. Colombe is Latin for—"

"Dove, yes, I figured that out."

"So, you think Dad left the company to Brandon and me in his will?"

"I do. It seems like Halcyon hasn't had control over the company or profits from it in the five years since he passed away. Seeing as how its grown into one of the leading green energy conglomerates in the country, this is obviously surprising."

"Obviously," I whispered, struck dumb by the revelations. "You needed guardianship of me so you could gain control of the company when you found the will. It would be a complete embarrassment to the Constantines for a Morelli to takeover a lucrative company that should have belonged to them."

Tiernan's silence was answer enough.

"That's why you took me in," I whispered as my thoughts stampeded through my head, creating enough clamor to make my ears ring.

Through the cacophony, I couldn't make out what Tiernan said next.

"I have to go, I'll call you back later," I said swiftly before ending the call and tossing the phone on my bed.

I couldn't tell Tiernan that Caroline had been trying to make me a Constantine. He'd go ballistic in a way I was sure both he and the Constantines would not recover from. He would also undoubtedly insist I return to Lion Court immediately, but I refused to leave without checking Lane's locked office.

I grabbed my robe from the chair and tugged it on as I darted from my room and down the grand staircase to the main floor. Lane's office was in the left wing of the house, on the opposite side of Caroline's like a matched set. Of course, it was locked, but I had an idea how to open it.

Henrik answered my call on the first ring.

"Anca," he said, his rich baritone pouring through the line like molasses. "Are you calling to have Ez come pick you up? We miss you."

I froze for a moment despite my urgency to properly absorb his words. When I spoke, my voice was whisper soft, "Miss you too, Henrik. But I'm not coming home yet. I've got some things to figure out…like how to open a locked door without a key."

His laughter boomed in my ear. "Of course, you do. I told Tiernan we weren't good influences on you and Brando."

"You're the best," I insisted, holding the phone to my ear as if it was Henrik himself.

"Does this mean you are coming back to us?"

My heart ached at his vulnerable sincerity. "Yes, it does. Just as soon as you help me break into Lane Constantine's office."

"We might have to change our nickname to The Gentlemen and A Lady at this point," he teased before sobering. "All right, give me the details of the door."

A few minutes later, the phone tucked between my ear and shoulder, my tongue pressed between my teeth as I concentrated, I pressed a bobby pin I'd twisted into an L-shape into the bottom of the lock and then jimmied a second piece above that, pushing deep enough to engage the tumblers.

It took me five minutes and approximately twenty tries to get the damn door open, but finally it gave with an anti-climatic *snick*.

"I'm in!" I squealed.

Henrik laughed and clapped. "You'll be an

international jewel thief in no time."

"Gotta dream big," I agreed, giddiness bubbling in my blood like Champagne. "Okay, I've got it from here, thanks, Henrik. And, um, could you not tell Tiernan about this yet? I'll explain everything later."

He hesitated for a moment. "You're safe?"

Warmth flooded my chest. "Yes, Henrik." At least for now.

"I'll keep your secret then, on the condition that you're home tonight. Brando's organized a Christmas play to welcome you home."

Laughter burst from me at the thought of my little brother directing Tiernan, Walcott, Ezra, and Henrik in some kind of Christmas theatre. "You're kidding."

"Not at all. Tiernan's the Grinch," he added, waiting as I almost split my side laughing until saying, "Kid's a little genius. He waited until after his episode the other day to ask Tiernan and the guy couldn't say no."

I shook my head even though I still felt sick that I'd missed two of Brando's seizures since I'd been with the Constantines. "I can't wait to see it. To see all of you."

"Tonight," he said, a promise and a demand.

"Tonight."

I ended the call and slipped the phone in the pocket of my robe before turning the ornate gold door knob and pushing into my father's office.

The scent hit me immediately, a muted smokiness from the Dior cologne he always wore mixed with the leather of richly bound books. Instantly, I was taken back to being a girl rushing into Dad's arms whenever he arrived back home with us. The feel of his strong arms closing around me, his murmured laughter as he squeezed me tight and pressed his nose into my hair.

"My little dove," he'd murmur into my ear as if it was a secret.

A sob lodged itself in my throat, but I forced it down with a hard swallow and turned my attention to the contents of the room.

It was a large space dominated by floor to ceiling book shelves in glossy mahogany that matched the palatial desk in the middle of the space. There was a fireplace directly behind that topped by a mantle lined with framed photos and above that, a painting that took my breath away.

It was, by far, Picasso's most iconic dove painting. Titled simply *Dove*, it was a white bird on a black lithographic ink wash. The starkness of the background made the fragile creature starkly beautiful, utterly pure. The simple print had become the basis for the symbol of the Paris Peace Conference in 1949 and from then on, a notable motif for peace around the globe.

And one of the five original prints was hanging above the mantle in my father's office.

A crater opened in the center of my chest at the thought of Dad sitting there every day with a symbol of his peace, a symbol of *me*, watching over him.

There had been an awful melancholy residing in my heart since the moment I realized Dad didn't live with us the way normal dads did, the moment I realized he had another family that would always demand more of his time than he could ever to give to us. I wondered, as any child would have, what was wrong with me? Why couldn't I be better enough to make him want to stay? Why wasn't our love enough?

For almost eighteen years, I worried that I was fundamentally flawed. That it was somehow my fault that Dad always left and no amount of maturity as I grew older and tried to analyze it from an unbiased lens could rid that tiny kernel of doubt at the centre of my personality. I'd grown around it, learned to hide from it and shield it from others.

But until this moment staring through bleary

eyes at the simple beauty of Picasso's *Dove* over Dad's desk, at the center of his great domain, I had believed Lane Constantine was a liar. That every time he told me I was his dove, his little haven of peace, every time he told me how much he loved me, he was holding something back like a secret or untruth.

Now, I knew he'd meant it.

Every word.

Every time he put his reputation and livelihood on the line by carving out time to be with Aida, Brando, and me it was because he wanted to. No. Not want. Now, I understood that what had driven Lane toward Aida and the family they made together wasn't so simple, so easily given up as base desire.

It was something with its own force, a singular gravitation pull. No matter how far Dad was from us, he was always in our orbit, circling, waiting for the next time the stars aligned and he could be with us again.

I understood that then, looking at that painting, crying so hard I could barely breathe, but I understood it too, because of Tiernan.

That magnetic compulsion to be near him, to love him when everything in our lives seemed to conspire against us. The terrifying enormity of the emotions his very presence had evoked in me from day one, the way every moment with him made me feel as if I was on fire. The way I knew he would always bleed for me, when I was sad, if I needed a champion to fight for me, to prove to me that every inch of him was mine to have, and I would do the same for him.

I choked on a sob as forgiveness bloomed in my throat like a thorny rose.

It was so much easier to understand Aida, her depressions when Lane was gone, her euphoria when he returned to us, even her distraction and neglect of Brando and I. She didn't truly exist unless she was with Lane and I wondered, if I'd been able to see Dad here at the Constantine Compound with his other family, he'd been the same. I'd like to think so.

When Dad died, Aida didn't get out of bed for more than a bathroom break for over a month. And even when she dated again, it was with mercenary intent, to better our lives, not heal her broken heart. She knew, I thought, that Lane had been it for her.

So fucking romantic and so tragic.

Lane and Aida. Tiernan and Grace.

I resolved right then and there with more conviction than I'd ever felt before, not to let

Tiernan and I end on such a devastating note.

"Bianca?"

For a moment, I thought it was Dad calling to me and my fragile heart pounded like ram against the cage of my ribs as if it could break free and go to him.

But it wasn't Lane.

Of course not.

And no one should have been home.

I whirled away from the painting to face the man at the door.

Beckett Fairchild stood there in a smart overcoat with that bright red scarf he'd worn at Aida's funeral. Despite his dark hair, his pale eyes and facial features resembled Dad slightly.

"What are you doing in here?" he asked.

The words weren't accusatory even though they could have been. I was quite clearly trespassing on a sacred space in a house where I was merely a precariously placed guest. Instead, he seemed genuinely curious, almost saddened by the sight of me crying in my pajamas in front of a dead man's painting.

"I-I thought I heard something coming from behind the door and I got scared," I explained after clearing my throat and dashing the wet from my cheeks. "I'm sure thieves just wait for the family to leave so they can try to break in."

A small smile tugged at his mouth, but he also cocked a brow. "Yes, well, there is a very good security system in place. Monitors on most on the windows and doors in the house."

Alarm rang through me. How had Tiernan stolen in and out of my bedroom if that was the case? I had to think there wasn't a monitor in my room.

I shrugged. "I'm not used to all this. I come from a small town where breaking and entering is pretty common."

Beckett nodded, his movements easy and casual, but there was a shrewdness in his eyes that made the hairs on the back of my neck stand on end. He jerked his chin at the *Dove* painting. "I think Caroline mentioned that you are an admirer or art? It's an exquisite piece, but I can't say I've ever seen anyone cry over it."

"I'm a seventeen-year-old girl," I played it off with a self-deprecating shrug and a little grin. "We tend to be overly emotional."

"Mmm," he hummed in the way Caroline did, in the way Dad used to do sometimes too. As if they knew better than you, as if you were as transparent as wet silk. "You know, Lane was moved by doves too. Later in his life, he had a peculiar kind of fascination with them. It seems you have a penchant for them, too?"

His gaze cut to my wrist and I was annoyed to realized I'd been rubbing my thumb over my dove tattoo.

I tugged my robe back over the mark and crossed my arms. "I'm sorry, can I help you with something? The family left for some charity breakfast half an hour ago."

"You can actually, I was looking for you."

I blinked at his carefully blank expression. His stillness and implacability reminded me of Tiernan, predatory and deceptively dangerous. "What could you want with me?"

He laughed, a short sharp sound like he was making fun of himself. "To explain all that, I need time and, honestly, I'd rather discuss this outside of the Compound. You know, in this house, the walls have ears."

Instinctively, I looked around the room, which made him laugh again, softer this time.

"Why don't you get dressed and meet me in the foyer in ten minutes. I'd love to take you somewhere."

"I don't get in cars with strangers," I quipped.

Another ghost of a smile. "It's a good thing I've known you since you were born then, Bianca

Laney Belcante. Get dressed, if you aren't down in fifteen minutes, I'll leave without you."

He turned on his heel in a magnificently dramatic fashion, black overcoat billowing out behind him, and disappeared down the hall.

CHAPTER FIFTEEN

Bianca

BECKETT FAIRCHILD DROVE a silver Aston Martin the exact same model as the one Tiernan had used to take us to Lane's Memorial Gala at The Met. I was surprised he didn't use a driver the way it seemed most residents of Bishop's Landing did, and that he handled the car with finesse as he drove too quickly around the looping curves of the city on our way onto the interstate highway.

"Where are we going?" I asked as I tugged my cashmere skirt farther down my tight-clad thighs.

He glanced at me and I realized for the first time that he had beautiful, deeply green eyes. "I'm curious, you don't seem to remember me."

I frowned at his non-squitter, but decided I'd know soon enough. "You were at my mom's funeral."

"Yes."

"Why?"

His jaw clenched, a muscle spasming there. "I knew Lane all my life. Our fathers were distant cousins who worked together closely over the years and when they had sons a few months apart, it seemed obvious to throw us together. We were so different, but I think growing up together wore down our sharp edges and we fit together well."

I didn't say anything because the air in the car was ballooning with pressure, pushing on my body like a trash compactor.

"We were brothers by choice," he continued, almost to himself. "I would have and *did* do anything for him. Including keeping the secret of his mistress Aida Belcante and then, later, his beloved Bianca and Brando."

"Does Caroline know?" I asked, unable to mask the terror in my voice.

"It's good to hear you have the sense to fear her," he said. "I couldn't quite know if you were as utterly brave and stubborn as Lane could be or just silly and naïve in accepting an invitation to stay at the compound."

"I'm going to be honest and say it was probably a combination of the two," I admitted.

Another of those whisper-smiles. "It seems so

obvious to me that you're his daughter. I've wondered how Caroline could be so blind, but then again, love makes fools of us all and Caroline loved Lane very much."

I winced slightly, rubbing my thumb over my tattoo in a gesture I'd taken up to comfort myself. Growing up, I'd believed in fairy tales, in princes on white steads, damsels in high towers and villains with nothing but evil intentions, but coming to Bishop's Landing had taught me that no one was just hero or a villain. My prince charming was most women's nightmares, my villain one of society's most lauded matriarchs. And I might had started out a naïve damsel in distress, but that wasn't how I was going to end up.

No one was going to save Brando and me, but myself.

"Do you know why she took me in?"

"I've got my own speculations, but Caroline is a complicated woman. I've known her since she was enamoured with Lane, long before he even noticed her yet, your guess is probably as good as mine."

Beckett maneuvered the car in and out of traffic easily, well over the speed limit. It was obvious we were heading into Manhattan, and I was curious where we would end up.

"Is it true?" I asked, taking a chance in trusting him because at this point, it seemed like he had been keeping my secrets even longer than I had. "Did Lane leave Brando and I something in his will?"

Beckett sighed. "It's complicated. Lane was fairly young and in perfect health when he died. He was also the kind of man, in the position he was in, who believed he would live forever." His laugh was a tangled note of loss and bitterness. "Do you know how he passed?"

"Aida only ever said he had a heart attack." Even though, it had taken weeks of pestering her to get an answer.

"He'd just had his annual checkup with one of the top doctors in the city, including an echocardiogram that came back perfectly sound." He shot me sidelong glance filled with mystery. "There are some people who think he was murdered."

The words impacted with my gut like a sucker punch, breath exploding from between my lips.

"Who would have done something like that?" I asked with the last of the air in my lungs.

"A great many of people. Lane was one of the most powerful men in the country, Bianca. His holdings totalled the *billions*. A man like that has enemies."

"The Morellis," I surmised, blinded momentarily by the idea of Bryant—of Tiernan?—murdering my father.

"Yes," he said cautiously. "But there are other options, too. A few years before he died, Lane and I started a rather successful green energy technology innovation and investment company."

"Colombe Energy."

"Exactly." He reached over and patted my thigh in a grandfatherly way. "Inspired by his daughter."

"He was the one who taught me about green energy, not the other way around," I said. "But it is nice to know he named it for me."

"He started it for you," Beckett corrected as we crossed the Queensboro Bridge into Manhattan. "Lane loved all his children. You could say a lot about him, but he was a good father who loved his kids more than anything. But raising you and then Brando was different for him. He couldn't give you the money and connections he could give his legitimate children. But he could give you a better world. Not just a cleaner one, one that stood a chance against global warming and the climate crisis, but a better world for *you*." He paused. "No matter what happened, he wanted you, Brando and Aida to be secure. So, he created Colombe Energy with the intention to give it to you."

"What?" For the third time in thirty minutes, I was breathless. "Can you do that? Just...*give* someone a company?"

Beckett laughed. "It's not as easy as simply handing it over, no, but he had contingencies in place. Winston was his heir at Halcyon, but Lane made sure Colombe Energy was separate from the holding company so he, and Caroline, wouldn't be able to intervene when the time came for you to take it over."

"As in *run it*?" I couldn't fathom it. Dad had always encouraged me to apply to New York University, even knowing as he must have how precarious a situation that would be for him, but he didn't urge me to choose between studying art conservatism or business. The idea that he would leave an entire business to me was just...shocking. Especially after we received absolutely nothing when he died.

Beckett nodded. "Only if you wanted to." He laughed. "Lane wasn't above blatant nepotism. If you want to pursue art, he was prepared to sell his majority shares of the company to you."

"Who runs it now?"

"Me," Beckett admitted. "As I said, Lane and I started the company together. I worked in energy long before I became CEO of Colombe Energy."

"Did he tell you all of this?" I asked as we passed The Met on our left and turned down a side street. "How could he have thought so far ahead, but let us nothing in his will?"

"It was...complicated as I said. Caroline watched his finances very carefully. She was—is—a very jealous woman. He did talk about drawing up a separate will for you, Brandon, and Aida, but when he died, there was no trace of it."

I hesitated as we drove a few blocks away from Central Park and descended into underground parking beneath a glass fronted skyscraper. Even though Beckett hadn't told Caroline about my existence, even though he was being forthright with me, there was something about his manner that raised my suspicions.

I'd learned that no one did anything in this world for nothing.

So what did Beckett Fairchild want?

"Come on," he interrupted my thoughts as he parked and opened his car door. "We're here."

I followed him out of the car and into the

underground elevator, watching as he pressed the button for the uppermost floor of the building.

"Tiernan Morelli found out about me," I started slowly as I watched the floors tick by. "Obviously, you must have known that when he showed up at the funeral."

Beckett made an unintelligible noise in his throat. "Yes. I was there to make sure you and Brando ended up with the right people. When Tiernan showed up...I admit, I was at a momentary loss of what to do. He acted quickly."

"He wanted to use Brando and I to embarrass the Constantines."

"I gathered that when we saw you crying on the floor of The Met at Lane's Memorial Gala. He didn't go through it, though."

"No, he didn't." I agreed, ignoring his searching look as I continued to watch the floors count off on the display above the doors.

Finally, we hit the last story and the doors opened.

"Welcome to Colombe Energy," Beckett gestured wide with his arm as he stepped into the foyer of the company offices.

Immediately before us there was a reception desk backed by a wall of running water, the name *Colombe Energy Investments* attached to the glass.

It was beautiful, the entire space, right down to the stylized dove in a green tree that was their logo.

It was Christmas Eve so the offices were empty as Beckett led me through the space beyond the wall where bull pens were bracketed on all sides by closed door offices. At the very back left corner a door was marked with the name 'Constantine.'

"We have the money to be uneconomical," Beckett said with a wry grin as he produced a key and unlocked the door to Lane's old office.

Unlike Lane's space at home, this was fairly devoid of his personality. The filtered air held no remnants of his scent and there was no Picasso painting hanging in a position of honor. I was more than mildly disappointed.

"Why did you bring me here?" I asked softly as I walked around the office, ending up at the large glass and metal desk Dad sat at.

There were three frames on the desk, one of Caroline and Lane on their wedding day years ago, both beaming brightly, another of Lane and his sons all in preppy golf clothes on a course by the ocean, and finally, one with his daughters where he sat crouched at a kid's table pretending to have tea.

None of Brando and me.

Of course, there couldn't be.

Caroline probably visited him here. His kids. His friends and associates who couldn't know about Lane's other life, his mistress and love children.

Still, it burned in me like an untended lit match.

"Lane wanted this office to be yours one day and, if you want it when you've finished university or traveling the globe or whatever it is kids do these days after high school, it's yours if you want it." His voice was softened by sympathy as he watched me look at those framed photos. "Open the drawer, he left it unlocked the last time he was here."

I sat in the large leather chair at the desk and bent to open the drawer on the right side. The mechanism was sticky from disuse, but with a firm tug, it pulled out and into my lap.

Photos and memorabilia.

The drawing I'd made of him, Aida and myself for Father's Day when I was six or seven, the certificate of academic achievement I got in eighth grade, a photo of me on my first day of kindergarten. A photo of Brando in Dad's arms, his face suffused with tenderness and awe, and another one of him hugging Mum from behind, his hands on her pregnant belly, his lips to her smiling cheek.

When I looked up through tear-glossed eyes, Beckett was sitting heavily in a chair across from the desk, rubbing his hand over his face.

"He loved you so much," he told me. "Sometimes, I've wished that men were taught the same words women seem to have for their emotions." He sighed and looked out the window at the metropolis spread out beneath us. "Lane wasn't the father he wanted to be. We both weren't. Sometimes after a long fucking day at work, we'd have a drink here in the office and lament all the things we should have done differently in our lives. Having you and Brando wasn't one of them, but not being there for you...it killed him. Living with regret like that, it's like a knife in the chest every day."

"You speak from experience," I croaked through my tight throat, still thumbing through the paraphernalia in Dad's draw, moved beyond to tears by further evidence of his love for us. There was a little collection of stapled receipts that caught my notice because the first one declared Lane's purchase of Picasso's *Child with a Dove* from a Sotheby's auction in London. I slipped them into the pocket of my coat when

Beckett wasn't looking.

"I do," he agreed, slumping in his chair so he could tip his head back as if he needed his words to be closer to God. "Lane and I both made poor choices, Bianca, but at least he made his for love."

"And you?" I asked, intrigued despite myself. I didn't know who this man was or why he was helping me. That niggling question of *why* continued to gnaw at the back of my thoughts.

"I was just an arrogant prick," he said on a bitter laugh. "Arrogance runs in the family. I thought I could have it all and nothing bad would ever touch me. It was just a one-night stand, but it had been a long time coming. Flirtations for years at functions. A curiosity that ignited one night over too many martinis."

"Why are you telling me this?" I asked, sitting straighter because I could sense the anvil about to land on my head. "Why are you helping me?"

"I'm helping you because Lane was my best friend, my family, and I'd do anything for him. Even after death." He heaved a massive inhale then expelled it harshly through his nose. A dark lock of hair fell into his face, over his green eyes, and for a moment, I thought he looked like someone I knew. "I'm helping you because I hope you'll help me too."

I narrowed my eyes at him. "I'm not sure I

have much to offer."

"I think you do," he countered, leaning forward with surprising verve, bracing his forearms on his thighs to look me dead in the eye over the desk. "You have the heart of Tiernan Morelli."

Alarm clanged inside me like warning bells.

"Hardly," I said, voice cool and easy. "He hates me, but he loves my little brother. I think that's why he puts up with me."

"No," Beckett countered. "I don't think so. You see, Bryant has been abusing Tiernan his entire life and until recently, Tiernan remained as loyal to him as a beaten dog. Only now, after *you* were threatened, did Tiernan break things off with Bryant in a rather spectacular fashion."

"That's a bit of a leap in logic," I admonished, channeling my inner Constantine.

"Maybe," he shrugged. "But the moment I found out, I've made a point to watch Tiernan, to be there however I could, and it's obvious that he cares about."

"The moment you found out what? What do you want with Tiernan's heart?"

"Hopefully," he said, his handsome face broken open with honesty and devastation. "A place in it alongside you one day. I know what it is to be a bad father, Bianca, because Tiernan is my biological son."

CHAPTER SIXTEEN

Bianca

I LEFT COLOMBE Energy in a kind of waking dream. New Yorkers hurried home with the last of their Christmas shopping, bright lights popping brightly in my periphery, seasonal music spilling through open shop doors. None of it registered.

Because Beckett Fairchild had dropped a massive secret on my shoulders and he expected me to carry it without guilt or remorse.

"I've wanted to tell him," he said back in the office when his announcement was met with my shocked silence. "I've told myself a thousand times I would but, well, you know Tiernan, he isn't exactly Mr. Approachable."

I'd blinked at him, unmoved.

Tiernan was intimidating as hell, but that wasn't excuse not to tell him the truth. And knowing him as I did, I understand that if he found out I had discovered this secret without confiding in him, whatever tentative romance we were developing would be snuff out irreparably.

"I didn't know," he said, looking out the window as if he couldn't bear me witnessing his pain. He was a tall, regal man, but his shoulders had caved in, his head hung low. "I didn't know for years. It was only one night with Sarah after years of dancing around each other. We used protection. I wanted her to leave Bryant, but..." His face spasmed and anger crossed over it. "We fought about it. She told me it was all just a play to make Bryant jealous, to hurt him the way he hurt her for loving Caroline all those years."

"Unless you found out yesterday, you still waited too long to tell him."

His lips thinned, but he nodded. "Why do you think I'm asking for your help? I never married. I never had a desire to after Sarah, but I always wanted kids. I'd like to know Tiernan."

"I have to go," I said, jerking away from Lane's desk. "I don't know why you thought I could help you and even if I could, I won't. Do you understand what it's like to feel you've been abandoned by your own parent?" An edge of hysteria crept into my voice, turning it hard, the metallic sound ringing out through the empty offices. "Do you know how that sits in a person? Gnawing away at every good thing that ever comes to them because they can't believe they deserve goodness when even their own parent neglected them? It's a fucking *disease* and you—" My finger shook as I fixed it at him. "—You infected him with that. There is nothing I can do to change that. If you want his acceptance or forgiveness, it's on you make it right with him."

"But can I?" Beckett countered, dragging hands through his hair the way I'd seen Tiernan do when he was agitated. It was disturbing to realize there were so many like tells that spoke of their resemblance: the green eyes, different shades but so vivid, the strong jawline that was squared off at the corners, and the hands with the same wide palms, thick fingers. "How can I make this right when it's been wrong for thirty years?"

I shrugged and realized I was still clutching a photo of Lane, Brando and me when my little brother was newly born. Dad and I were bent, blond heads together, over a swaddled baby with twin expressions of reverence on our faces.

"I'll never forgive Lane for leaving us in the dark," I whispered the truth, the words carving up my throat like knives. "Even seeing this, even knowing he left provisions for us. Even knowing what it's like to love a person to the point of madness. I'll never forgive him for letting me believe he didn't care. For leaving Aida broke and broken, for never being a parent to Brandon. Never."

I sucked in a deep breath, struggling with my own despair and Beckett's, whose face was crumpled and damp like a used napkin.

"But I love him. I love him because he's my dad and human beings are programmed to love their parents, but also because now, I know." My hand trembled as I flapped the photo in the air. "I know he loved us. I know he thought of us all the time and wanted the best for us even though he put us all in a position where we could never have the best. He used to be my hero." I choked on the word then laughed. "But now I know he was just a man. I used to think his life here, all of this and all of you, was a fairy tale and now I know it's all just a beautiful nightmare."

A quivering silence descended, punctuated only by my harsh breath as I struggled with my rage and sorrow.

"If you want Tiernan to know you're sorry, if you want him to know you love him, words will *never* be enough. True love in action." I lifted my eyes to his. "What are you willing to do to win your son's heart?"

I'd left after that, leaving Beckett behind me staring out the window at New York City as if it had the answer to my question. It was getting late, the sun falling deep behind the metal gates of the city's skyline, but I didn't go to Grand Central Station to catch the train back to Bishop's Landing or order a car to take me home.

Beckett's revelations had stirred a restlessness to life inside of me that burned through my limbs like an abundance of lactic acid. My legs took me out of the building and down the street to the right, heading toward Central Park and the place that had come to symbolize so much in my life. The Metropolitan Art Gallery.

I needed to see *Child with a Dove* again. As if that would make of all the chaos I'd witnessed since moving to Bishop's Landing.

It was oddly empty in the marble foyer, only a few families with bored kids milling about the space, a handful of couples nuzzling on benches in front of the more romantic paintings like Pierre-Auguste Cot's *Springtime* and Jean-Léon Gérôme's *Pygmallion and Galatea*. My heels clicked against the smooth stone floors as I rounded the corner into the large room that housed Picasso's first blue period painting.

The frame stood empty on the wall, a small white sign affixed to the blank space within that read *Under maintenance*.

Given how Tiernan had cut the canvas from the frame, I wasn't entirely surprised by, but my heart still rattled against my ribs at the loss of it. I'd felt so irrationally sure that it held the answers to all of Lane's unanswered mysteries.

My body sagged with sudden exhaustion and I staggered to a bench in the middle of the room to rest for a moment. When I sat, a crinkle of paper drew my attention to receipts I'd spirited away from Lane's desk at Colombe Energy.

I stared at them blankly, flipping through a receipt for *Child with a Dove*, another for *The Dove* that hung in his home office, and finally, the last one, the original *Le Rêve*.

The Dream was one of Picasso's later paintings, a portrait of his beloved mistress it was rumored he began and finished in a single day.

A sob bubbled up from my churning gut and caught at the back of my tongue.

Lane had called Aida his dream.

If he'd bought the painting, I had to believe it was for us, for me. Yet, I hadn't seen it in any of The Met's galleries, at Colombe Energy or in the

Constantine Compound. If the painting was the missing piece of the puzzle, a trio of paintings for the trio of Dad's other family, I had to find it.

"Excuse me," I called to a passing museum employee who stopped for me. "Is Picasso's *Le Rêve* on display here?"

The woman retrieved a phone from her pocket and looked up something on the display. "It was a number of years ago, but not since then."

I nodded casually, but my mind was whirring. If they'd taken the painting down, it was no doubt in storage somewhere beneath the museum. I wasn't some kind of cat burglar with the skills to break into the vault of The Metropolitan Art Gallery, but maybe I didn't have to.

I had something more powerful than thievery on my side.

"When will *Child with a Dove* be back on display?" I asked, affecting wide eyes and a trembling lower lip. It was a look Aida had perfected over her life and I hoped after years of witnessing its powers, I could pull it off too.

"It's scheduled to be rehung after our Christmas closure," the woman replied after checking her screen again.

"I don't suppose there's a way to see it now?" I asked with my most Aida-like smile. "My father was actually the one who donated the painting to the museum."

"Oh." Her eyes lit with interest. "You're one of the Constantine children?"

My smile widened even farther, cutting painfully into my cheeks. I extended my hand the way I'd seen Caroline do, with cool civility and a touch of condescension. "I am. Dad actually bought the painting for my twelfth birthday."

"Awe," she gushed. "That is incredibly sweet. I can't imagine my dad buying me anything more than a pair of socks for my birthday."

I laughed with her then shrugged. "Some of us are just born lucky, I guess. Is there any way you could help me? He passed away five years ago and we just celebrated the anniversary. I suppose with Christmas and everything, I'm feeling a little melancholy and nostalgic. It would mean a lot to me...and my family."

The dark-haired woman stepped closer as she made a soft clucking noise with her tongue. "Let's see what we can do, shall we? Mr. Klemm is our floor manager today, why don't we find him?"

I beamed at her. "That would be perfect."

"A CONSTANTINE, YOU say?" Mr. Klemm asked

me with a severe frown on his heavily wrinkled features. "May I see a form of identification, please?"

My heart wedged itself at the base of my throat, thudding so strongly I felt I might throw up all over Mr. Klemm's sensible loafers. Somehow, I managed to hand over my driver's licence.

"I use a different last name," I attempted to explain even though I knew I'd be hauled out of their on my ass for attempting to impersonate one of the most famous families in the city. "But my father is Lane Constantine."

Mr. Klemm's small eyes were nearly lost in the folds of skin hanging under his bushy brows, but he managed to pin me with them after glancing at my ID. Without saying a word, he started to tap on the keyboard of his computer. We were in a cramped office on the main floor we'd reached through a maze of corridors and the little room smelled of dust and pickled vegetables.

My knee juddered under the desk with nerves I couldn't begin to squash. I felt so close to something, to knowing what Lane had clearly always intended me to know.

"I see," Mr. Klemm said after a long moment, his jowls quavering as he picked up an old

258

landline phone and punched in a number. When he raised it to his lips, he covered the speaker with a hand so I couldn't hear his low murmur into the receiver.

With my luck, he was probably calling the police. I'd have to use my one phone call to contact Tiernan and he'd be livid as hell I'd gone off searching for answers without him.

"Ms. Bianca Belcante," Mr. Klemm snapped in a way that made me wonder if I'd missed his first few attempts at garnering my attention. "*Child with a Dove* is currently in our restoration section with the head of department. I informed her that you wished to see the painting and she has offered to allow you access. If you'd like to follow me, I can hand you over into her supervision."

Sweat broke out on my brow as my heart set to racing. "Yes, please, Mr. Klemm. That would be amazing."

He peered at me again with flat-lined lips but nodded and proceeded to usher me from the office.

I followed him deeper into the hive of the museum, giddiness eating at the edges of my excitement and anxiety. I'd always been fascinated by one of the most famous museums in the world and dreamed that one day I might work The Sherman Fairchild Paintings Conservation Center so to see it now was an incredible experience.

Mr. Klemm stopped at door, glanced over his shoulder at me, then entered something into a keypad before opening it.

It took me a moment to follow, because I could glimpse the light pouring in through the glass walls and massive oil paintings propped on easels at the center of the room.

"Wow," I breathed despite myself as I stepped into the room. "This is a dream."

"I always thought so too," a female voice agreed from my right.

I looked over to see a beautiful older woman with a softly creased face smiling at me as she walked over in a lab coat. She was wearing gloves to protection whatever she had been working on, but she plucked those off in order to shake my hand.

"It's wonderful to meet you, Bianca," she surprised me by saying. "I've heard so much about you from your father. My name is Emelie Fairchild."

My eyebrows cut hard into my forehead. "You knew my father?"

She laughed, grey eyes twinkling. "I knew him

very well, he was my brother's best friend all their lives."

I blinked into her green eyes, hit by the realization that this woman was Elias's mother and Beckett's sister. Before I could curb the impulse, I took a step away and let her hand drop from mine.

Her expression flickered. "Mr. Klemm, thank you for delivering Ms. Belcante. I'll take over now and make sure she is seen out securely."

"But—"

Suddenly the warm, unassuming woman seemed every inch the Constantine wife she was. "That's enough, Mr. Klemm. I thank you."

The older gentleman grumbled but saw himself out without protesting further.

"I just came to see the painting." If Emelie was a Constantine, even just by marriage, there was a huge chance she would tell Caroline what I'd been doing at The Met. "I have a passion for Picasso."

Emelie's eyes sparkled in the descending white light of the winter evening. "Yes, I've heard. There's no need to be concerned, Bianca. Between Lane and, now, Elias, I know you're a good woman and I'm happy to finally have the opportunity to meet you."

"Caroline doesn't know I'm here," I tested.

She nodded easily, waving her hand. "Not to worry. Where do you think Elias gets his rebellious nature from? Our part of the family has long born the black mark of Caroline's displeasure. I won't find it in my heart to capitulate to her dictatorship now."

"Thank you." I wasn't sure I could trust her, but the damage had already been done. She knew I was there to see *Child with a Dove* and, it seemed, she knew I was Lane's love child.

"Come," she encouraged, holding out her hand to me. "Let me show you the painting. It was damaged badly, but of course, the cameras malfunctioned the evening of the party so we don't know exactly what happened." She paused, casting a glance at me as she led us to the corner of the large room. "You wouldn't know anything about that, would you?"

I shrugged, but her small smile told me she suspected I had something to do with the damaged painting.

"I was with him when he bought it," she told me as we stopped in front of the portrait. "It was an unlisted item at the auction, but he'd had feelers out for years about Picasso's dove paintings. He told me they reminded him of someone special."

I nodded, my heart in my throat as I took in Picasso's blue period masterpiece. I'd never been so close and the details were exquisite.

"He bought *Le Reve* that day too," she continued, oblivious to the way my entire body reacted to her words.

"Is it here?" I asked breathlessly. "I'd love to see it."

"It's in storage. Lane and Caroline had donated countless items over the years to The Met. What's not on display is housed in the vaults below the museum."

"Do you have access?" I asked, as if I didn't care, as if I was just bored and it was the only thing I could think of to ask.

By the way Emelie's eyes gleamed with curiosity, I didn't pull it off.

"I do," she said slowly. "For the Constantine family, not much in The Met is off-limits. We've been patrons for decades."

"I'd love to see it," I reiterated.

Emelie studied me for a moment. "As an art lover or as Lane's daughter?"

"Both," I said honestly, gambling everything on that moment. "I think he might have left something for me in the portrait. He's done it before."

To my shock, she laughed delightedly. "Oh yes, that sounds like Lane. He loved to play games and create riddles. All right, Bianca, let's see what your father left you."

THE STORAGE VAULTS beneath the museum were a maze of security procedures and cramped corridors, but Emelie navigated us through them with ease. She chatted easily the entire time, talking about art resurrection projects, speaking about the internship program they had for undergraduates in the field because Lane had mentioned years ago that I had an interest in the field.

Inside my chest, my heart burned like a banked coal.

I barely breathed as Emelie finally stopped at a marked door and entered a code into the keypad before pushing the seal door open.

"Be careful not to touch anything," she warned as I stepped into the cold, filtered air of the temperature-controlled room. "If you don't have the key for the cases, the alarms will sound."

I nodded mutely, struck dumb by the cases of art sealed in the chamber. There was a small collection of Degas sketches in one case and a large painting I somewhat recognized as a Frida Kahlo sketch in another.

I turned slowly, my eye catching Le Reve instantly, snagging on the bright colors and surreal lines. The mistress was blonde like Aida, dozing in a red chair in a way that was both sensual and romantic. The love Picasso felt for his subject was apparent in every line of her body.

My dream and my dove, Lane would say.

I wondered for the millionth time what endearment he would have given Brando if he'd had the time to watch him grow older.

The case was all glass based on a metal platform with a keyhole in one corner. I stepped closer and bent, studying the small slot as my hand went into my deep coat pocket and curled around the key Tiernan had found behind the *Child with a Dove* painting.

"If I open the case with a key, will the alarm go off?" I whispered to Emelie, my entire focus on the gold framed painting.

"It shouldn't," she murmured, her eyes hot on the back of my head.

I nodded slightly, tongue between my teeth as I took out the key and carefully slotted it into the mechanism. When it fit smoothly inside, a sob burst from my lips.

This was it.

The dream within *The Dream*.

The click of the lock opening was loud in the still room but the glass door swung open soundlessly as I pulled it back.

"Stop," Emelie said, making me jump in my skin. I whirled around to face her, ready to do battle for what lay beneath the painting, but she only stepped forward to pull a pair of protective gloves from her pocket. "Put these on if you want to touch it."

After I dragged them on, she placed a gentle hand on my wrist. "May I check the painting for you? I don't want any damage done to the canvas."

All I could do was nod as I stepped back to watch Emelie reach into the case and carefully lift the painting so she could flip it over, replacing it on the easel so that the back was to us. She carefully undid the latches securing the frame then pulled out a pair of pliers from her lab coat to coax the frame support from the backing. As she peeled it back a flurry of thin papers fell from the gap in the layers to line the bottom of the case.

Before Emelie could move, I wedged myself on the gap between her and the case, dropping to my knees to collect the papers.

"What is it?" she asked, breathless with excitement. "I did the inspection on the work myself when it as donated…these must have been added after it was already stored here."

I wasn't listening.

My eyes were glued to the papers, a collection of them scrawled with Lane's loose, loping scrawl. A stapled set of documents lay in the debris as well, officially presented with the header of a law firm I recognized from the papers Caroline had tried to have me sign just days before.

I collected them all almost frantically, trying to order the handwritten pages so I could finally read the goodbye I'd never been able to have with my dad.

> *My doves,*
>
> *There is no way to say goodbye to the ones you love, but as I think on it, I believe that is for a reason. We never truly say goodbye to the people we love because we live on in each other's hearts and minds long after one of us might be gone. Maybe it is the delusions of an aging man, but I like to imagine you all thinking of me as you go on with your lives. I have no plans to die soon, but if I do I hope Aida, my love, that I am able to take care of*

you beyond the grave. Since the first moment I met you, I wanted to give you the life you dreamed of. I know I failed in that regard, but you never made me doubt that our love was enough. That and our beautiful children are the two best gifts this wealthy man has received. To be loved for me alone, and not my riches. You, my dream, have been the escape that has kept me sane these many years. I wish I could thank you properly for that. Instead, I will just have to say for the millionth time, I love you and even in death, I will never stop doing so.

It's especially difficult to write this letter when my youngest boy is still only a baby. I have to believe we will have a lifetime of memories to create together, but just in case, Brandon, my son, never doubt how much I love you. How proud I am to be your father no matter what you go on to accomplish in life. You will be a better man than I have ever been just by virtue of having a mother and sister who also love you more than life.

And finally, my sweet dove. I hope you will include me in your vivid dreams, think of me when all your waking ones come true as I have no doubt they will. Of all my children, there is none so pure as my dove.

The world is a hard place, hard even when you are wealthy and powerful, and as much as I have tried to shield you from that, I know one day I will fail and all the ugliness will seep in. I am not afraid for you when that day comes because I know purity of heart does not equal weakness. You are strong, Bianca, stronger even than you know. Your future will be a beautiful one even if I have no part in it, even if I am not around to witness it. I have no fear in my heart for my daughter. You have all the best parts of your mother and me, and, truthfully, I am already in awe of you.

I have been unfair to you, my family, battling against what I felt I should do and what I knew in my heart was right. The day is coming when I hope to make a change for good, but if fail, please know, you all have always been my dream

Love always,
Dad

Tears rained over the pages, smearing the ink in a way that horrified me, but I couldn't stop the deluge. I was a crier by nature so there was no way I could contain the impulse when I had a letter for my dad in my hands. My chest ached and stomach heaved as if his words were rearranging my insides. In a way, they were, because I finally knew just how much Dad loved us, how much he'd thought of us and wanted the best for us. He was a conflicted man, deeply flawed, but seeing evidence of his foresight for us after years of believing he'd left us desolate and unloved resolved his hero status in my heart. Every girl wanted to love her dad and Lane had just given me reason to revere him for the rest of my life.

He'd given me his last words and hopes, his last dreams written on flimsy sheets of paper I wished I could cast in stone so they would never fade.

After I read the letter for a second time, I turned my attention to the stapled sheaf of papers and lost my breath to the enormity of the declaration written there.

"Oh my God," I whispered looking up at Emelie with round eyes.

"Did you find everything you thought you would," she asked kindly, offering me her hand to help stand. "Any life changing revelations?"

I curled the papers into my chest and grinned so widely it hurt. "Absolutely."

CHAPTER SEVENTEEN

Bianca

I VISITED LOMBARDI & Ghorbani law offices in the city on my way home to Bishop's Landing. The day had taught me a valuable truth about people and life. There were very few people who were all good or all bad, and few deeds that could fit solidly in one corner of that spectrum. My dad had called me his dove not because I was all good and all pure, but because I had a strong heart and he believed it wouldn't lead me astray.

And it hadn't.

My heart had led me to Tiernan Morelli, to a man that yearned for family and deserved peace more than anyone I had ever known.

And I was going to give him that. That happily ever after I'd promised him.

Even if it meant exacting revenge.

The plan I loosely formed the night before

took concrete shape now that I had Lane's hidden will. The potential to exact a pound of flesh from Caroline Constantine was in my power to enact and I was just foolhardy enough to try to see it through.

Happily, the moment I crashed into Elena's offices and harassed the receptionist for an appointment, Elena took one look at my harried appearance and promised to help me.

Three hours later, I was opening the door to the Constantine Compound with my heart lodged like an animal stuck in the pipe of my throat. I knew without a doubt Tiernan wouldn't approve of my plan, so I hadn't told him. Instead, I'd texted Henrik again to tell him I would be late. Now, I was stepping into a potential minefield with only Elias and his mother as back up.

I checked my phone one last time to make sure they were in place and then stepped into the expansive foyer of the Constantine's mansion.

A mess of noises floated through the open archways leading deep into the house. The tangled voices of the Constantine family and the chime and clink of dishes as they finished their Christmas tea and present exchange.

Despite my resolve, the decision I'd made to eschew my Constantine roots and focus on my future with one particular Morelli, I felt a momentary burn in my gut to be included in the family's festivities. I'd dreamed of being in this house with this family for so long that the idea still haunted me like a mirage.

But the miraculous thing was that whatever residual yearning I felt for the Constantine was surpassed tenfold by my longing for Brando, Tiernan, and The Gentlemen of Lion Court. I couldn't breathe without thinking of Tiernan, without wondering how he was and if he was thinking of me. It was madness, but it was ours, and I couldn't wait to finally go back to a house that felt like a home and make a life with my brutal and beautiful lover.

"Bianca?" my voice drifted down the hall a moment before the *click* of tall heels reached me.

Seconds later, Caroline appeared in the arch-way in a gorgeous navy silk dress that made her look fifteen years younger than she must have been with six children. Her hair was perfectly coiffed and clusters of large diamonds glittered at her ears, throat, and wrists. She was absolutely extraordinary, every inch of her beautiful and immaculate. But there was something about that perfection that was almost repugnant.

It made you wonder what she was hiding

beneath it.

"I thought you were unwell?" Caroline asked, stopping a year yards away from me as if I might be contagious. "But when Cook took soup up to your room, you were gone. Where have you been? If you were with that filthy Morelli, I expect you to turn around and leave immediately."

I sniffed miserably, forcing tears to my eyes. "I-I'm sorry, C-Caroline. A man called me today saying he had something he needed to tell me." I looked up at her with wide eyes. "I h-have something I n-need to confess."

Caroline studied me for a moment, her haughty regard cool and careful. Only when I began to cry in earnest did she move forward with a kind of cooing noise that didn't around natural in her mouth.

"Awe, you sweet thing," she said, unconsciously using a version of Tiernan's endearment for me. It made me want to claw her goddamn eyes out, but I had to maintain the façade if I was going to pull this off.

When she was close enough, I launched myself into her arms, hugging her tightly as I cried into her shoulder. She was stiff as a plank of wood in my embrace for a brief moment before she softened enough to pat me lightly on the back.

"What's happened, Bianca?" she asked, genuine interest in her voice.

"N-not here," I begged, pulling away to wipe my nose. "I don't want anyone to hear us."

She considered me for a moment then nodded. "We'll go to my office."

I smothered my smile in her shoulder, sobbing there for a second. "Thank you," I hiccoughed.

She led me down the hall, comforting me almost robotically when one hand steering me by the shoulder as I continued to sniffle into my cupped hands. When we reached her office, she pushed me into one of the twin velvet chairs before her desk then locked the door after us.

"Now, stop crying, Bianca, and compose yourself. What has you weeping so uncontrollably?" she demanded as she settled her bottom against the front of her desk and looked down her nose at me.

"I'm sorry," I whispered through my raw throat, because I truly had cried a lot that day. "I'm just so overwhelmed and I feel so *awful*," I wailed. "After you've been so good to me."

"Start from the beginning," she insisted, flashing me a terse smile when I looked up at her for comfort. "What happened?"

I dashed at the wet on my cheeks but allowed my lip to curl under in a pout the way Aida used to do when she wanted something. "A man called. He said he'd been searching for me for years, but it wasn't until I came to Bishop's Landing that he found me. H-he…" I cried loudly again, almost choking on the forced sob. "He said my dad left me something in his will."

Instantly, the air the room charged, suddenly pulled into a high voltage outlet. Caroline shivered so delicately, if I hadn't been watching her, I would have missed it.

"Oh? This is the father who passed away some time ago?"

I nodded miserably, refusing to meet her eye. "The thing is…" I sucked in a deep breath. "The thing is, Lane Constantine was my biological father. He and my mother had an affair a-and they had Brando and me." I squeezed my eyes shut, tears springing from the compressed corners. "I should have told you sooner, but Dad always spoke so highly of you and his other children a-and I was s-so desperate to me you all. T-then you were so kind to me and I just felt *awful*."

Caroline was silent as I wept for a moment, but there was calculation in her gaze as she looked out the window at the perfectly manicured yard blanketed in snow. It was tinted nearly the same pale blue as her eyes in the descending dusk.

"I don't want it," I told her desperately, lunging forward to clasp her hands tightly, forcing her to look down into my miserable face. "I don't want it, honestly. I-I know I don't deserve it and you've b-been so kind to me. I just want to stay here with her and get Brando and then we could be a family."

When Caroline shifted, I clung tighter, my voice a high, pleading whine. "Please, Caroline, I'm so sorry I was grateful before. I want to be a proper Constantine more than anything."

"Well," she said finally, pushing my face out of my stomach where I'd pressed my tear stained cheek. She tipped my chin up with two cold fingers so I was looking into the mask of her benevolent face. "This is certainly a shock, Bianca. How am I supposed to react to this horrible accusation?"

"I-I have the papers," I scrambled back, tossing a copy of the will on the table. The real one was safely with Elena back at her offices. "You can see, I'm telling the truth! But I don't want it, I promise. I just want don't want to be alone anymore."

My words ended on a soft whimper that

wasn't hard to produce because the words were true. I didn't want to be alone anymore. I didn't want to have fight alone, be alone, live alone.

I wanted it all with Tiernan because I knew no one else in the world would fight for us and our family as much as he would.

"You understand you wouldn't be able to tell anyone about this," she said carefully, flipping through the pages I was certain she had already seen before. "This could bring disgrace on our family and I won't have that. If you want to stay here with me, you'll have to sign a non-disclosure agreement. You could never have been Lane's bastard, but you could be a real Constantine cousin," she promised sweetly, dipping down to smile in my face. "I'm willing do to that for you, sweetie."

I almost laughed into her saccharine face, but I swallowed it down and presented a tremulous smile instead. I'd learned a lot from Caroline about acting in the weeks I'd lived with her.

"You would?" I breathed, grasping her hand tightly in my own. "Really?"

"Of course," she soothed, smoothing my hair back from my sticky, red face. "If you want a place in this family, I can give that to you. All I ask is that you keep my husband's mistakes a secret."

Mistakes.

Brando wasn't a mistake. He was the best human on the face of the planet and the world would be a lesser place without him.

I wasn't a mistake either, even though recently I might have been convinced otherwise.

Lane had wanted us. In the end, he'd believed we were the only choice for him.

Tiernan wanted us. Even though loving us both ostracized him from his father permanently. His words reverberated in my head, *loving you was the best mistake I ever made.*

"I can do that," I agreed easily, shaking my head so hard it started to ache. "And I meant what I said. I don't want anything. You can have it all back."

"Hmm?" Caroline asked as if she couldn't remember what I was referring to, but I knew better. The hand at her side clenched tight then carefully unfurled.

"I'll sign whatever papers you need to take control of it yourself," I gushed. "Do you still have those guardianship papers?"

"I haven't been able to add Brandon's name to the agreement yet," she cautioned, and it was a test, a metal detector held over my words.

I swallowed thickly then bowed my head. "But you'll promise to get him here as soon as you can?"

Through the curtain of my hair, I witnessed Caroline's lightning flash smile.

"Yes, yes, I'll make sure of it. For now..." She stood and rounded the desk, producing papers from a locked drawer. "I still have the old agreement. Why don't you sign it and we can get the ball rolling on this? I'd love to be able to introduce you to my children as our beloved cousin right now as an early Christmas present."

I grinned. "Really? Yeah, let's do that."

Caroline grabbed the Mont Blanc pen on her desk and laid out the papers for me over Lane's will on the desk. I reached for the pen just as a knock came at the office door.

Caroline frowned, glancing between the door and me. "You sign and I'll get the door, sweetie."

I nodded but as soon as she walked beyond me to the door I sent her back a vicious glare. Of course, I knew who was at the end. Elias had texted her as soon as Caroline had taken my bait.

"Oh, Emelie," Caroline said with polite surprise, then warmer, "Beckett, darling. I thought you couldn't make it tonight?"

I had no idea why Beckett was with Emelie,

but I took advantage of the distraction none the less and switched out Caroline's papers with the ones Elena had drawn up for me that afternoon. I tucked Caroline's guardianship papers in my canvas bag.

"We were stealing some goodies from the kitchen and thought we overheard someone crying," Emelie explained from the doorway. "Is everything okay in here?"

Caroline laughed lightly. "Oh yes, Bianca is just overwhelmed by her Christmas present."

Beckett peered around the door and waved at me. "Hello, Bianca! Elias will be happy to see you."

"Hello," I returned, grabbing the papers as I walked over to greet them properly. I handed them over to Caroline along with the pen. "I think they just need your signature."

"Oh, sign those already and get back out here," Emelie exclaimed, waving her glass of champagne as if she'd had too much to drink. In reality, she'd arrived only twenty minutes before Elias and I had. "Perry was just about to make a toast and then we thought about a game of charades."

Caroline frowned. "I don't think we are quite done—"

Beckett stepped forward, just a little too close to Caroline. Her eyes flared wide for a moment when he took her elbow in a gentle hold and rubbed his thumb on the inside of her arm. "Come out and have some fun, Caro. I want to see you smile at least once tonight."

I blinked at the palpable energy between them, understanding what Elias had said about rumors flying around the nature of their relationship.

So, why was he helping me dupe Caroline, now?

A small grin played with the edges of her full mouth and finally she sighed. "Oh fine, Beckett, but you must know you are the worst influence."

He laughed heartily, taking the pen from my grip and giving it to her before presenting his back for her to use as a table. "I'm as pure as they come. And chivalrous too."

Her grin widened into a smile was almost sweet. I felt a pang of something like empathy for her, wondering what it must be like alone on the throne of a family built on secret and lies.

It wasn't enough to change my course, though.

Excitement burned through me as she bent over his back and signed her name to the line beside me with a neat little flourish.

"Done," she announced.

Beckett turned and caught her around the waist playfully. "Excellent, now come out and play with the rest of us. Em, can you take care of those? Caro, do you need them scanned?"

"Yes, scanned and sent to the lawyer," she agreed, but her voice was slightly breathless as Beckett pressed her into his side.

"No problem," Emelie agreed, eyes twinkling as she stepped into the office with me.

"We'll make the announcement later tonight, Bianca," Caroline said, almost as an afterthought, her mind clearly on Beckett and the return of a fortune she'd believed had been wrongfully stolen from the family. She looked as giddy as a woman like her could be. "For now, let's toast with champagne."

"Yes, we certainly have cause for celebration," I agreed with a broad grin as I followed her out of the office, closing the door on Emelie who was about to seal Caroline's fate.

I TOASTED WITH the Constantines, but I didn't stay to mingle even though Tinsley was there with a gorgeous older man named Magnus who I was incredibly curious about. I went up to my borrowed bedroom and carefully packed the few things I felt comfortable taking back with me to Lion Court.

Even though we had somehow pulled off the heist of a lifetime, I knew I wouldn't feel safe until I was back at Lion Court.

I was just descending the last of the stairs into the hall when Caroline's voice caught me off guard. When I peered up through my hair, she was standing at the mouth of the hall leading to her office with a look of shock on her face.

"I certainly hope you aren't going to visit Lion Court," she warned. "Remember, you're a member of the household, now, Bianca. Adherence to the rules is paramount as a Constantine."

"Oh, I know," I promised her, dark glee blooming in my gut. "Obedience is everything. I know what happens to those who disobey you, Caroline."

That animal stillness settled over her again, prey sensing it's been targeted by a predatory threat.

I grinned at her as I stepped off the last stair. "You know, I couldn't for the life of me figure out why you'd want to take in an orphan girl without social grace or standing. At first, I thought, maybe she just hates the Morellis *that* much. Enough to take anything she can away from them…"

I shifted the strap of the canvas Metropolitan Museum of Art bag I'd bought in the gift store that day. Caroline's eyes tracked it carefully.

"But if you really hate them that much, taking guardianship of the wayward ward of the Morelli black sheep wouldn't exactly be a coup d'état. You wanted something else. And today, I found out what that was."

Caroline released a dainty exhale that on any-one else, I might have called a snort. "You're very dramatic, Bianca. And very wrong, I might add. I'm a generous woman, you can ask any of my children or acquaintances."

"Do you really think Tinsley would say so?" I asked, referencing the daughter she'd shipped off to boarding school who now lived with her much older boyfriend. "Or your ex-body guard, Ronan?"

I knew from Elias that Caroline's previous enforcer had left his employment in the Constan-tine family and switched sides to the Morellis.

My words hit home. I watched fascinated as Caroline stiffened, every inch of her still except for the minute rise and fall of her chest.

"You can play pretend all you want, but I was

raised in the pastures and poverty of rural Texas, I know bullshit when I smell it." I smiled beatifically at her. "You wanted me because you knew Lane Constantine left a considerable fortune for me in his will."

Caroline shot a quick glance down the hallway, her jaw tight enough to crack her molars. Her eyes were narrow, twin flecks of ice, as she slowly stalked toward me.

"Now, Bianca, I don't know what delusions you are under, but I wasn't aware of my husband's heartbreaking indiscretions, let alone the existence of his offspring. That you would be so indelicate about my feelings in this deeply saddens me. I'm afraid given your clearly unstable nature, I can't have you reside in this house any longer. Not when you could be a risk to my children—"

"I'm leaving anyway," I informed her coolly, stepping toward her to counter her predatory approach. A flicker of disbelief shadowed her face as my clear confidence. "I got what I came for."

Her laugh was bitter exclamation of villainous triumph. "You received nothing. Do you not understand what happened when you signed those guardianship papers? I am effectively in control of your property until you come of age, and that includes Colombe Energy. Did you really think I'd ever give the daughter of a whore the name Constantine let alone gain control of an entity that was never Lane's to give away. Winston is in charge of Halcyon now and he is the only one who should be running CEI. The thought of *you* having access to our reputation and fortune is laughably pathetic."

I laughed, almost delighted by her. "Do you know what's so funny about this situation? I never cared about the money. All I wanted, most of my life, was to be accepted into my father's family. To truly be a part of his life."

Caroline's hard laugh fell between us like the clatter of rock. "Powerful men often have mistresses. They mean nothing to them. A way to blow off some steam. To do the dirty, despicable things a well-raised woman would never allow him to do her. They're whores," Caroline said steadily, but her eyes, they *seethed*, steaming like ice under scorching sun. "And so are their bastard children."

Rage coiled inside me, suffocating my control until it threatened to die. "You can call my mother and me whores if it makes you feel better. Clearly, my dad thought more of us than that because he left control of Colombe Energy Investments and a small fortune in stock options in multiple Halcyon companies to *me*."

The color leeched from her face, draining visibly from forehead to the faintly lined neck above her silk collar. It brought me immense satisfaction. I wasn't a vindictive person, but this bitch deserved everything I could dole out after what she did to Tiernan, how she made Elias feel, what she intended to do to Brando and me. I couldn't know for sure, but it was fairly obvious she intended to steal our inheritance and leave us destitute once more.

"Well," she hissed between her clenched teeth. "I've rectified that situation. Now, that I am your guardian, I'll revert everything back to its rightful place. As for you, Bianca, I'll make sure you are shipped off to a nunnery. I've heard there are delightfully austere convents in the Midwest that will suit my needs nicely."

So, she had intended to ruin Brandon and I. I couldn't blame her exactly, it wasn't often someone got the better of Caroline Constantine, let alone her own husband.

"You knew about us," I continued as if it was story time and the matriarch of one of the most powerful families in the country wasn't trying to roast me alive with her gaze. "You knew about us and it drove you mad, didn't it? Maybe you even confronted Lane about it, tried to get him to break it off with Aida, but he never did, did he? He loved her, loved us, until the day he died and this will proved it. Did you always know he intended to include us?"

Her lips rolled under and pressed tight, a vault locked tight. I didn't need her confirmation. It was obvious she'd known and disapproved. Had she destroyed dad's will and he'd made provisions in hiding the extra one for me? Or had he simply written mine as a provision to the first, hoping to keep us from Caroline's infamous fury?

In any case, I doubted I would ever get the answers and now, it didn't really matter.

"I'm not going to a nunnery, Caroline. Quite the opposite actually. I'm going back to Lion Court and Tiernan Morelli." I looked at her with pity and watched as it seemed to douse her with cold water, making her bristle even further. "As for the issue of my guardianship, those papers you signed? They weren't the same ones you had drawn up. After I found Lane's will today, I stopped by Lombardi & Ghorbani law offices and had them draw up an agreement of my own." I paused for dramatic effect because I wanted to relish catching Caroline at her own game. "You signed an agreement to give Colombe Energy Investments with a very generous ten-million-dollar endowment in memory of Lane Constantine."

Just as quickly as the color drained from Caroline's porcelain skin it returned, vermillion red sweeping her features. When she spoke, her entire body seemed to vibrate with the strain of containing her fury.

"That will *never* hold up in court, you thieving cunt."

I shrugged, but my heart trilled like an alarm in my chest, urging me to get the hell out of the Compound and away from the scorned woman before me. "Actually, I think it will. You see Emelie and Beckett Fairchild were witnesses to your signature. I think if you ask them, they'd be willing to swear an oath in court to that affect. Really, Caroline, you should be kinder to your family members, resentment can fester for years."

For one single second, Caroline seemed utterly bewildered, her eyes scouring my face as if searching for clues. How could innocent and naïve little Bianca Belcante from backwater, Texas have duped her so horribly?

I grinned because for once in my life, I felt the headiness of being the one in control. It was made all the better by the fact that it was Caroline's own pride that had been her downfall. If she'd ever given me an ounce of respect, she wouldn't have fallen prey to the lion in the guise of a lamb.

Of course, as my own pride surged through my blood like an aphrodisiac, my ruin followed swiftly in its path.

Because Caroline Constantine didn't know how to lose gracefully, she'd never had to before.

Caroline Constantine only knew how to fight.

I gasped as she lunged forward and clutched a swathe of my hair in a tight fist. As I tried to pry her off me, her grip tightened and she started to pull me by the hair up the stairs. A scream tore through me as her other hand tangled in my locks and used them like reins to manoeuvre me off my feet. I feel with a brutal crash to the edge of the marble stairs, the pain punching the air from my lungs.

Still, I tried to scream, breathless. Tears streamed down my cheeks as she hauled me up the stairs one at a time. I could feel my hair tearing out at the roots, hot blood seeping over my scalp. Her own hair was dishevelled, white silk skin splotched with the red of her exertion.

Just as I successfully tore one hand free from my hair, Caroline stepped back, angled herself and swung one Manolo Blahnik pump straight at my temple.

Stars exploded like a super nova in head and a moment later, I passed out.

Chapter Eighteen

Tiernan

S HE WAS LATE.

The sun had set over an hour ago and still, Bianca was missing from Lion Court.

It took everything in me to play calm while The Gentlemen and I baked my grandmother Zelda's diablo cookies and gingerbread men with Brando all afternoon waiting for Bianca to arrive, but the moment the sun set, I started going out of my skin with frustration and fear.

Where the fuck was she?

"I spoke to her this morning, T," Henrik murmured as we finished icing the last of the cookies. Brando didn't want just ordinary gingerbread men, so Walcott had ordered a set of superhero themed cookie cutters. Henrik was putting the last touches on a vivid green Hulk cookie, his thick fingers deftly and delicately decorating the hero's face. "She's fine."

"You spoke to her this morning?" I asked, almost ready to bite my friend's head off. "Why did she call?"

"She needed help opening a door."

"A locked door, I presume. What the fuck was she getting into? You don't think it's a bad fucking sign that we haven't heard from her since then? She should have been here an hour ago," I muttered under my breath, careful to keep the decibel low so Brando wouldn't hear me at the other end of the island where he sat on the counter babbling happily to Walcott and Ezra.

Henrik chuckled. "It's good to see you like this."

"What?" I barked. "Mad as a fucking hatter?"

"In love," he countered. "In love with a good woman who has made you a better man."

I scoffed, but my heart wasn't in it because it was with Bianca where ever the hell she was getting up to trouble.

"Mind your own fucking business."

"I'm too busy minding yours." Henrik laughed. "Santo made contact with Bryant. Apparently, the old goat is interested in what he has to sell, especially if it has something to do with the Constantines."

I snorted. "He's utterly transparent and he doesn't even give a fuck because he thinks he is too powerful to be taken down."

I'd had the idea to use Santo as the bait luring Bryant into our trap because the two already had an established relationship. Even though Santo was an underboss in the Belcante crime family, Bryant was just arrogant enough to believe he could control the man and greedy enough to believe anyone would betray someone for the right price.

All that remained was constructing the right cage to lock Bryant into.

I'd tapped out just about every single one of my resources searching for information on the Constantine's Halcyon operation that might tempt Bryant, but so far, nothing. Winston Constantine had his business locked up tight as a nun's vagina.

Henrik's phone chimed with an incoming message. I grabbed his wrist before he could even fully pull the device from his pocket and checked the screen myself.

> **Bianca:** *I'll be late. Tell Tiernan not to worry. I'm just getting his Christmas present wrapped up tight.*

Anxiety spiked through me like adrenaline, urging me to storm out the door and chase after her, where ever she was. I knew my little thing was up to no good, because she had more courage than sense most of the time.

"If she's not home in two hours, we go after her," I growled to Henrik who only nodded at me with his own concerned frown. "We don't just have Caroline to worry about. Bryant has been too quiet. The fact that he hasn't tried to have me maimed or killed is fucking disturbing."

"For now," I said a little louder so Brando could hear me. The kid was the only cure for the madness raging inside me. "I think it's time for someone to get ready for bed."

"Anca always lets me stay up 'til midnight on Christmas Eve," Brando declared somberly, his fat curls shivering as he nodded along with his words. "It's way too early for me to sleep."

I arched a brow and fixed him with my coolest stare. "You wouldn't be lying to me, would you? Because Santa skips houses where little lying boys live."

Brando pursed his lips as he studied me for sincerity. "How about I just stay up for one more hour?"

A smile cracked my stern mask, but I didn't

try to curb it. "How about we do one more Christmas activity, you take a bath because you stink like sweaty gingerbread men, and then you go to bed after that?"

How a seven-year-old kid could bargain with me better than seasoned mafiosos and accomplished businessmen was beyond my understanding. But Brando grinned as if he'd won the lottery, slipped off the counter onto the green stool we'd bought for him and then scampered over to me to shake my hand. I took it soberly in mine for a firm shake.

"Bianca always reads me *'Twas The Night Before Christmas*," he told me with a sly look. "And she lets me eat all the cookies I want before bed."

"Lies," I warned, pinching his sides to make him squeal with laughter. "I've done my own research, buddy, and too much sugar can trigger one of your episodes. You don't want to be tired on Christmas, do you?"

He frowned, considering it for a moment. "No, I guess not."

"Wise man." I took his little, icing sugar sticky hand in mine and tugged him into the front parlor we'd put one of the Christmas trees in.

Ezra followed with a plate of cookies, Walcott with a tray of mugs filled with hot chocolate (with Baileys for the adults) and Henrik with his pink guitar. We all settled into the couches, Brandon tucked under my arm with his feet up on Ezra's thick thighs.

Something uncoiled inside me, a tension I'd lived with for so long I hadn't realized it even existed until it released itself. This was the Christmas tableau I hadn't had since I was a boy, my family cozying up around the tree, happy and full of seasonal treats. Brando leaned his entire weight into my body, cheek to my chest as if I wasn't some monster to be feared but a man who would always support him and protect him. It was the truth, but it moved through me like a religious revelation. I felt changed by the simple act of his implicit trust in me.

There was no way in hell I'd ever let anything happen to this boy who had already lived through so much misery in his short life. I would love him every single fucking day until the end of my days and then I'd haunted him here in Lion Court after I bequeathed it to Bianca and him to make sure he was fine for the rest of his life.

"I'm happy you're here," I told him in a voice as raw torn flesh as I reached into my chest to rip a piece of my heart off to place in his keeping.

"Me too," Brando said, yawning widely so I could count all of his tiny teeth. Picasso jumped up onto the couch and curled over the length of his body. He rubbed a hand over his dog's head and sleepily looked up at me. "If Anca was here, it'd be the perfect Christmas."

"She'll be back soon," I promised, smoothing a hand over his riotous curls before I picked the book up off the coffee table. I'd found a box of old Christmas things in one of the unused rooms in the house and the old book was at the bottom, a second edition that was crumbling at the edges.

Henrik played the guitar softly as I read the book to Brando. Ezra held both of his small feet in each massive hand as if Brando was his touchstone. Walcott sat in the chair across from us snapping photos on his phone when the mood struck him.

It was so sweet, it was almost enough to make me sick.

But it didn't.

Far from it.

By the time I finished, Brando was dozing on my chest, drooling slightly into my cashmere sweater. Ezra offered to take him upstairs, but I wanted to be the one to do it if Bianca wasn't there.

I ran a warm bath because the kid really did smell and he was sticky all the way up to his elbows with sugar, floor, and icing. He barely opened his eyes as I sat him in the swirling bubbles, propped up with one of my hands while I used a bowl and washcloth to gently clean him with the other.

"Tiernanny?" he murmured, huge blue eyes opening slightly to fix me with his stare. "Do you love me?"

I dropped the bowl into the tub. "Why're you asking me that?"

He blinked. "Well, Mom loved us and she took care of us, too. You're doing a good job even though I'm not really your kid. Does that mean you love me, too?"

A tumble of tangled words rolled up my tight throat and onto my tongue, but I couldn't untangle them enough to speak eloquently. Instead, I just nodded slightly as I retrieved the bowl beneath the suds and set it on the side of the bath so I could soap up his blonde curls.

"I guess that means I love you very much," I grumbled.

Brando nodded sagely, as if he'd known all along. "That's good. I really love you, too. At first,

I thought you were kinda scary like The Hulk, but you know, you're both really nice guys when you're not angry."

My laugh was slightly choked. "Tip your head back, bud." Carefully, I rinsed his hair, holding the back of his skull in my palm.

"You love Bianca too, right?" he asked with his eyes closed, trusting me to hold him upright. "But it's different because you like to kiss her. That's what boys and girls, or boys and boys, and girls and girls do when they like-like each other."

"How do you know so much about that, huh?" I teased as I finished up and pulled the plug.

Brando shrugged as he stood up to get out of the tub. "Lots of girls in my class think I'm cute."

This time my laughter rang out through the black tiled bathroom, echoing all around us. When I recovered, Brando was grinning at me.

I shook my head, engulfing his small form in a massive towel.

"I bet they do. Yeah, I guess you could say I like-like Bianca and I think she's very cute." My tone flattened, deepened as I chafed him all over then sat on the rim of the bath to pull him into my lap so we could talk face to face. "Actually, I love-love her."

"Because she makes you smile?" he asked.

It was astonishing how simple and profound a child's logic could be.

"Yeah, kid, because she makes me smile and I hadn't smiled in a very long fucking time."

He nodded, tucking his head under my chin sleepily. "I knew you guys would end up together, you know. The heroes always end up together in the comic books."

I stared blankly ahead as his words filtered through my guarded heart.

The heroes.

This beautiful boy with a heart like an untouched diamond thought I was a hero and that I deserved the woman who had been his beacon in the dark for every one of his seven years of life.

If that wasn't an honor, I didn't know what was.

And those words spoken by a young boy somehow meant so much more than anything my father had ever said.

A lifetime of hatred felt so insignificant in the face of an ounce of kindness from Bianca and Brandon. It was almost enough to turn me into an utter fucking sap.

Brando fell asleep in my arms as I carried him to his bedroom with Picasso tight at my heels because the dog went everywhere his master did.

It was only when I'd tucked him into his Spiderman sheets that the heavy door knocker clanged throughout the house.

By the time I descended the stairs, Walcott had already greeted the guest and let him into the hall.

Beckett Fairchild stood there looking pale as a spectre.

"Tiernan," he said, but I already knew what his next words would be. "Caroline is holding Bianca prisoner at the Compound."

CHAPTER NINETEEN

Tiernan

THE CONSTANTINE COMPOUND was lit up like a flare in the dark bowl of the night sky. The snowy drive was raked with tire marks from the cars coming and going from the great house to celebrate Christmas Eve, but none remained outside the garage to the left of the main structure. All was still, not even a fucking mouse stirred.

But across the street from the gates, I waited in the warm dark of my SUV with Henrik, Walcott and Ezra armed to the fucking teeth beside me.

Behind us, first one, then two, then three black SUVs rolled up and parked.

If I was going to storm the Constantine Compound and get Bianca out safely, I sure as fuck wasn't going to do it without backup.

I got out of the car without a word to my men, who followed silently as I crunched through the snow to the car behind us where Carter waited against the hood.

"Brother," he greeted, his his expression calm. "Are you sure you want to do this?"

I thought about Beckett Fairchild's frenetic energy standing there in the foyer of my house. The wrath that ignited as he told me about Caroline dragging Bianca to her room by her hair and the locking her in her room like a princess in a fucking tower.

Clearly, Caroline didn't understand that if anyone was going to lock that princess in a tower, it would be *me*.

If she hurt Bianca irrevocably, I'd kill her where she stood.

"Apparently, Bianca somehow tricked Caroline into endowing the business she inherited from Lane with ten million dollars," Walcott informed him, pride rich in his voice.

"You're kidding," Carter said. Walcott shook his head, and Carter laughed again. "I can't wait to meet this girl. But this won't be easy. I've done a little recon for you. They have security posted everywhere, but they're weak on the right side."

I held up a hand, silencing him. "I've snuck in

before. The oaks on the left side of the property eclipse the wall, if you're a good climber, it's easy enough to get over."

"And you're a good climber?" Walcott asked drily.

"Mom would get so angry when he came in with skinned knees and ruined trousers." Carter said, his eyes bright with memories. "Didn't you break your elbow or something falling out of some tree?"

"My collarbone."

Carter grinned. "Yeah, that was hilarious."

"As heartwarming as this is, can we please get back on track? She's spent enough time in that fucking prison."

"There could be backlash," Carter warned. "Is she worth this much to you?"

"She's mine." I wanted the words to emerge calmly, cool as ice. Instead, they burned up my throat on the way out. "She's mine and Caroline took her from me."

"Ah," Carter said, something like amusement in his dark eyes. "So it's like that. The heartless Tiernan Morelli has fallen."

"Call it whatever you want. Bianca and I belong to each other and I won't let anyone, let alone a Constantine, take her from me." I'd fight anyone and anything, even my baser instincts and cruel inclinations, to keep Bianca with me forever. Not just keep her, but love her. Cherish her. Bring her as much peace and joy as I knew she was capable of giving me.

"Never thought I'd see the day," Carter said.

"Caroline will rue the fucking day," I growled, letting the lid open on my rage just slightly so some of that scalding steam could hiss through and relieve the pressure. "Let's go."

It took some coordination.

Henrik, Ezra, and I went over the wall on the left side. The first two Gentlemen slunk through the shadows at the high wall encompassing the gate until the reached the gates so they could disable the two guards stationed there. On the right side, Walcott and Carter took care of the two men on patrol of the grounds before they went to the back entrance of the house.

I walked straight to the front door and knocked.

As soon as the door opened and a man in uniform emerged with a gun in his hand, I disarmed him viciously, breaking his arm with a great *crack* like timber snapping. He howled as I twisted that arm behind his back and handed his discarded gun over to Carter. Caroline was there at the top of one curving staircase as I frogged marched the man into the foyer. Her hair was down around her shoulders, face bare of makeup, her body robed in light blue silk. I'd never seen her without the armor of designer fashions and perfectly coiffed hair.

Standing there, she looked younger, almost innocent.

Caroline Constantine wasn't innocent of anything though.

"Caroline," I roared, my voice echoing through the grand hall, multiplying tenfold as it bounced off marble floors and vaulted ceilings. "I'm going to give you one fucking chance to hand over Bianca Belcante before my brothers and I show you just how savage Morellis can be."

As if on cue, there was a crash from the back of the house and seconds later, Carter and Walcott came trotting up the hall into the foyer. They gathered behind me, a fierce wall of brotherhood and masculine fury at my back.

Through the voracious concern and rage taking pieces out of me, I was aware of a warmth in my chest that spoke of awe and gratitude.

To have brothers, blood and found, surrounding me was a dream I'd always thought too impossible to even hope for.

Caroline stared down at us, the only crack in her composure the slightly shaking hand she pressed to her chest. "Ah, two strapping Morelli males. What an honor. I'm afraid I'm not receiving visitors right now, so you'll have to leave the way you came."

A harsh laugh barked from my throat. I shoved the disabled guard into Ezra's keeping and rushed the stairs, taking them two at a time until Caroline was in my reach. She gasped with genuine fear as I crashed into her. Losing her balance on the stair, she fell backward and I caught her with a hand fisted in the collar of her robe, my other hand a fist cocked back ready to land a blow.

"Do you know how many men I've beaten with these hands?" I asked, almost conversationally but for the rasp of my growling words. "I've beaten street scum and politician's sons, boys who were barely men and men old enough that one push of my finger propelled them into their graves. Do you know, Caroline?" I dipped down, my snarl eclipsing her entire world view. "I've never beaten a woman. Not because of any moral barrier, but because usually, they take one look at the scar on my face and the threat of certain death in my eyes and they agree to tell me everything I want to know."

"You're just a thug," Caroline spat, gathering the tattered remains of her dignity to her. It was obviously hurting her, though. She kept trying to push herself off the floor as she struggled to free herself from my grip. "Bryant's pet monster."

"Not any longer," I promised. "Now, no one is leashing me. No one decides when enough is enough. Can I tell you a secret?" I leaned even closer, my words a hot hiss against her ear. "I was raised in violence and I love to speak its language. Would you like to see how fluent I am in blood and fury?"

She licked her lips once, twice, as if surprised by their dryness. "No. I do not."

"I didn't think so," I said, almost sullenly. "Maybe some other time, but I hope for your sake we never meet again. Because if we do, it will probably be because you tried to steal from me again. And if you ever come for Bianca again, or Brandon, I will tear you apart with my bare hands and a crow bar. I'll pull off your fingers and toes, crack open the cage of your ribs just to see if there is a heart in there after all. Do you hear me, Caroline?"

Pale brows knit over her arctic eyes. She didn't want to capitulate, her pride warring with self-preservation. Once, I would have admired her for it. But now, I pitied her. Only a woman with no one to lose would chose pride.

"I hear you," she said softly.

Fury still boiled hot in the pit of my gut, but looking to Caroline's face, that pity I felt surged even stronger. There was a strange parallel between Bryant and Caroline, two massively powerful heads of powerful families who had sat so long on their respective thrones that they'd both lost perspective. It wasn't about wealth and reputation. It was about taking care of family.

Suddenly, like a puncture wound punched into my chest, the rage rushed from my lungs.

I dropped Caroline to the floor and looked up at the hallway leading to the only woman that really mattered in that moment.

"Go get Bianca," Carter murmured, jogging up the stairs to keep an eye on Caroline. "I've got this."

I went.

I ran so hard my heart threatened to burst like an overripe tomato. Ezra, Henri and Walcott chased me up the stairs just in case I need them. Beckett had told me which door in the hall was Bianca's and when I tested it, it was locked.

"Tiernan!" Bianca's muffled yell came through

the door.

I closed my eyes for one precious second, letting the sweet sound sluice through, dissolving some of my monumental wrath.

"Hold tight, sweet thing," I shouted.

Henrik was already bending to try his lock picks at the doorknob, but I placed a hand on his shoulder to pull him away. Instead, Ezra and I stepped up to the door. I held up three fingers and counted down.

On one, we kicked at the wooden door.

It caved in on a crashing, creaking groan then slammed against the ground. I planted a foot in it as I darted into the room and came to an abrupt stop.

Because there she was.

My peace, my love.

Zip-tied to the post of that antique bed like an animal, forced to her knees to take the pressure off her wrists. Her beautiful dress was torn at one shoulder, scratch marks carved deeply into the skin there. I could see the crusted blood at the roots of her pale hair, the dried trail of it down the sides of her neck, one single line of it dripping all the way into the crease between her breasts.

And my vision went red.

I turned on my heel without thought, driven

by the instinctual violence that Bryant had bred into me like a virus, a disease I'd never be rid of. Walcott and Henrik held me back, arguing loudly with me.

I couldn't hear them over the roar of blood in my ears like the call of a lion. I was all animal. All beast. Ready to tear Caroline apart with my claws and fucking teeth.

"Tiernan," a sweet voice called, pulling me back to myself slightly.

Still, I pushed against my men, elbowing Henrik to get past him.

"Tiernan!"

"She needs to fucking *die*," I roared so loudly, I had no doubt that the bitch could hear me all the way down in the hall. I wanted to hear me and piss herself in fear. "Do you hear me, Caroline? I'll fucking *end you*."

Ezra stepped in front of me, his face in the gap between Walcott and Henrik. He raised his hands calmly, expression placid, and signed, *"Bianca needs your kindness more than you need to hurt Caroline.*

That, combined with one more ringing call of *Tiernan* from Bianca, diffused the rabid tension in my limbs. As my mind cleared, I felt almost shaken, weak and vulnerable.

Because I was.

It was a vulnerable thing to realize someone had hurt the one you loved. To understand that you hadn't been there to protect them and they'd been mistreated.

My eyes burned, dry and hot as coals in my skull as I abruptly changed direction and jogged over to Bianca. Her eyes were massive, wide and fathomless as a winter lake under a midnight sky.

"Tiernan," she breathed this time, lower lip turning under into that pout I'd lived for since the day I met her. In anger, in sorrow, I loved that mouth in all of its expressions. "Thank you for coming."

And then she burst into tears.

"Hush, my sweet girl," I murmured over and over as I took a knife out of my boot and made quick work of the zip ties Caroline must have had one of her guards use on Bianca.

"Hush, my love," I chanted softly as I pulled her free and straight into my arms.

She clung to me like a burr, like something that was made to stick and never let go. Her hands in my hair, mussing it as she caressed me fitfully before fisting her hands there to secure me close.

I held her so tightly I could feel her frantic

heartbeat in my own chest, taste her tears on my cheek. It took me a moment to realize that some of that brine was my own, a hot tear tracking down my scarred cheek to the corner of my mouth.

The taste of it was bittersweet.

I hadn't cried since the day Grace died and I wasn't ashamed of crying now, holding the woman who had reminded me about the goodness of life and the grace of loving.

"I love you," I told her for the first time even though the emotions had been clogging my chest for weeks. "I love you and I'll never let anyone hurt you ever again."

"I know," she sobbed, soothing me even as she sought comfort from me, a hand massaging my neck. "I never felt safe until you forced me to come to Lion Court."

I laughed, the sound harsh with relief and tears. "Best decision I ever made."

She pulled back just enough to smile beautifully at me, face tear-stained and flushed. Her hand cupped my scarred cheek, her thumb tracing the rough line of it. "I think you mean the best mistake you ever made."

When I chuckled, she ate the laughter off my tongue with her own.

Chapter Twenty

Tiernan

CARTER FOLLOWED US back to Lion Court to make sure we were settled.

I had handed Bianca off to Ezra who carried her gentle as a babe up to the stairs to my bathroom where Walcott was already drawing her a bath and now I stuffed my hands in my pockets as I lingered with my brother.

"You didn't have to come," I started, as if that was thanks enough.

Carter snorted.

I glared at my little brother, but a fond smile twitched my lips. I'd always remembered Carter as a fucking rogue, and it was good to see that hadn't changed with time.

"If you ever need me," I tried again, clearing my throat of the dust I dredged up with the gratitude. "I'll be there for you. Whatever.

GIANA DARLING

Whenever. You need a weapon, well, I think my skillset speaks for itself."

"We don't need a weapon," Carter said. "We need a brother. Leo's getting married to Haley Constantine next month, and you should be there."

"Brothers." I grinned, shaking my head. "I never thought I fit in, but the Morelli men seem to have a thing for Constantine women."

"Not me," Carter quipped happily. "I'm glad to escape that drama."

"I'm sure you'll have your own," I warned with dark delight.

To my shock, he slung an arm around my shoulders to put me into a mock headlock.

I let him.

Because this casual, playful embrace meant everything about over a decade of stony silence.

"Come over here," I offered, swallowing a momentary fear that he would ice me out again. "We're opening presents in the morning, but we still have to talk about Bryant. He's been too quiet and I want to strike before he does."

"All work and no play," Carter said, clucking his tongue. "I can drop by for a bit. Bryant expects me for dinner, but I could swing by around four." He lingered for a moment, staring at me as if waiting for something to happen.

"What?"

"I missed you," he said simply, as if he wasn't sticking my knife in my chest. "I always wanted this for us. A brotherhood."

"Yeah," I said, the word all rasp. "Come here."

He came, stepping into my open arms for a tight, quick hug. When we broke apart, we both avoided eye contact, mildly embarrassed by the show of affection.

"I'll see you tomorrow," he muttered, turning to leave. "Enjoy having your woman back. She'll need you after today."

"She needs me every day," I countered arrogantly.

He rolled his eyes, closing the door on his murmured laughter.

As soon as he was gone, I turned and jogged up the stairs.

BIANCA SAT ON the edge of my large free-standing bronze bathtub with Henrik knelt before her like a knight before his queen. He was gently cleaning the blood from her neck and chest with a washcloth. They didn't notice me right away, so I watched with my heart thumping away in my throat as Bianca reached up to plant her hand on Henrik's bald head. As if she needed to touch him to make sure he was real.

"I knew Tiernan and my Gentlemen would come," she whispered hoarsely, her lids low with exhaustion.

Walcott emerged from the walk-in closet with a towel and one of my old boxing hoodies for her to change into. When Bianca swayed suddenly, he dropped both to the floor to catch her from falling back into the tub.

I knew without clarification that Ezra wasn't there because Bianca had asked him to check on Brando.

Now that Bianca had started to teach me the language of love, I could see it so clearly when before, I'd been utterly blind. There was love in the way they touched each other, the tangible weight of it in the air like odorless smoke, the look of it on their faces as they interacted.

I felt all of it mirrored in me, reflecting back at them.

It made me feel both good and like a good man.

It didn't eradicate the bad things I'd done, the cruel things I had no doubt I would still do because it was in my nature to be cruel, but it softened me in profound ways I was only just discovering. And softening, I knew, wasn't bad because Bianca had the softest heart of anyone I'd ever known.

As if she could sense my gaze, her beautiful eyes opened and fixed on me. I watched with a kind of awe as slowly, she smiled. It was the same smile she had looking at a beautiful piece of art, or at Brandon. A smile like a sunbeam shot straight from her soul.

Fuck me, there was soft and then there was *too* soft.

I pushed off the doorframe and stalked toward, vibrating with the need to touch her and take care of her.

"Enough," I almost barked, more severe than I meant to be. "Leave us now."

Without hesitation, Henrik and Walcott left.

And I was alone with Bianca.

She watched me with those wide eyes as I knelt at her feet the same way Henrik had, as if I was pledging allegiance to her. First, I removed her high heels, scuffed from her ordeal with Caroline. Fury fizzed up my spine like a lit sparkler but I breathed deeply, grabbing a handful of Bianca's honey-sweet scent to move beyond it and focus on her. It was intensely intimate to kneel there and take off her shoes, almost servile. It felt right somehow, to do this for her, to show her the humbleness and enormity of my love in such a small act of service.

She gasped when I traced the underside of her foot with my thumb, following the steep arch to her ankle and then up, up her smooth calves to her thighs. The momentum of my hands drove her dress higher and she braced her hands on the lip to raise high enough for the fabric to hitch to her waist. I loved that she closed her eyes on a flutter, trusting me as I pulled the garment over her head, leaving her in a small pair of plain white cotton underwear. It made me smile to see that she still had the cheap panties she'd worn in Texas, as if a part of her could never quit that part of her life.

I wouldn't want her to.

Her nipples furled tight and pink as rosebuds and all her naked flesh had my cock thickening in my trousers. But this wasn't about that.

It was about comfort.

She braced her hands on my shoulders as I picked her up, my hands spanning nearly the entire width of her waist beneath her ribcage as I settled her into the warm, bubbling water in the tub. A soft sigh feathered through her lips as she sank back, resting against the back, her little feet with blue painted toes peeking above the bubbles beneath the faucet.

I watched her for a moment, memorizing her peaceful features as if I'd never get a chance to do so again. But having her caged at Caroline's and now, still threatened by the furious revenge of Bryant Morelli, had instilled a fear in me that gave birth to edgy appreciation. I was bound tightly by my determination to be grateful for every fucking inch of her, every single day.

I hadn't been grateful for my siblings the first time I'd had their love and I hadn't been grateful enough of Grace or grateful for as long as I wished I could have been for our baby.

I wouldn't make that mistake again.

"You're staring at me," she murmured softly without opening her eyes.

Her wet hand emerged from the bubbles to find mine on the copper rim. Our fingers tangled, my darkly tanned hand with its callous and scars, and Bianca's tapered, sweetly gold fingers. I loved the contrast, loved even more knowing that though she seemed weaker than me, softer than me this way, she had fathomless strength of her own.

"It's my right, isn't it?" I asked, a sliver of my usual arrogance worming itself into my tone. I settled more comfortably on the floor and reached over to draw a fingertip down her straight nose. "To look at you in wonder."

A small smile curled over her lips. "As my guardian?"

I chuckled. "I think we're well beyond that. Though tying you to me in every conceivable way is enticing."

"I don't think I can be your ward and your girlfriend," she teased, finally opening her eyes to reveal their midnight blue sparkling. "I think there's actually a few laws against it."

I scoffed, raising her hand to my mouth to softly nip at the ends of her fingers. "You're well over the age of consent and you'll be eighteen in three months."

"I will. What will you do then, when you no longer have any legal ties to me?" she joked, but a flush that had nothing to do with the warm water worked its way into her cheeks.

"Hmmm." I sucked her ring finger into my mouth, watched her eyes go black. "I'm sure I'll think of something."

"Get in here," she ordered, sitting up a little, tugging on me like she couldn't stand another second without me close. "Get in here with me."

I stood, but she wouldn't let go of my hand. "It's tough to get undressed with your hand in mine."

She shrugged, eyes glittering with mischief.

I shook my head then shrugged too and stepped one foot into the tub. She squealed with surprised delight as I sank into the water in my shoes, fully dressed in the dismantled black suit I'd worn all day. Immediately, she wrapped her arms around my neck and her legs around my waist, plastering my clothed form to hers.

"Impatient hussy," I taunted even as I wrapped her up in my arms and kissed the corner of her smiling mouth.

"Arrogant jerk."

"No arguments here."

Her laugh sounded so fucking sweet, I had to taste it with my tongue. Almost instantly, the kiss exploded with heat and furious need. Bianca clawed at me, pulling closer as if she could press me into her body forever. I peeled her hands off, banded an arm around her waist, and flipped us so I was on the bottom. She gasped as I dragged her up my body by the hips until she was forced to brace herself on the tub behind my head. I sank into the water a little more and there it was,

Bianca's gorgeous, damp pussy, the soft blonde curls springy.

She tried to say something, protesting maybe because my shoulders pressed her wide open for my gaze, but I silenced her by parting her folds with my tongue. She remained awkwardly stiff for only a moment more before I mouthed her clit between my lips and sucked. Then, she melted, every bone in her body softening like butter under the heat of my ministrations.

I ate her softly at first, sampling every inch of her like a fucking delicacy. When she started moaning and writhing, humping gently against my mouth in a way that made me throb, I increased the intensity until I was slurping up the juices running down her thighs, biting at the soft skin beside her groin and tonguing hotly at her entrance. I was insatiable for her, inconsolable with need to devour every inch of her beautiful body.

I slanted my gaze up her body, beyond the heavy slope of her chest to her shattered expression. She closed her eyes, tipped her head back so her long, wet hair trailed in the suds, and brought her hands up to play with her breasts as she began to properly fuck into my mouth.

There she was, the good girl giving way for

my wanton slut.

I fucking loved it.

My fingers bit into her plush thighs to keep her still as I broke her apart with my tongue. When she came the first time, she bowed so forcefully I worried her spine would snap, but the second time, she melted into my mouth so fully I couldn't breathe and I didn't even fucking care.

"Tiernan," she begged, pulling at my shoulders, her wet fingers slipping. "Please, I need you inside me. I want to come again all around you."

A ragged groan tore through me, ripped from my tight groin up over my cum-covered tongue. Without replying, I tugged her back down into the water.

"Thank God," Bianca murmured like a prayer as her hands scrambled to undo my pants and peel the wet fabric away from my straining erection.

When she finally managed, hands shaking with an eagerness that made me leak precum, she fisted my dick and immediately settled herself over me. She sank down forcibly, taking me all the way to the root even though it must have stretched and burned. Her groan was long and low, an animal sound that moved through me like a drug.

"I have to fuck you," she explained almost

desperately as she planted her hands on my wet shirt and started to do just that, rocking her hips hard back and forth. "I have to feel you come inside me and know I'm yours."

"What a filthy girl," I praised, curling my hands over her hips to help propel her hard up and down on my aching cock. "I love to hear you talk dirty for me. Love to know you're a slut just for me."

"Yes," she hissed, bending to kiss me, her hair a wet, fragrant curtain all around us. "I love how hard you take me. How much you make me want to bend and break open for you however you see fit."

"Fuck." I curled up slightly to take one of her swinging breasts in my mouth, biting then sucking at her hard nipple as I held her still in the air and fucked up into her.

"Fuck," she echoed on a breathless scream as I hammered her at just the right angle to make her shake apart like an earthquake, every inch of her quivering with the raw energy of her orgasm. Her sweet pussy clamped around me, milking me hard until I had no choice but to fill her up with my hot cum.

Our fierce groans and gasping moans faded into breathless sighs as we both spiraled down from the height of our climaxes like feathers floating on a down draft. My little thing hugged me tightly, burying her face in my neck even though it meant her chin was in the now-tepid water.

"Walcott is *not* going to enjoy cleaning up this mess," I said, my eye to the water, suds, and overturned jar of bubble bath that coated the bathroom floor.

Bianca giggled in my arms and it shocked me that such a simple sound could live inside my chest like some eternal flame.

"I'd live and die for that laugh," I told her in a raw voice as I curled my hand around the back of her neck and pressed another to the vulnerable base of her spine. "I'd live and die for you."

"I know," she murmured, pressing a kiss to my pulse point, the *scritch* of her lips harsh against my stubble. "But let's hope you never have to, okay? I promised you a happily ever after."

I chuckled. "You did. I suppose a large part of that was taking revenge against Caroline like you did."

She stilled, her voice filled with caution. "Are you angry?"

"No. How could I be when I've wanted the Constantines to pay so badly for so long that I stole two orphan children to do it myself?" I asked darkly.

To my surprise, she laughed. "Good. Really, I just wish you could have seen her face. She was white as the snow outside. I thought she might faint."

Wicked satisfaction seeped through my chest and mingled with the pride there. "Clearly, I've corrupted you."

"Clearly," she agreed happily, nuzzling me. "But only because there was something in me that already yearned for corruption."

"True," I murmured, squeezing her neck. "I recognized the darkness behind those velvet eyes."

"And I recognized your goodness," she countered, pulling back to stare me dead in the eye so that I could see the sincerity there. So that I couldn't hide from it. "No one is all good or all bad, and together we're the best combination of both."

I kissed her then, a seal of red lips like a wax on an official stamp.

On silent agreement, we broke apart and got out of the lukewarm water. Bianca peeled me out of my wet clothes and we dried each other off, still unable to keep our hands off each either even though the lust had cooled to reverent affection.

She giggled when I hauled her into my arms and, both of us naked, stalked into my bedroom where I lay her down in my bed. Instead of joining her there, I took a step back, taking a mental photo of the perfection that was Bianca Belcante's lush femininity in my dark space. A space that had symbolized my isolation for so long.

"Aren't you coming to bed?" she asked, lazily arching her pale gold body in a bow, breasts tantalizingly presented.

"Not yet," I murmured. "Put on the clothes Walcott left out for you then get back into bed and wait for me."

I wanted to give my girl the last gift she need-ed to rid herself of the turmoil of the day and the days before. So, I turned on bare feet and padded down the long corridor to the opposite side of the staircase to a familiar door with a plaque reading 'Brandon.'

The door swung open silently, revealing a lump under the sheets topped by a riot of sleep-mussed curls and a little grey apostrophe of sleepy dog pressed up to his side. I swallowed thickly past the emotion that rose in my throat as I thought about Brando growing old in the room, graduating from elementary school into high school and beyond, going to college to make something of himself without worrying about money (because I had so much and it was all his if he wanted it) or familial expectations (because I had none and all I wanted was his happiness). I thought about adding kids down the line, filling more of the empty, forgotten rooms in Lion Court with blonde headed Morelli-Belcante children. I thought about us all together on Christmas Eves like this one and decided it would be a tradition to spend the night together snuggled up in my huge bed, our united warmth against the cold winter night, our collective breath in harmony, our dreams shared behind our closed lids.

A family.

That was what we were.

That was what we would be.

My throat constricted so tightly I could barely breathe as I sat on the edge of Brando's bed and pet a waking Picasso.

"It's okay, boy, you can come with us, too," I promised as I gently gathered Brando's sleep-heavy, warm body in arms and hugged him to my chest.

He woke just enough to curl into me, murmuring, "Tiernanny?"

"Right here."

"Is it time to open presents?" he asked, rubbing at his nose with a small fist before tucking it under his cheek. "Anca told me we got presents when I was a baby, but we never had as many as what's under the tree downstairs."

I tugged his body farther up in my arms, placing his cheek against my healing shoulder, my hand on the back of his downy head. "Not yet, buddy. But there are so many presents, you might have to spend all morning opening them. Picasso will have to help because your hands will get tired."

A sleepy giggle that was more a murmur of breath. "That sounds fun."

"It will be." Fun on Christmas morning for the first time in a long time for everyone in the household. "And guess what, I have an early present for you right now."

Brando blinked open one eye as I walked us down the hall, Picasso's nails clicking softly on the hardwood. "What is it?"

I grinned at him, but didn't answer.

A moment later, I didn't have to.

Because we were pushing open the door to my chambers and suddenly Bianca was there, scrambling to her knees in the bed on a sharp inhalation of breath.

Brando stirred in my arms, turning his head until his gaze settled on his sister, the woman who had been his parent and best friend for all of his seven years. A woman he hadn't seen in weeks.

Immediately, they rushed to each other. Brando slithered out of my arms, his little feet hitting the ground already running. Bianca stood on the bed, running across the blankets so that when her little brother launched himself up at the mattress, she caught him in her arms and hauled him right against her chest. They folded into each other in a way that was beautiful to watch, puzzle pieces slotting together. It was clear they had embraced like that a million times and intended to a million more. That the bond they shared was the purest love. And like Bianca and Brando themselves, their purity didn't make them weak and fragile, but strong as diamonds.

I stood there for a few long moments as they clutched at each other, silent tears streaming down their cheeks. Bianca checked him over, turning his head, running her hands over his limbs, whispering questions and laughing in a bittersweet way about how he'd grown in her absence.

Picasso sat on my feet, his tongue lolling as he watched the scene with me. I placed a hand on his head as we watched the two people we guarded with our lives reunite.

Finally, Bianca curled my oversized sweatshirt over her hands and used them to dry Brando's tears.

"Have you been happy?" she asked, the words aching.

Brando nodded, his movements still slow with sleep. "Walcott bought me a kitchen stool and Ezra taught me more sign language so now I'm going to be better than you and Henrik let me paint his toenails *pink* and Tiernan—" He stopped abruptly as if he'd run into a wall, peeking back over his shoulder to look at me. "Tiernan and me missed you, but we had fun, too."

"Good," she whispered brokenly, her eyes filling with tears again as she hugged him to her and looked at me over her shoulder.

"Thank you," she mouthed.

I shook my head, because she didn't need to thank me. Taking care of Brando was entirely selfish. He had every man in the house wrapped around his little finger.

"I thought we could have a Christmas sleepover," I suggested as I rounded the other side of the bed and got beneath the covers, pulling the sheets back for Bianca and Brandon to join me. "When I was young, Leo used to let all of us sleep with him on Christmas Eve."

The shadows playing over Bianca's face deepened with sadness for me, knowing I'd lost that after my twelfth birthday.

"Don't be sad, sweet thing," I murmured as she and Brando crawled up the bed and joined me under the blankets. Brando instantly pressed himself tight into my side and grabbed for my hand as he grabbed for Bianca's. "This is better than anything I ever thought I'd deserve."

Bianca curled into Brando to mimic my pose, both of us parentheses around him. She reached over his head across the pillows to tangle one hand with my own, her cheek resting on her bicep. Picasso jumped on the bed and curled up at Brando's feet, propping his chops on his white-capped feet to watch over us.

"We used to sleep with Mom sometimes," Brando slurred as sleep came for him. "I miss her, but I'm happy we get to live here now. With you and The Gentlemen."

"Me too, kid," I said, but he was already asleep.

"I miss Mom, too," Bianca said, her eyes twin pools of darkness in the dim yellow light spilling in from the bathroom. "But I have to believe this was meant to be. Us. This family."

"It was," I agreed. "We were always meant to belong to each other. It makes it better, honestly, to look back at those years of anger and loss and bitterness. To believe everything happened to lead us here." I squeezed her hand. "I won't lose you, Bianca. Not fucking ever. It makes me goddamn grateful I'm older than you because honest to Christ, I won't live another day without you."

She made a soft nose in her throat, eyes already closing with exhaustion. "You won't have to. I'm not going anywhere. None of us are."

Chapter Twenty-One

Tiernan

"**O**H MY *GOD!*" Brando exclaimed for the fortieth time that morning, discarded wrapping paper piled about around him like colorful snow drifts after a blizzard. He held up the limited-edition Spider Man figurine I'd found at auction for an absurd amount of money given it was a fucking toy. His ecstatic expression made it utterly fucking worth it. "Look at Spidey!"

"Wow," Bianca gushed, as she had been all morning, sitting beside her brother so she could be the first to share in his joy. "That's amazing, Brandy boy."

He jumped to his feet and did a little shimmy, like his joy couldn't be contained. Then, with an ear-splitting holler of happiness, he rushed around the mounds of presents and into my lap where I sat on chair with a vantage point that let me watch the Belcantes properly enjoy the presents. I laughed as he squirmed in my arms, thanking me loudly as he patted my cheeks with both hands. Picasso barked along with him, prancing amid the packages.

It was fucking chaos, but fuck me, I loved it.

And by the looks of synchronized joy on Ezra, Henrik, and Walcott's faces, they felt the exact same way.

"You're welcome, kid." I tickled his sides to hear his delighted squeal then gently pushed him off my lap so I could stand up. "Do you think it's time for Bianca to have a present of her own from me?"

"Of course!" he crowed, jumping with both hands in the air.

Maybe Chef Patsy shouldn't have put out the Diablo cookies and gingerbread men we'd made yesterday for a pre-breakfast snack while we opened presents.

As Brando darted over to Ezra, jumping into his lap so the big man could help him open the package, I went around the massive tree to collect one of the two presents I'd stashed there for my girl.

When I emerged with a massive brown paper-wrapped package that was bigger than Brando himself, Bianca looked up at me with eyes just as wide and excited as her brother's.

I carefully placed it on the floor in front of her, waiting until she gripped the edges before I let go and moved around to her back. I pressed myself into her, moving her hair away from her neck to press a kiss there.

"You once told me that your dad called you his dove because you brought him peace," I murmured, palming her hips. "Well, you and Brando are my peace, too. I thought this was a fitting symbol of that."

She trembled under my fingers as she started to peel off the paper. The edge of a heavy gold frame appeared and then, with one long *rip*, the entire wrapping gave way to reveal the painting.

A Picasso.

One I had Henrik hunt down to a private gallery in Spain. I'd offered an exorbitant amount of money to pry the thing from the reluctant owner, but it was worth it.

Because Bianca's breath whooshed from her lungs and she stood there blinking at her favorite artist's painting *Two Doves with Wings Spread*.

"Two doves," I whispered as I hugged her back against me. "My Bianca and Brando."

The force of her emotions bowed Bianca's

head, her hair shimmering forward like a gold curtain to obscure her face. Still, I didn't need to see it to know she was crying softly, her shoulders shivering with the movement.

Walcott stepped up to hold the painting so Bianca could spin in my arms and look up into my face. The painting was pretty enough, I guessed, but nothing could eclipse a single look from Bianca's blue suede eyes.

"Tiernan," she said, searching for words, and then, not finding any sufficient, she rocked to her tiptoes and kissed me soundly in front of our entire family.

The men whooped and hollered, clapping as if we'd just exchanged marriage vows.

I tipped her head back gently, aware of her abused scalp, and deepened the kiss, claiming her mouth with teeth and tongue. She moaned, clasping me as if I was the only thing that kept her afloat. When we broke apart, I grinned wolfishly at her while she reclaimed her equilibrium.

"I feel badly I only got a bottle of that expensive water you like and new gloves," she muttered, blushing. "It's just I felt like I was using your money to buy you a present and it felt a little wrong. Next year, when I get Lane's inheritance sorted out, I'll get you something special, too."

"At the risk of sounding like an asshole, I really only wanted you. You and Brando and my men like this on Christmas morning."

"Not an asshole," she said, kissing me again. "At least, not right now."

Everyone but Brando, who was too busy playing with his new toys, chuckled.

All the presents had been given now except one, but this I wanted to give to Bianca alone so I jerked my chin at Walcott who immediately announced it was time for brunch and started to usher everyone into the dining room. When Bianca tried to move, I locked her in the circle of my arms until we were alone in the messy room.

"There's one more."

"Tiernan—"

"Hush," I ordered as I sat down on the couch and pulled her over my lap. "Or I'll have to give you a Christmas spanking." When a flush spilled down her chest, I chuckled. "I might have to do that, anyway."

She squirmed in my lap. "Okay," she agreed, slightly breathless.

My little thing was such a greedy girl.

I ignored the tightening in my groin and handed the present I'd kept in my back pocket all morning. It was a small-ish, flat velvet box wrapped in white paper.

The same one Walcott had found and given me to gift Bianca with the night of Lane Constantine's Memorial Ball.

Bianca took the package gently, unwrapping it carefully the way one might diffuse a bomb. When she reached the velvet box, she caught her full lower lip between her teeth and opened the thing with a soft *snap*.

Instead, nestled in plush silk, a diamond encrusted, heart-shaped locket twinkled brighter than the star Ezra had helped Brando fix to the top of the tree.

Bianca's hand flew to her mouth, covering the open O of it. When she raised her eyes to mine, they sparkled even brighter than the trinket.

I spoke as I gently lifted the heavy necklace from the box. "You know my maternal grandparents left this house to me. Eamon and Zelda were eccentrics, wealthy because Eamon's father started an enormously successful shipping company in the early 1900s. They had four children, but they still managed to travel the world and seek out adventure. They died two days apart, first Eamon from heart disease and then Zelda from an undiagnosed brain tumor." I held Bianca close as she shivered at the reminder of her own mother's aneurism. "My Mom talks all the time about how in love they were. Even as a boy I could see it, as tangible as the sun."

"Eamon gave Zelda this locket when he fell in love with her and she wore it every single day for the entire forty years they were married." I opened Bianca's hand with one of my own and gently placed the locket in her palm. "Now, I'm giving it to you."

I didn't know how to say I wanted her to wear it for the next forty years, fifty years, sixty years, too. I didn't know how to tell her I planned to make every dream she'd ever have come true if it was inside my power to do so. I didn't know how to tell her that her presence in my life had changed it irrevocably in a so many ways, I knew I'd discover new ones for decades to come.

So, I just placed that locket in her hand and muttered, "Open it."

Bianca took in a shuddering breath and gently placed her thumbnail inside the split in the silver to pop open the mechanism.

Inside, written on a tiny piece of paper in my cramped script because I wanted to write it myself even though my dyslexia made my writing crap, one word was written.

You.

"You carry it with you," I explained. "Now, you'll always know."

"Carry what?" she breathed, almost distracted by the emotions moving through her.

"My heart."

"Tiernan," she whispered, her eyes wide and dark as they lifted to mine, her lashes trembling and mouth a soft, heart-shaped opening of wonderful surprise. "I'm honestly speechless for the first time in my life."

"It's yours," I shrugged, trying to make light of the gesture I'd spent weeks imagining. "I don't how to take it back. I know it doesn't make up for the loss of the necklace Lane gave you that I destroyed, but I hope you can accept it, love it even, in a different way."

"I love it in *every way*," she said, suddenly fierce, turning into me to claps my face in both hands, the locket caught between her palm and my scar. "I love you in every way. And I will for forty years or fifty years or however long life will let me have you for."

"Thank fuck," I cursed on a relieved exhale that filled me with giddy joy. My head fell forward until our foreheads connected. "I was planning on keeping you captive here if you said no, anyway, but this is much easier."

She laughed against my mouth and then kissed me through it. And even if she'd only given me that single moment for Christmas, it would have been more than enough.

✧ ✧ ✧

IT STARTED EARLY that afternoon.

Brando would have called it my Spidey-sense, but I called it intuition honed by years of dangerous living.

It was the sense that everything suddenly rest on a blade's sharp edge, ready to split apart or fall off into oblivion.

The first inkling ignited when the doorbell chimed throughout the house and moments later, Walcott ushered Beckett Fairchild into the now-cleaned living room where Ezra was patiently helping Brando build the Avenger's Tower in Lego, while Henrik and I played chess, teaching Bianca by explaining our own moves.

Everyone stilled at the sight of the dark-haired, green-eyed man whose large body took up much of the doorframe.

"Happy Christmas," Beckett said into the stunted silence. "I'm sorry to interrupt, but I wanted to make sure Bianca was well after the...events of yesterday."

"I'm fine," Bianca assured him, standing up to greet him with a hug. "Please, come in and visit for a while. I take it after what happened, you aren't exactly invited to the Constantines' for Christmas."

The older man's grin was more of grimace. "Not exactly, no."

Bianca sat beside him on one of the velvet couches and surprised me by taking his hand. "I didn't expect you to witness the signature and I won't be angry if you don't want to appear in court, if it comes to that. I know you and Caroline have…history."

I narrowed my eyes at the mysterious subtext of their conversation, a low growl ready in my throat because I didn't like seeing my little thing with a secret connection to another man.

"Yes," he agreed, clasping her hand back gently, patting their joint embrace with his other hand in a kind of fatherly way. "But I hope my *future* is with you…and yours."

"That isn't up to me," she warned, eyes darting to the side, toward me, for a fleeting second.

Beckett cleared his throat, straightening his broad shoulders in the expensive black suit he wore even though it was Christmas Day. I myself was in black jeans and a black cashmere sweater

Walcott had given me as a gift from Brando.

The door chimed again, probably Carter. He was going stop by to talk about my plan for Bryant before he headed to Morelli Mansion for Christmas dinner. Walcott excused himself, but my focus remained on Beckett who turned to stare at me for a long moment.

I stared back, eyes narrowed with hostility.

No matter his reputation as a kind and charming man, there had always been something about the man that got my hackles up.

"Tiernan, may I talk to you for a second?"

Before I could answer, Santo Belcante strolled into the room with an armful of presents, grinning over the top. "You got room for one more in this fucking creepy ass house?"

Bianca laughed as she went to him, offloading some of the presents. "If you come bearing gifts, of course."

She led Santo to Brando and bent down to make quiet introductions.

Brando frowned at the mysterious man and I caught his indignance. "I don't care if you're our real uncle. We aren't leaving here. I don't want to go with you!"

"Hey," Santo said, hands raised in the air as he crouched beside Brando and Bianca. "I've got no intention of taking you away if you're happy here, okay? I just want to be friends, if you've got room for one more?"

Brando studied him with knotted brows for a long moment before finally looking at Bianca who nodded at him. "Do you like superheroes?"

Santo thought about it seriously for a moment then said, "I think my favorite has to be Batman. I like that he doesn't have any magical powers, just courage and smarts."

Brando nodded. "He's not as cool as Spider Man, but I guess you could stay and play with me for a while."

Santo bit off the edge of his smirk. "Thanks. I'm just going to talk to Tiernan for a second and then I'll come back, okay?"

Brando agreed, already turning back to Ezra and their Lego set.

I jerked my chin at Santo, knowing why he'd come, and then addressed Beckett's previous question. "I've got some business to attend to, but if you wait around, I could make time."

Beckett frowned, but I was already leaving the room with Santo on my heels, leading the way to my office. As we crossed into the hall, Carter stood just inside the door tossing his coat and scarf to Walcott.

I collected him on our way to my office and took up position behind my desk while the other two men settled in. There was a furious look on Carter's usually amicable face and he cracked his knuckles anxiously.

"What is it?" I asked him.

"Bryant won't tell me exactly what he plans to do to you," Carter spat, his face flushed with mounting fury. "He worries I'll have some kind of 'misguided' brotherly empathy and he won't take the risk. He's determined to ruin you, Tiernan."

"He's taken everything from me for years. He won't take what I have, now," I promised darkly. "Santo, you already contacted him. Tell us how that went?"

The mafioso leaned forward on the couch at the edge of the room, a lock of overlong hair falling into his face. "He's interested. I was understandably coy about what the fuck I was offering, but I promised it was information on Halcyon."

"Fucking Bryant," Carter muttered.

"It's Dad," I said. "What the hell did you expect? He's tried to ruin aspects of all of our lives. He won't back off until we put a fucking muzzle on him and it has to be one that sticks. If we can entrap him with Santo's intel, then we can blackmail him. We can control him, keep him in line."

"Will that even work?" Santo asked, sharp teeth gleaming in the light from the fireplace. "At this point, will anything short of death stop him? In my experience, men with that level of power never go quietly into oblivion. They need to be in control."

"Are you willing to kill your own father?" Carter asked me incredulously. "Getting away with murder isn't easy and the cost isn't cheap, trust me."

"I'd kill the fucker in a heartbeat," I said calmly, because I would. Bryant had proven himself to be a rabid dog, I knew he wouldn't be fully silenced unless it was with a bullet, but there were two reasons I wouldn't risk it. "But Mom doesn't deserve to be widowed by her own sons, even if Bryant treats her like shit, she loves him."

"She'd be better off," Carter said.

I shrugged. "Yeah, but you want to take that choice from her? I sure as hell don't. I don't feel comfortable taking our father from our sisters, either. He's a bastard, but at the end of the day, he's their father and we are hardwired to love our parents. Besides, I have a family that needs me now. I won't risk going to prison and having that all ripped away just for the satisfaction of ending Bryant."

"It's a close call." Carter sighed heavily. "Ultimately, I agree. Bryant lives. But seriously, Tiernan, I heard him talking to cousin Charles about targeting your 'assets.' If he's waited this long for revenge against you, you know it's going to be big. Lucian, Leo and I can try to talk him down later tonight at dinner, but he's set against you now."

I had no doubt.

Bryant was the one who taught me only to land the first punch if you were sure it would knock the opponent out for good, otherwise you risked retribution. Our father practically had a whole fucking rule book written around the concept of revenge and I knew he planned to throw the whole fucking thing at me.

"I can arrange a meeting with Bryant anytime," Santo offered. "I just need something tangible to give him, or he'll smell bullshit a mile off."

We fell silent, each of us knowing the entire crux of our patriarchal takedown hinged on that one thing.

And then, in the silence, came a tentative knock at the door.

Before I could tell whomever it was to fuck off, Beckett Fairchild peeked his head around the door. "Hello?"

"We're having a private conference, Beckett," I barked. "Wait your damn turn. I said I would make time for you."

Beckett glowered at me, an expression I'd never seen on his face that was surprisingly effective. "No, I'm afraid I have to speak to you *now*, Tiernan."

He closed the door behind himself and confidently stroke into the center of two Morelli men and a well-known mafioso as if his skin was made of titanium armor. I watched with some amusement as he braced his hands against my desk to lean over to me.

"I won't apologize for eavesdropping, because I have exactly what you need."

"I won't apologize for cutting out your tongue so you can't pass on anything you so innocently overheard," I responded with a wolfish smile as I pulled a knife from the top drawer of my desk and set it on the table between us.

Beckett didn't even glance at the weapon, his vivid green eyes hooked through mine. "There's no need for that. If anyone is going to cut out my tongue, it will probably be your father after I go with Santo to sell him information about Colombe Energy Investments."

His words ignited a nuclear silence, the air ballooning with pressure.

"And why the fuck would you do that?" The words rumbled through my chest as I stood and flattened my own hands on the desk, leaning over it to snarl in Beckett's face and match his pose.

There was something wrong about this, something that made the hair on the back of my neck stand on end.

"I have my reasons," Beckett replied, not backing down in the face of my ire.

"If you want to help us so badly, you'll share them."

He stared at me with such intensity, his eyes started to redden from the strain. "Lane was my best friend, my brother by choice. I promised I would look after Brandon and Bianca, and I failed. This is my way of making it right."

I didn't believe him for a single second and based on Carter's scoff, he didn't either.

But… "You understand that going with Santo very well might result in Bryant sensing a trap and putting a bullet in your fucking head?"

I waited for him to shy away from the stark truth, but Beckett just rolled his shoulders back and fixed me with that jade green gaze. "You spoke of the people you love as reason not to kill your father. Well, I have my own loved ones and I'm willing to do this for them."

Our stand-off was cut short by the vibration of my cellphone and the simultaneous metallic ring of the landline going off throughout the house.

Walcott must have picked up the house phone, but I let mine ring for a long moment while I stared down Beckett Fairchild, searching for cracks in his conviction.

I found none.

Instead, he seemed to grow even larger, swollen with conviction.

Finally, I broke eye contact and answered my cell without looking at the screen.

"Hello?"

A moment later, Walcott burst through the office door, his face beneath the molten scarring white as snow.

"Tiernan," my head of security at the casino said in a voice trembling with anger. "Someone set off a bomb at *Inequity*. No one was there because it's Christmas, but the casino... it's fucking gone."

I stared across the room over Beckett's shoulder at Walcott as the cold fury crept through my veins like ice, freezing my resolve in place, clarifying my mind.

"Well," I said to Carter. "It seems Bryant landed his first punch. He took out my club in New York."

A ripple of shock ran through the room. We all knew Bryant was capable of disgusting deeds, but he'd never taken it quite so far against his own family.

"Okay, Beckett," I said the cold knife of my anger cutting a smirk into my face. "Welcome to the fucking club. I don't give a shit anymore, if you can help us take down that fucker, you're in."

CHAPTER TWENTY-TWO

Tiernan

OF COURSE, BRYANT was too much of a suspicious asshole to meet anywhere outside of his control, so the exchange was scheduled to take place two days after Christmas at the Morelli Mansion.

A place I was essentially banned from.

Happily, I had a very loving, alcoholic mother who was all too willing to sneak her favorite son into the building from the separate entrance to her wing of the house. It had its own security system, only the video monitors played in the central security room at the heart of the house and if the guards were too busy watching for the arrival of Santo and Beckett, I'd be able to slip inside without any fanfare.

There was no fucking way I was going to miss the takedown of Bryant Morelli. It was glaringly and darkly funny to me thinking back to when I'd believed Bianca was my enemy when all along it had so clearly been my own father who hated me and hunted my joy down at every single fucking turn my life took.

Now, he'd taken *Inequity* from me.

An underground club and casino that had taken me a decade to make into what it was today, a well-known, elite's haven for sin and indulgence. It produced enough revenue in one month to keep an entire small town afloat for a year.

Bryant thought it would be a devastating loss, a crippling financial setback. He'd always assumed because of my dyslexia that I was all brawn and no brain, but whatever I lacked in reading ability was more than made up for by my talent with numbers and a natural business acumen I'd probably learned from the prick himself.

Inequity was the obvious diamond in my crown, but I had many other ventures hidden in the shadows that Bryant was none the wiser to. Thanks in large part to those and Henrik's investments, I'd have *Inequity* up and running in a new location before the year was out.

Bryant had landed a punch, but it hadn't knocked me out. It had only stirred up a lifelong history of bitterness and wrath that tangled inside me like a payload I was ready to catapult at my father.

To my shock, it was Lucian who waited in the SUV idling in the driveway that morning while I said goodbye to my Belcantes. I crouched before Brandon so I could accept his hug on his level and Picasso took the opportunity to jump onto his hind legs to lick my face. Brando dissolved into laughter, encouraging his dog to attack me with kisses.

It was just the kind of silliness I hadn't had in my life for decades and just the kind of silliness I found my heart warming over. It almost hurt, the frozen organ de-thawing after so many years of arctic existence.

Bianca watched us with her pouty lower lip caught between her teeth, her hands wringing behind her back. There was anxiety in every inch of her, but when I caught her eye as I rose she smiled valiantly.

I caught her around the waist, bending to kiss her forehead. "I'll be fine. You forget, I'm most people's worst nightmare."

Her laugh was half-hearted. She preoccupied her nervous hands by smoothing them down my black compression shirt, tracing the hard ridges of my pecs and abdominals beneath the stretched fabric. "A beautiful nightmare." She corrected, finally looking up at me with luminous eyes like morning sunlight on lake water. "My nightmare, okay? Don't let anything happen to you."

"I'm only going for the satisfaction of seeing the fucker get caught at his own game. Much like *you* did with Caroline, my savage little thing."

Finally, a grin that warmed her entire face. She rocked to her tiptoes and cupped the back of my neck with one hand, tracing my scar with the thumb of her other hand. "This is the last of it, okay? No more scars, no more battles, no more heartache. I'm going to give you the happily-ever-after you deserve."

"Happiness isn't free, Bianca. It demands payment and I'm willing to pay whatever toll it demands in order to be with you. In order to keep you safe," I told her and the words were harsh, but my tone was gentle because she was still young, still pure even after being exposed to the filth of Bishop's Landing. Pure in a way I knew she'd stay pure forever.

Bianca kissed me in response, as if I was a sailor going off to sea for God only knew how long. As if she was willing to live and die spending the rest of her life in that single kiss.

My heart ached and thumped, stretching and

growing and warming like a struggling bloom under the sunlight of her love.

I left after that, not turning back even when Brando called goodbye again because I didn't want to think about what would happen if we failed in our plan. What would happen if Bryant ever got his filthy fucking hands on my sweet Belcantes.

I got into Lucian's car, slamming the door behind me, a scowl affixed to my face that I knew wouldn't dissipate until I returned home to Lion Court. Ezra got into the back on the other side, the only man I was taking with me because he was the best man I had in any dangerous situation.

And we were off.

"I wasn't expecting you," I told my eldest brother. "I don't expect you to fight my battles for me. I'm not a kid."

"No," Lucian agreed. "God knows I've got my own shit to deal with, but if I've learned a goddamn thing over the last few years, it's that family matters. So, here I am."

I caught his eye in the rearview mirror. "I'll be there when you need me."

He shrugged as if he didn't give a fuck either way, but the fact he was helping me at all spoke volumes.

"I know he deserves jail. Or worse. But it would harm the family irreparably for him to be publicly punished that way," Lucian informed me as he raced through the icy streets, the wiper blade's working hard to clear the windshield of thickly falling snow. They made a *whomp-whomp* sound that mimicked the brutal beating of my heart. "That would harm everyone. Morelli Holdings. Mom. Our sisters. So we'll back this house arrest."

"Not to mention the tell-all book he would probably write if we didn't have him under our control. We'll keep the entire thing under wraps. It's strictly need-to-know. And no one but us brothers need to know about it." I produced the cuff Henrik had secured and programmed for us from the leather satchel I carried. "I've got the tracking device."

Lucian looked in the rearview mirror at the large device. "That's fucking massive."

My grin was twisted like heated metal as I raised it to my throat. "I had Henrik order a large one instead. It seemed fitting for an animal like Bryant."

My brother chuckled sinisterly, the sound linking between us like a tangible display of our bond. It was a bond built on more than just revenge, though. We were brothers in arms against a tyrannical dictator who had brutalized us for years. We were forged from the same fire, honed to sharp points by the very same man.

And together, we would bring him to his motherfucking knees.

The rest of the drive was silent, a mounting tension seeping throughout the car until Ezra had to crack a window so we could breathe easier. We parked around the corner from the Morelli Mansion in Mr. Andrew Gibson's driveaway, a friend of Carter's who'd agreed to hide the car. From there, we collected our gear and tromped through the crunch of snow to the back gate of our family estate.

To our collective surprise, our mother was the one to great us at the gate. She was bundled up in a huge cream suede coat with the fur-lined hood pulled up over her auburn hair, only her mercury grey eyes bright in her flushed face. Her silly dog, Sheba, was curled against her chest, but she still stepped forward to embrace me in a hug that was edgy with even more desperation than usual.

"Tiernan," she said, turning her face into my chest, closing her eyes. "You've been neglecting to visit."

"I've been busy," I murmured, but I hugged

her back. Even though my mother was weak-spirited, nothing like my sweet Bianca with her sharp claws, she was the only member of my immediate family who had loved me consistently my entire life.

"I'm scared for you," she said, ignoring Ezra and Lucian as they slunk through the narrow gap we created in the frame of the gate and onto the property. "Bryant, he…he's very angry with you, my sweet monster. Dr. Crown had to stay for three days while he tended to your father after what happened at The Met."

"Good. It's too bad the asshole didn't just keel over and die."

"Tiernan!" She pulled away, her face pale with shock. "That's your father you're talking about."

"Yes," I hissed, the violent wind whipping the word into her face like the crack of a slapping hand. "The same man who gave me his scar. The same man who drove Grace to kill herself and our unborn child. The same man who isolated me from my siblings, who wouldn't let me go to school because my dyslexia and the scar *he* gave me made me a disgrace to his family name."

I heaved in a cold breath that helped bank the heat of the fury crackling in my chest.

My voice softened and I took Sarah's gloved

hands in my own, tugging her close to protect her shivering form from the worst of the wind. "The same man who essentially locked you in the east wing and forgot about you as soon as you'd pushed out the last of his brood. The man who drives you to drink too much and pop pills like M&Ms."

"I don't..." she started to protest instinctively, but the words withered under my fierce glare. "Well, I suppose this had to happen one day. The son must always try to break free from his father."

"Not just one son," Lucian finally interjected, staring at our mother like she was a gnat beneath his shoe. "I know you don't have much time for us, and I don't really give a fuck. But you can't imagine we'd have much sympathy for you. You chose this life. Not just for you, but for your children. No wonder you need those pills to sleep at night. Bryant's crimes are on you just as much as they are on him."

Sarah quaked hard in my grip as if Lucian's words were sundering her in two.

"Quickly, let's go inside," I urged, leading her forward through the gap in hedgerows into the snow covered back garden. "They'll be arriving any second if they aren't here already."

"Who?" Sarah asked.

We ignored her, jogging through the grounds to the east wing's back entrance where Sarah's favorite bodyguard waited at the door. Up the stairs into her opulent set of rooms, the parlor made even more lavishly feminine by the presence of three enormous men clothed in black who set up station on her antique coffee table.

"Carter should have set up cameras in the office yesterday," Lucian murmured as Ezra flipped open his laptop and started to pull up the feed.

A moment later, the two men grinned as video popped up on the screen. The room was empty. Ezra pressed a series of controls and a grainy sound feed erupted in the room.

Sarah winced as she handed her coat off to me so I could hang it for her. "What in heaven's name is all of this? You said you were coming to visit me."

"I'm here, aren't I?" I countered, tossing her coat on the back of a gold chair before joining my brothers around the computer.

"They're here," Lucian noted as Carter's microphone spilled smoothly through the speakers, revealing Bryant was leading Santo, his men, and Beckett up to the office.

"But what are you *doing*?" she hissed, high

color sluicing down her neck. She hated any sign of neglect and there I was, eschewing her for something to do with Bryant.

The air around her popped and fizzed, a tantrum brewing.

"Tiernan!" Her voice was shrill as a tea whistle.

"Shut her up," Lucian demanded, casting a cold look at her.

I understood my brother's apathy toward our mother. Sarah had stood by too many times in the past when Bryant took his fists and belt to us. It was a hard thing to forgive and even loving her, I wasn't sure I could ever forget her negligence.

Even loving her, enough was enough.

I stalked over to her, watching as her expression changed swiftly from anger to a pleading kind of neediness.

"Tiernan, sweetie," she began then swallowed the rest of her words, turning ashen when Bryant's voice came through the mic.

"Ever thought you'd see the inside of the enemy's camp, Beckett?" he was jeering, taunting him because of his close relationship with the Constantines. "When I heard you were turning on them, I had my suspicions. But it seems you and Caroline had a falling out over Christmas?

How unfortunate you both."

"Who?" Sarah breathed, but I didn't have to answer because he did.

"My reasons for doing this are my own, Morelli, but don't forget for one moment that I do not like you and this is *not* a social call," Beckett replied with icy civility.

A moment after he spoke, Sarah fainted.

Luckily, I was close enough to lunge forward and catch her before she hit her head on the edge of the bar cart. Still, her shoulder hit the corner, sending two martini glasses shattering to the floor beside us.

"Fucking hell," Lucian growled. "Get her under control, Tiernan."

I lifted our mother into my arms and deposited her on a pink tufted chair. There was a vial of smelling salts on the sideboard I retrieved to wave under her nose until she slowly blinked back into consciousness.

"What was that?" I demanded as soon as she was cognizant. "Why did you react so poorly to Beckett Fairchild?"

I watched her throat move with a painful swallow, her hand fluttering to cover it from my gaze. "Be a darling and fetch me my pills. I need them."

"No. Tell me why the fuck you fainted at the sound of his voice?"

Something was building inside me, sucking everything I was back into a looming wall of water that seemed to threaten my very existence. That tingle of premonition sparked down my spine and urged me to shake Sarah's shoulders lightly as if I could rattle the answer loose.

"Tell me!" I demanded when she only blinked into the distant.

Her grey eyes cut to mine, wide and opaque as stone. "I-I'm just scared for you. What if Bryant discovers you're here?"

"Lie to me again, Mother," I growled, my teeth set on edge. "You'll be reminded why you call me your monster."

"You would never hurt your mother," she gasped.

I arched a brow in cold challenge. Of course, I would never hurt my mother, but I wasn't above making her sweat in order to get my long awaited answers. "I'm here today to hurt my father. What makes you think I'd hesitate with you?"

Of course, I had no intention of hurting her, but I was done, that wall of water curling high over my sense of self. There was no hope of reining it in. At this point, I could only hope it was crash down soon, ridding me of this poisonous anxiety.

Bryant's voice came again. "So sensitive, Beckett. I expected bigger balls on a man with your reputation."

His rough laughter echoed through Sarah's parlor.

"Please," she breathed as if she was asphyxiating. "Get me a drink, Tiernan."

I took mercy on her, pouring a large tumbler of straight vodka. She took it gratefully, her hand trembling so badly as she raised the glass to her lips that alcohol spilled down her chin into the collar of her cashmere hoodie.

"I met your wife once," Beckett said. "She was a lovely woman."

Sarah whimpered, clutching the empty glass in both hands like a life preserver.

"Ha!" Bryant snorted. "That must have been a very long time ago."

"Enough with the misogyny, Dad," Carter protested mildly. "I don't think Santo Belcante needs to hear about the dynamics of our family, hmm?"

"Who is Beckett to you?" I demanded of Sarah. "You have three seconds to tell me."

"Tiernan," she protested.

"Three."

"Tiernan, sweetheart, you don't understand—"

"Two."

"Tiernan!"

"One." I warned. "You owe me the truth, Sarah. Tell me now or I swear to fucking *God* that I will never visit you again. You'll waste away in this suite, unloved, unwitnessed and when you die, one of the servants will discover you and no one will go to your funeral."

"Stop!" she said, dissolving to tears. "No good was ever going to come of it, Tiernan. Don't you understand? It was a *mistake*. A stupid, vengeful mistake I made because your father could never love me. Do you understand what that's like?"

"How dare you ask me that?" I murmured darkly.

She ignored me, hysteria settled so deeply inside her that I wasn't sure she could even see me anymore.

"Beckett, he was so beautiful, so kind. And he was close with the Constantines, basically one of them. He liked me and I was lonely, aching to stick it to Bryant for neglecting me for so long."

"You slept with him," I said the words aloud even though they'd been sitting inside me since the moment she reacted to Beckett's name.

Sarah blinked at me, fresh tears raining down her cheeks into the vodka-soaked neck of her shirt.

"He's my father." Something was wrong with my voice, the words fell dead between us, thunking to the floor. "Does he know?"

When she didn't respond immediately, I surged forward, looming over her like that tsunami wave inside my chest, caging her in. "Does he know?" I roared.

"Yes." The word exploded from her lips. "Yes, h-he started hounding me about it about six years ago. Said he'd run into you and seen your eyes. Fairchild eyes. He cornered me in Bergdorf's one day and I confessed. He made me!"

The wave crashed into me, obliterating everything inside my chest, drowning my heart, my sense of identity, everything I'd ever known. I tumbled under the driving wave, cycling in the churning water unable to draw breath.

Suddenly someone was pulling me away from a wailing Sarah, tugging me to my feet and pushing me onto a sofa. It was Ezra. He crouched before me, his hands moving frantically.

Tiernan, you need to focus. Take a deep breath. Your mother doesn't matter. Who your father is doesn't matter. What matters is making life safe for

Bianca and Brando, for all of us.

I fell forward, elbows to thighs, face in my hands as I struggled for breath.

Vaguely, I was aware of the deal going down over the monitor. Of Bryant agreeing to buy the proprietary ultrasound technology developed by Colombe Energy before the company could go public with it.

The rich echo of satisfaction in Bryant's voice did more to calm me than Ezra could.

The son of a bitch thought he was king of everything. No, not king. God. He believed everything good in life was owed to him and if it wasn't given freely, he was happy to take it. He was a bully, pure and simple.

He'd bullied every one of his children to some extent and he'd fucking terrorized me.

He'd treated Sarah so badly she was driven into a rival's arms. The irony wasn't lost on me that Bryant had forced me into Bianca's life, too.

We'd all allowed ourselves to be victims for too long, to let a fucking villain reign supreme over our lives and it was past time we took him off that corrupt throne.

Before I knew what I was doing, I was on my feet, stalking out of Sarah's parlor.

Voices erupted behind me, calling me back,

but I was already jogging down the hall, racing down the stairs to the main level to charge up the opposite staircase leading to Bryant's domain.

His fucking throne room.

My gun was in my hand, raised steadily despite the violence seething in my gut like a pit of agitated snakes. When I kicked in the office door, everyone inside froze.

Beckett sat in a chair to the far right before Bryant's desk, his face caught in horrified shock as he stared at me leveling a gun at Bryant.

Carter was behind our father's shoulder where he sat at his desk, the very same position I'd taken up in that very room for my entire fucking life.

Santo stood off to one corner, closing a duffel bag filled with stacks of cash as if a madman hadn't just stormed the room.

And Bryant.

My fucking piece of shit fake father who'd made my life a living, breathing nightmare?

He took one look at me, tipped his head back and roared with laughter.

Cold teeth bit between my shoulder blades, right where Bryant had me tattoo the tally marks of the lives I'd taken for him.

"Tiernan," he crowed. "What excellent timing. I just made a nice little deal with some friends here to see out the humiliation *you* were supposed to dole out to the fucking Constantines."

"You didn't do shit expect for dig your own grave, you son of a bitch," I said, the words cold as ice cubes clinking against my teeth, my hands steady as I narrowed my sights on his rotten fucking heart. "It was a goddamn set up."

Bryant's laughter dissolved into a chuckle, his black eyes fixing on me with igniting anger. "I very much doubt you could pull that off. You're about as dumb as they come, son."

"I'm not your fucking son," I barked, clicking the safety off my gun, the small sound echoing too loudly.

"Maybe not, but I am," Lucian said from behind me, slightly breathless as he reached the landing with Ezra and took up at my back. "Think of it as a belated Christmas gift, Daddy-O."

"Sorry we didn't get you a card," Carter quipped as he stepped away from Bryant's right hand side and rounded the desk to join us.

"You fucking disloyal idiots," Bryant spat, getting to his feet even though I took a step closer and then another, right next to Beckett still frozen in his chair, two feet from pressing my gun into Bryant's chest. "You think you can just get away with this? I own you all and I own everything you think is yours."

He pierced Lucian with that soulless gaze. "I gave you Morelli Holdings. Don't you think I could take it away? You think I don't know about Elaine? You think I couldn't have her relapsing in a second? You know, son, they put absolute poison in drugs these days. It wouldn't be unusual if poor little Elaine overdosed on fentanyl."

"Fuck you," Lucian snarled. "That's the last time you speak her name or I'll cut out your tongue."

Bryant shrugged easily, as if there weren't four angry men focused on him with violent intent. "And Carter? You think I don't know about what you get up to overseas? You don't think I could blow the whistle on you anytime I damn want?"

Carter didn't give him the satisfaction of replying. Instead, he took his handgun from his shoulder holster and calmly clicked off the safety before training it at Bryant's head.

Our father chuckled, seriously perverted delight suffusing his features as he clapped his thick hands. "Look at the sons I've raised. Angry, violent men. Tools. My tools. It's almost funny to think you would try to stage a rebellion. You breathe because I allow you to breathe. What I allow you to have, I can take away like this." He snapped his fingers then sat back in his high leather chair, getting comfortable before he turned his gaze to me once again.

"You don't believe me? Look at Tiernan. Here he stands looking victorious, so ready to hurt the man that raised him knowing he wasn't his own son, knowing he'd never be good enough to live up to the family name. Such lack of gratitude when I gave him everything."

I shifted uneasily, because he seemed so certain.

"Look at him," he urged again, looking around the room. "He doesn't have any idea that as we speak, I'm taking away the last thing that matters to him."

Fear impaled me straight through the chest like a thrown javelin. I staggered under the weight of the blow, pain and fury exploding through every inch of my body.

"What have you done?" I asked through numb lips.

Bryant grinned, all teeth and red gums. "I told you those old McTiernans shouldn't have given you that house. I never liked the independence it gave you. So I've taken it away."

Whatever logic or control that locked the

beast inside me in chains to the bottom of my soul snapped with a serious of painful jerks, my torso quaking with the impact. There were no thoughts in my brain. No reason. No boundaries.

Only pure, distilled agony and cold, bone breaking fury.

I was on him in a second, lunging across the desk to tackle him, dragging him from the chair to the ground. He fought me, maybe, but it was futile. I didn't feel his nails rake my skin, or his teeth bite hard into my forearm. I was made animal, made heathen by this fury. Brandon's Hulk had nothing on the strength and brutality of my emotions as I started to pound Bryant Morelli into the ground. My fist connected with his chin.

At first, no one tried to stop me. Distantly, I could hear them arguing about what to do, but nothing registered.

Nothing except the fear that Bryant had taken my Belcantes from me the way he'd taken everything else.

"What did you do to them?" I roared so powerfully, the words tore up my throat and left blood on the back of my tongue.

"I told you not to fall in love with a Constantine," he rasped. "I warned you nothing good would come of it."

As if on cue, somewhere in Bishop's Landing there was a fierce roar and then an echoing, resounding *boom!*

Everything in me stilled, flash frozen with fear. I looked over the desk at my brothers, their eyes wide with shocked horror.

No.

No. No. No.

The framed family photo that excluded me, the one I'd thrown a dagger into, had been reframed and placed back on his desk. I reached for it then, slamming it on the corner of the wood so the glass shattered and rained down beside Bryant's face. My fingers pinched the edge of one long shard of glittering glass and I raised it high over my father's face.

"You'll fucking pay for this," I whispered through my ravaged throat, my entire body quaking with so much rage there was no way to purge it but through violence. "Every day for the rest of your life you will live locked up in this house like the animal you are. We're taking *everything* from you, you fucking psychopath. No more fucking freedom. We are going to watch your every move to make sure you never interfere with our lives for your own agenda again. And if I go back to Lion Court and find my family dead,

I'll string you up right here in this forsaken room and I'll take strips off you every single day until you bleed out and die."

There was no more laughter in his face, only a sick, descending kind of realization. His eyes darted around the room, searching for a savior in any of his sons.

No one moved a fucking inch.

And I wasn't going to waste any more time on the pure evil that was Bryant Morelli.

I wanted to slam the shimmering, blood-smeared glass down at his face. I could barely hear over the lion roar of vengeful hatred in my fucking broken heart. I wanted it to split open flesh and muscle, to dig into the bone of his cheek and jaw as I carved the same path his belt buckle had once carved in me.

But that was exactly what Bryant had trained me to do. He raised and groomed me in the language of violence so I could be his ultimate weapon, but I was done being *his*. He had taken everything from me to make me believe that my bitterness and rage was justified, that all I was and all I had left was the tool of my trade, my weaponized body.

And that wasn't true anymore.

I had my brothers, again.

The Gentlemen, Ezra behind me and Henrik and Walcott with my two most prized possessions.

Bianca and Brandon.

Even if—my thoughts hiccoughed over the idea—even if they were gone, Bianca would never condone Bryant's murder. She wouldn't want that blood on my hands or years in jail wasted away as a consequence.

She would want me to find my way back to joy.

And that meant ending the cycle.

Choosing grace instead of violence.

The biggest fuck you I could give Bryant was to step away from everything he'd tried so hard to teach me.

So I threw down the piece of glass and stood up even though it was the hardest thing I'd ever fucking done.

"Step away from Mr. Morelli, Tiernan," a new voice warned from behind me.

I barely heard him, but suddenly Beckett was behind me, slotting himself between the desk and my body, blocking me from the door.

When I looked up, there were two Morelli guardsmen at the door. They'd knocked out Ezra who lay crumpled at their feet.

One of them had their gun trained on me.

The other was holding Bianca.

My heart stuttered to a smoking, crashing halt.

"I'm okay," she assured with a faint smile even though the guard had her in a chokehold. "But Tiernan, I think they blew up Lion Court. I just went to the gate because Tilda was there—"

"Enough," Bryant's warbled voice cut through the room. "If you want her to live, get off."

I moved away from Bryant slowly, watching the guard with Bianca, watching Bryant as he staggered to his feet and slumped in his chair dabbing at the blood spilling from his split lip and chin.

He looked at me for one single second that seemed to last a life time.

There was no empathy in that gaze, no warmth or love. Just an empty chamber where goodness went to die.

And I knew what he was going to do because he was just that fucking evil and only a psychopath would harm an innocent like Bianca.

"Kill her," he demanded.

But I was already moving, darting around Beckett and the desk, running at the guard threatening the best fucking thing that had ever happened to me, the only woman kind enough and strong enough to love a monster like me.

The guard, a man I'd worked with countless times named Ethan, raised his gun at me and fired.

The bullet tore through my still-healing shoulder.

I didn't stop.

It all happened so fast, my focus intent on Bianca, but I knew Lucian and Carter were engaged with the other guard, that Beckett was doing something to Bryant.

I was six paces away, so fucking close.

Ethan fired again.

The bullet cut through my side like a flaming arrow. A grunt of savage pain blasted across my tongue, but I couldn't stop now.

Nothing could have quelled the momentum inside me driving me toward Bianca.

It was gravitational.

Even if I fell, I'd do it after reaching her.

After saving her as clearly as she'd saved me from a life of pain, misery and loneliness.

When I was two steps away, my right hand chopped at the inside of the guard's wrist and the other grabbed the barrel, forcing the gun back at a painful angle. I was slower than normal, sluggish with pain, and he was able to fire another shot before I could turn the gun fully away from me.

It nicked the side of my neck, a blazing trail of fire that threatened to swallow me whole.

I fell to the ground, but the gun was in my grip, torn from the assailant.

Immediately, Ezra, who'd been coming to on the ground, scissored his legs and took the guard to the ground. He crawled over him, pressing his forearm to the man's neck while he struggled.

My vision swam and I fell to the side, landing hard against the side that had taken a bullet to the belly and shoulder. Breath exploded out of me, black spots spiraling through my vision.

I struggled to stay conscious because Bianca wasn't safe yet.

But I should have had more faith in my little thing.

Because she bent to me, shucking her coat to press it against my seeping neck wound. She was murmuring to me, but I couldn't hear anything. When she pressed my hand over the jacket to stem the flow, I applied as much pressure as I could and when she bent to kiss me, her tears hot as blood on my face, I tried to kiss her back.

A moment after that, I closed my eyes against the surging pain and lost my fight to stay awake.

CHAPTER TWENTY-THREE

Tiernan

FOR A MOMENT, when I first swam back into consciousness, I thought I'd been buried alive. That Bryant had won, as he always had in the past, and I was buried six feet beneath the earth. My limbs were weighed down by some incredible force, the pressure on head almost agonizing.

But then I realized I could breathe easily.

That I could peel back my dry, sticky lids and open my eyes.

The light stabbed my corneas, digging ice picks into my brain, but after a moment I regained my vision again.

There was yellow thread spilled all over my chest.

No, not thread.

I tried to work through the fog of my

thoughts and realized it was hair.

Golden hair.

Two heads of it perched on my chest.

Bianca and Brandon.

They were squeezed onto the hospital bed I lay in like two parentheses curved around my body, protecting me, comforting me even in my unconsciousness.

The way Bianca and I had lain with Brando in my bed on Christmas Eve.

My mouth was parched, but that wasn't why my throat started to burn as I stared down at those halo haired Belcantes.

They were safe.

They were here.

With me.

Because they were mine and they wanted to comfort me even if I wasn't aware of it.

I raised a heavy, trembling hand and cupped the back of Bianca's head just to touch her.

"They spent the last two days in the waiting room," Walcott's voice said.

I looked up, expanding my world beyond the hospital bed to take in the rest of my surroundings.

Walcott, Ezra, and Henrik all sat crammed together on the ledge of the window. Beckett and

Sarah sat in separate chairs pulled up to either side of the bed. Carter stood near the door, my youngest brother beaming at me.

They were all here.

Everyone.

My chest throbbed and I knew no amount of morphine would ease the ache.

"What happened?" I croaked.

The rumble of my voice through my chest woke Bianca, who peered up at me sleepily before her mouth fell into an 'O' of surprise. She squealed softly, an elated sound, and then gently pressed a kiss to my chin.

"Oh my God," she breathed, kissing me there again. "If it wouldn't hurt you, I'd kiss you all over. I'm so happy you're awake."

I laughed hoarsely then stopped on a wince when it pulled at stitches in my neck and side. "Rain check."

Bianca smiled so widely, it almost blinded it me more than the light had. She shook her head, as if to free herself of an enchantment I'd cast over her, and reached over to the bedside tray to grab a cup of water. She raised it to my lips and I happily sucked it all back.

"What happened?" I asked again, clearer now.

Bianca sighed, ducking her head against my

chest and stroked the fingers of one hand lightly over my jaw.

"I was taken by Bryant's men when Tilda showed up at the gate and asked to speak with me. She'd been crying and I should have been smarter, but my first thought was to help her. Comfort her. I hadn't thought to wonder if she was crying because Bryant had forced her to lure me out of the mansion. I hadn't known he was blackmailing her with the affair she was having with a married oil tycoon." When I growled with anger beneath her cheek, Bianca looked up at me. "Don't be angry with her, Tiernan. People do desperate things when they're threatened."

Henrik picked up the thread of the narrative then, thumping his first against his chest in a gesture that spoke of his happiness to see me alive. "We were lucky. The idiots Bryant sent tripped the silent alarm. Walcott hurried Brando and Picasso into one of the cars and got them out of the house while I went after the intruders. I caught them in the back parlor. My guess is, they intended to fix the bomb to the gas tank downstairs, but they never made it that far so when they heard me coming they put it on the piano."

Terror slithered through me at the thought of my family if Bryant had succeeded. Lion Court was an old house and I didn't like the odds of them surviving that kind of blast.

"It went off when I was tackling the last one in the backyard. I could feel the blast of heat even twenty yards away. It took out the back-right corner of the house. So, we won't be living there for a while."

"I've already got crews clearing up the debris and an architect drawing up plans for rebuilding," Walcott assured me, as if that mattered.

As if anything mattered but the two blondes settled safely in my arms.

"Bryant?" I demanded, fresh rage surging through me, eating at my drug-induced mellowness.

Carter was the one to explain then, stepping forward to clutch my feet in his big hands, as if he needed to touch me to ground himself.

It filled me with something warm and liquid, like my blood had been replaced with champagne.

Carter fixed his dark eyes on me. "He's in lockdown right now."

Bianca shifted her head on my chest to peer up at me with those vivid blue eyes. She touched her fingertips to my lips and clasped her heart-shaped locket in her other hand.

"I wish men wore lockets too so you could

wear it visibly every single day," she whispered.

"What?"

"My heart," she said softly, harkening back to the words I'd told her when I'd given her the locket. "There's nothing I wouldn't do for you, Tiernan. Your fight is my fight. You bleed, I bled."

Looking into her face then, I understood how dangerous love could be. Because she was right. There was nothing I wouldn't do for her, no line too far to cross, no price too step. I'd die and kill for her just as I lived for her now.

And I understood now that she felt the very same way.

That all the horror and pain I'd faced throughout my life was payment for this glorious woman. That I'd spend the rest of my life earning the gift of her.

"I love you," I told her, and it didn't feel like enough. "I'll tattoo your heart on my chest so I can wear it every day like you wear mine."

A slow, sweet smile like honey poured from an overturned jar. "I'd love that."

So would I.

"He isn't dead," Carter continued. "We caged him in the house with our men and set up the monitoring system."

"I'll stay there," Sarah said, leaning forward to pat my thigh, curling her hand around the muscle. "I-I want to stay. I'll keep him calm, make sure he doesn't get up to his old ways. You might have guards, but no one knows the old man like I do."

"You don't have to stay," I argued. "This is your chance to get away from him."

"I am," she said. "I'm thanking you, now. And asking if you can ever forgive me for keeping your biological father a secret."

My gaze skimmed over to Beckett who sat stiffly in the chair. His shirt sleeve was rolled up on one side, a bandage fixed around his elbow.

"If you want me to leave, I understand," he offered reluctantly. "But I'd very much like to stay."

"You were hurt." I jerked my chin at his elbow. "You didn't have to do what you did. I guess, now I know why you did it."

"He also gave blood for you," Bianca murmured. "There was a mass casualty on the interstate and they were running low on blood. One of the bullets hit your splenic artery and you'd lost so much blood."

I blinked at Beckett, reluctant admiration trying to wiggle its way through the walls of my chest.

He shrugged. "I had surgery recently. I knew my blood type and we were a match. It's not a big deal."

I looked into those green eyes, just a few shades darker than my own and I swallowed thickly. Trying to reason with the basic impulse of all children to love their parents. I knew better now. That family was what you made, not what you were born with. That sometimes, the people who loved you best didn't have to share the same blood as you, or even the same morals and outlooks.

Love transcended everything, if you let it. If you felt it.

But looking at Beckett, thinking about the years he'd been a patron of *Inequity*, the way he'd helped Bianca with Caroline and Lane's will, the way he'd stepped up *twice* to help me, I knew if I gave him a chance, he'd love me.

Bryant had been my father all my life and he'd never ever tried.

So I jerked my chin up at the man. "You can stay, if you want. But don't think this makes us best friends."

Beckett's lips twitched. "Never."

"Tiernan?" Brando's sleepy voice rose a moment before his head did, slumberous eyes blinking up at me. "Are you awake?"

"Are you?" I teased, pushing his hair back with one hand even though it hurt my shoulder. "Hey, buddy. I missed you."

His lower lip quivered, eyes filling. "You're okay?"

"Yeah, kid, I'm more than okay."

"You got shot," he informed me, as if I didn't know. "Three times."

"Yeah."

"You were trying to save Anca," he reasoned. "But if you do something like that again, I'm gonna have to be really mad because you can't leave us, okay?" He swallowed thickly and fisted his hand in my hospital gown. "Please don't leave us."

My nose itched with the urge to cry as I stared into the gentlest face I knew. I wrapped one of his curls around my finger and tugged. "I promise, Brandon, I'm not going anywhere. You, me, and Bianca are going to be a family forever."

"And Henrik and Ez and Wally?" he demanded.

"Them, too, of course."

"I always wanted a big family," he admitted, curling into me and casting an almost shy glance at Carter in the corner. "Are your brothers gonna be like my uncles, now?"

I looked over his head at Carter.

"Sure, we are," he agreed easily, then he bent forward. "Lucian and Leo couldn't be here, but you'll be seeing a lot of us in the future. I hear you like superheroes. You know, not to brag or anything, but I've helped save the world before."

Brando's mouth fell open. "Woooow. That's so cool."

Everyone chuckled, Brandon's charm melting the last of the cold tension in the room. Carter started entertaining Brandon with stories of his own adventures, and Sarah and Beckett struck up a tentative conversation in their chairs.

So, I took the momentary respite to urge Bianca's head back and kiss her deeply.

"You have hospital breath," she teased when we broke apart.

I growled, nipping at her lower lip until she laughed.

"I don't care," she whispered as if it was a secret. "Honestly, I don't even care about Dad's will or getting into NYU or about Constantines vs. Morellis. I don't care about anything except for you and my baby brother."

"You don't have to worry about us," I swore,

cupping the entire back of her head in one of my palms, loving the vulnerability of her resting her skull in my care. "We'll always be here. You can focus on graduating, on making new friends and growing up, and being NYU's brightest new student. You can have it all, Bianca, I'll make sure of it."

Her laughter feathered over my lips as she cupped my scarred cheek. "Whoever would have guessed that my nightmare would be the best dream I'd never thought to hope for."

I grinned at her. "Oh, I think I can remind you of just how much of a monster I can be when the occasion presents itself." She laughed again and the sound did more for me than the IV drip ever could. "So, is this it, the happily-ever-after you promised me?"

"Does it feel like it?" she whispered against my lips.

I kissed her again, sealing our lips around the words I didn't have to say. Laying there in that hospital bed, riddled with bullet wounds, bereft of my house and my club, but surrounded by people who wanted to love me, I'd never been happier in my entire godforsaken life.

✧   ✧   ✧

Thank you for reading BEAUTIFUL NIGHT-MARE! We hope you love Giana Darling's forbidden romance, the second book in the Dark Dream duet. You can read a bonus epilogue of Tiernan and Bianca by signing up for our newsletters here:

www.dangerouspress.com/nightmare

And Tiernan's older brother, Leo Morelli, has an epic romance!

The beast hides a dark secret in his past...

Leo Morelli is known as the Beast of Bishop's Landing for his cruelty. He'll get revenge on the Constantine family and make millions of dollars in the process. Even it means using an old man who dreams up wild inventions.

The beauty will sacrifice everything for her family...

Haley Constantine will do anything to protect her father. Even trade her body for his life. The college student must spend thirty days with the ruthless billionaire. He'll make her earn her freedom in degrading ways, but in the end he needs her to set him free.

The warring Morelli and Constantine families have enough bad blood to fill an ocean, and there are told by your favorite dangerous romance authors. See what books are available now and sign up to get notified about new releases here...
www.dangerouspress.com

ABOUT MIDNIGHT DYNASTY

The warring Morelli and Constantine families have enough bad blood to fill an ocean, and their brand new stories will be told by your favorite dangerous romance authors. These series are now available for you to read! There are even more books and authors coming in the Midnight Dynasty world, so get started now...

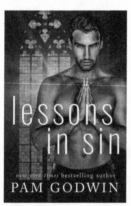

Love forbidden romance with an age gap?

As Father Magnus Falke, I suppress my cravings. As the headteacher of a Catholic boarding school, I'm never tempted by a student. Until her...

I became a priest to control my impulses.

Then I meet Tinsley Constantine.

"Taboo romance at its best! LESSONS IN SIN is another dark masterpiece by Pam Godwin!"

– JB Salsbury, New York Times bestselling author

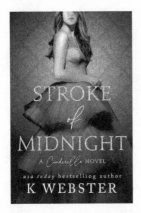

Meet Winston Constantine, the head of the Constantine family. He's used to people bowing to his will. Money can buy anything. And anyone. Including Ash Elliot, his new maid.

But love can have deadly consequences when it comes from a Constantine. At the stroke of midnight, that choice may be lost for both of them.

"Brilliant storytelling packed with a powerful emotional punch, it's been years since I've been so invested in a book. Erotic romance at its finest!"

– #1 New York Times bestselling author
Rachel Van Dyken

"Stroke of Midnight is by far the hottest book I've read in a very long time! Winston Constantine is a dirty talking alpha who makes no apologies for going after what he wants."

– USA Today bestselling author
Jenika Snow

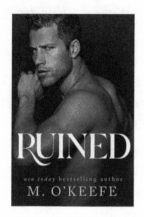

Ready for more bad boys, more drama, and more heat? The Constantines have a resident fixer. The man they call when they need someone persuaded in a violent fashion. Ronan was danger and beauty, murder and mercy.

Outside a glittering party, I saw a man in the dark. I didn't know then that he was an assassin. A hit man. A mercenary. Ronan radiated danger and beauty. Mercy and mystery.

I wanted him, but I was already promised to another man. Ronan might be the one who murdered him. But two warring families want my blood. I don't know where to turn.

In a mad world of luxury and secrets, he's the only one I can trust.

"M. O'Keefe brings her A-game in this sexy, complicated romance where you're left questioning if everything you thought was true while dying to get your hands on the next book!"

– New York Times bestselling author K. Bromberg

"Powerful, sexy, and written like a dream, RUINED is the kind of book you wish you could read forever and ever. Ronan Byrne is my new romance addiction, and I'm already pining for more blue eyes and dirty deeds in the dark."

– USA Today Bestselling Author
Sierra Simone

SIGN UP FOR THE NEWSLETTER
www.dangerouspress.com

JOIN THE FACEBOOK GROUP HERE
www.dangerouspress.com/facebook

FOLLOW US ON INSTAGRAM
www.instagram.com/dangerouspress

ABOUT GIANA DARLING

Giana Darling is a Wall Street Journal, USA Today, and Top 40 Amazon bestselling Canadian romance writer who specializes in the taboo and angsty side of love and romance. She currently lives in beautiful British Columbia where she spends time riding on the back of her man's bike, baking pies, and reading snuggled up with her cat, Persephone, and Golden Retriever, Romeo. She loves to hear from readers so please contact her at gianadarling@gmail.com if you have any questions or comments.

Join my Reader's Group:
facebook.com/groups/819875051521137
Like me on Facebook: facebook.com/gianadarling
Follow me on IG: gianadarlingauthor
Subscribe to my Newsletter: eepurl.com/b0qnPr
Follow me on BookBub:
bookbub.com/authors/giana-darling
Follow me on Goodreads:
goodreads.com/author/show/
14901102.Giana_Darling
Follow me on Twitter: @GianaDarling
Follow me on Pinterest:
pinterest.com/gianadarling

OTHER BOOKS BY GIANA DARLING

The Evolution of Sin Trilogy

Giselle Moore is running away from her past in France for a new life in America, but before she moves to New York City, she takes a holiday on the beaches of Mexico and meets a sinful, enigmatic French businessman, Sinclair, who awakens submissive desires and changes her life forever.

The Secret

The Consequence

The Evolution Of Sin Trilogy Boxset

The Fallen Men Series

The Fallen Men are a series of interconnected, standalone, erotic MC romances that each feature age gap love stories between dirty-talking, Alpha males and the strong, sassy women who win their hearts.

Lessons in Corruption

Welcome to the Dark Side

Good Gone Bad

After the Fall

Inked in Lies

Dead Man Walking

A Fallen Men Companion Book of Poetry:
King of Iron Hearts

<u>The Enslaved Duet</u>
*The Enslaved Duet is a dark romance duology about
an eighteen-year old Italian fashion model, Cosima
Lombardi, who is sold by her indebted father to a
British Earl who's nefarious plans for her include
more than just sexual slavery… Their epic tale spans
across Italy, England, Scotland, and the USA across
a five-year period that sees them endure murder,
separation, and a web of infinite lies.*

Enthralled (The Enslaved Duet #1)
Enamoured (The Enslaved Duet, #2)

<u>Anti-Heroes in Love Duet</u>
*Elena Lombardi is an ice cold, broken-hearted
criminal lawyer with a distaste for anything
untoward, but when her sister begs her to represent
New York City's most infamous mafioso on trial for
murder, she can't refuse and soon, she finds herself
unable to resist the dangerous charms of Dante
Salvatore.*

When Heroes Fall (Anti-Heroes in Love, #1)
When Villains Rise (Anti-Heroes in Love, #2)

<u>The Elite Seven Series</u>
Sloth (The Elite Seven Series, #7)

COPYRIGHT

This is a work of fiction. Any resemblance to actual persons, living or dead, business establishments, events or locales is entirely coincidental. All rights reserved. Except for use in a review, the reproduction or use of this work in any part is forbidden without the express written permission of the author.

BEAUTIFUL NIGHTMARE © 2022 by Giana Darling
Print Edition

Cover design: Damonza

CPSIA information can be obtained
at www.ICGtesting.com
Printed in the USA
LVHW091738250122
709349LV00005B/247